Murder at the Falls

The Creature Comforts Mystery series by Arlene Kay

Death by Dog Show

Homicide by Horse Show

Murder at the Falls

Murder at the Falls

A Creature Comforts Mystery

Arlene Kay

LYRICAL UNDERGROUND
Kensington Publishing Corp.
www.kensingtonbooks.com

LYRICAL UNDERGROUND BOOKS are published by

Kensington Publishing Corp.
119 West 40th Street
New York, NY 10018

All Kensington titles, imprints, and distributed lines are available at special quantity discounts for bulk purchases for sales promotion, premiums, fundraising, educational, or institutional use.

Special book excerpts or customized printings can also be created to fit specific needs. For details, write or phone the office of the Kensington Sales Manager: Kensington Publishing Corp., 119 West 40th Street, New York, NY 10018. Attn. Sales Department. Phone: 1-800-221-2647.

Lyrical Underground and Lyrical Underground logo Reg. US Pat. & TM Off.

First Electronic Edition: July 2020
ISBN-13: 978-1-5161-0932-6 (ebook)
ISBN-10: 1-5161-0932-5 (ebook)

First Print Edition: July 2020
ISBN-13: 978-1-5161-0935-7
ISBN-10: 1-5161-0935-X

Printed in the United States of America

To all those who further the human-canine bond with kindness and compassion.

Chapter 1

Call me grateful. Not a do-gooder and certainly no philanthropist, but someone who firmly believes in giving back and doing my part. Sounds crazy, I know, and pompous as well. My small share of Great Marsh, Virginia, was trivial in comparison with the mansions, estates, and megahomes of my affluent neighbors. That was fine with me. To an orphan, foster child, and army veteran, stability and self-sufficiency were the gold standard, priceless proof of beating the odds in a tough world. Every day I counted my blessings—Creature Comforts, a thriving business crafting leather products for dog and horse fanciers, and a host of pets and good friends to sustain me. Add in a jaw-dropping partner, Wing Pruett, and his darling daughter and my life was full. Unlike some of the moneyed malcontents haunting the local boutiques, I thanked heaven every day for those blessings.

Life was good for Persephone Morgan. Those good feelings left me vulnerable. When my pal, Babette Croy, dragooned me into joining a therapy dog program, I was powerless to resist. She had her ways. Babette, a socialite and local activist, used a cunning mixture of guile and guilt to manipulate gullible chumps like me into doing her bidding. Why else would I abandon my work, skip the morning gallop with my mare Raza, pack up my dogs, and trek twenty miles to an assisted living facility oddly named the Falls? Guilt and guile—you can't beat them.

My dogs, Keats and Poe, were perfectly trained and easily passed every test required by the Alliance of Therapy Dogs. Proper temperament was the key ingredient, and my boys were the poster canines for that. Still, Babette insisted that they accompany her and her border collie, Clara, to formal classroom sessions and be officially designated as Canine Good Citizens.

Only then, after being observed at three events, were we cleared for full certification. Those three sessions, a school, a library, and a children's hospital ward, were a piece of cake. My spirits were buoyed by the plaudits my guys earned for their impeccable manners. I felt virtuous and a tiny bit smug at my good deeds. Somehow, I had never factored assisted living facilities into the plan.

I parked my weathered Suburban and was immediately assailed by doubts. Not about my dogs. Keats and Poe were beautifully behaved Malinois war heroes with the medals to prove it. They were bred to herd sheep in Belgium, although the breed was more often seen now guarding military and police installations. Unlike me, they adjusted seamlessly to any human from cradle to rocker. Providing comfort to people in difficult situations was the official mission of the Therapy Dog program, and I envisioned my boys continuing to do just that at schools or somewhere equally innocuous. Our new assignment threw a spanner in the works. I vowed to try my best, but seniors were foreign territory to me. I'm an orphan who'd been deprived of the grandparent experience. Who knew if I could up my game enough to actually mix and mingle with the aged residents at the Falls and bring comfort instead of conflict?

There was no sign of Babette on the premises, or anyone else for that matter. I paused, confident that any moment the shiny red Mercedes would swing into the drive with Babette and her faithful border collie in tow. These excursions were tailor-made for Babette, a woman who never met a stranger. How I envied her ease with all kinds of people. Even though I'd faced bombs and brawls in Afghanistan, the prospect of confronting a group of pensioners was oddly unsettling. *Lose the pity party,* I warned myself. *Not everything is about you.*

I focused on the surroundings. The Falls was a gracious, multistoried complex set on a verdant site with glimpses of distant mountain peaks. If any institution could be termed "homey," this place would claim the prize. The architecture mimicked old Georgian construction, replete with generously proportioned windows and clapboard exterior. Wheelchair ramps were discreetly placed toward the back of the residence, affording any onlooker an unobstructed view of gracious living absent the painful reminder of infirmity.

On this breezy autumn day, the rocking chairs dotting the porch were vacant, so I signaled to the Mals and settled in. The slow, rhythmic pulse of the rocker soothed my spirits, lulling me into a light, languid sleep. I awakened with a start to find a tiny, birdlike woman of a certain age staring down at me. Hers was a smiling visage, impeccably turned out in a neat shirtwaist and patent-leather flats. Abundant white hair was piled on top of her head in a style reminiscent of another day.

"Caught you, didn't I?" she said with a sly grin. "Don't mind me. I do that all the time. Napping, that is. Soothing, isn't it?" She extended her hands palms up, speaking in a low, soft voice to my boys. "Beautiful creatures. What breed?"

"Malinois, a type of Belgian shepherd. There's a town of that name in Belgium. Don't worry. They're very gentle. Meet Keats and Poe."

She shook her head. "No worry. I love dogs. All animals, actually. They seem to sense it, don't they? That's one thing I really miss being in this place. Having my own pet." She grinned again. "Pardon my manners. I must introduce myself. My name is Magdalen Melmoth."

"Persephone Morgan. Perri, actually." For some odd reason I felt compelled to state my formal name, as if it were a validation, a type of credential.

Magdalen gingerly perched in a rocker adjacent to me. Her complexion was remarkably smooth despite her age, although the spots on her hands told a different tale. Bright blue eyes bored into me as she took my measure. "Persephone. Your parents must have been fond of the classics, dear. Your namesake was a great warrior."

I flushed, reluctant to admit the truth. What woman warrior flinched at the word "orphan"? After all, it was nothing shameful and certainly not my fault. Before I responded, an unlikely savior sped to my rescue. Babette Croy, swathed in designer denim and trailed by Clara the border collie, appeared on the scene.

"Well, I see you made yourself comfortable," she said. It was no accident that Babette had been voted Miss Congeniality on the pageant circuit and head cheerleader in college. Her glacier-melting smile and air of good cheer were infectious. She quickly introduced herself, Clara, and our mission.

"We're part of the Therapy Dog program." She plucked a paper from her capacious handbag. "Let's see. We've each been assigned a resident. Mine is Irene Wilson and Perri's—well, what do you know? You're Perri's partner, Ms. Melmoth. Isn't that something? Kismet or what?"

Few people could resist the onslaught of Croy charm. Magdalen's eyes twinkled as she surveyed my friend. "I understand it's a lot of work—getting your dog certified for that program. How kind of you to do it."

Babette shrugged in a failed attempt at modesty. "It truly is. Most people don't grasp that, Magdalen. Why, my Clara had to pass basic obedience, canine good citizen, and therapy training before they would even consider her. Perri's dogs were war heroes, so it was easier for them."

I forgave Babette for minimizing the accomplishments of Keats and Poe. She was a good-hearted soul who meant no harm even on the days when she tried every bit of my patience to the max. The general public was so accustomed to watching therapy dogs in action after national tragedies that many assumed any dog or well-intentioned owner could simply step right in without training. Au contraire. I recalled several duos who had started the program with us, flubbed the final test, and hadn't made the cut. Most pet parents didn't take that well. Not every dog or owner was suitable for therapy work, but rejection on any level was painful, particularly when it involved a volunteer assignment.

I checked my watch. Showtime was soon approaching and I had no desire to be late on day one. Punctuality was indelibly stamped into my genetic code. Call it a legacy of foster care or a military mindset, but Persephone Morgan was always on time. I plucked at Babette's sleeve. "Maybe we should register or something. I think some other people plan to join us."

Magdalen bit her lip, almost as if she were frightened. She slowly rose and pointed toward the entryway. "You'd better check in with Dr. Fergueson. They have all kinds of rules around here, and she's a stickler. Knows chapter and verse."

I felt strangely protective toward this elderly sprite even though we had never met before. Somehow, a bond had been forged between us, a connection made through our mutual love of dogs. I signaled Keats and Poe and rose to my feet. "No problem. I understand bureaucracy all too well. We'll find Dr. Fergueson and see you later."

"Nice meetin' you, Magdalen." Babette beamed another ray of sunshine. "Let Irene know I'm comin' her way. We're gonna have a real good time."

We entered the common room, a pleasant open space decorated with wing chairs and sofas arranged in conversation areas. A massive mahogany bookcase and assorted end tables tied the look together. The soft colors of green, yellow, and blue added a soothing touch.

"Hey, this is nice," Babette said, casting a weather eye around the room. "I was worried it would be a downer, but not so far." She lowered her voice. "And it doesn't smell."

"Babette!" Sometimes she went too far even for me.

"Oh Perri, chill. I mean that institutional odor. You know, like bleach or ammonia."

I was glad to see that several other members of our group had arrived. Safety in numbers, as the saying goes. Kate Thayer, a stocky matron with a ruddy complexion and a ready wit, was one of my favorites. Her Labradoodle, Gomer, as goofy as his name suggested, joined my boys for playdates whenever possible. Kate called herself a recovered librarian, although that was a vast understatement. Expertise in antiquarian books made her a sought-after resource for both universities and collectors from around the world. She was a talented musician and singer as well, and was seldom seen without her guitar. As Kate ruefully explained, none of her passions paid much, but they reaped big psychological benefits. The residents apparently enjoyed singing songs from their youth and tapping their feet along with Kate and tail-wagging Gomer. I was partial to music myself and looked forward to the sing along.

Although we'd never discussed finances, I assumed she had saved enough to live in relative comfort. Real estate prices in the Cleveland Park district, where Kate lived, were among the highest in the nation, and most properties there had listings well into the upper six-figure range. Pruett owned a town house just around the corner in Georgetown, another stratospherically priced residential area that was way too rich for my blood. I presumed through inheritance, divorce, or just plain good luck, Kate had managed to hang on to her homestead. She limped into the room, guitar in hand, leaning heavily on a cane. Today was a special day at the Falls. Once a month, special song requests were welcome, and following the performance by our dogs, residents would gather in the sunroom for a sing-along.

By Kate's side was Rolf Hart, one of my least favorite people. I'm fairly easygoing and try hard not to nurse grudges, but as in all things there were exceptions. Rolf's snarky rants against the military and those who served made an indelible, very negative impression on me. He was definitely an example of a pleasing book cover with inferior contents. There was nothing about Rolf's appearance to suggest the venal soul within. Tall, fit, blond and blue-eyed, he immediately registered on most women's radar. Initially, I even considered him attractive—until he opened his mouth. Real estate was Rolf's game, and despite his views, he apparently was very successful at it. According to him, he'd made his first million by age thirty and hadn't looked back since. Naturally, Babette had scoped him out, but quickly abandoned the hunt. As she later observed, people of means seldom bragged about it or even mentioned money. To do so was considered déclassé, a sign that Rolf was a social climber.

"Perri!" Kate beckoned to me from across the room. Gomer joined in greeting us by wagging his curly tail nonstop. Rolf's Borzoi, Portia, a lovely girl with class, manners, and a soft cream coat held her ground, staying friendly but aloof. She was the perfect counterpoint to her owner's brash ways and the only thing I gave him credit for. Even a hideous creature like Rolf might be redeemable through canine love. In view of his dog's name, I'd once asked him if he was a Shakespeare fan. To my surprise, he actually responded. Apparently, he had played Shylock in a college play and loved the experience. Against all odds, Rolf the Philistine was a season ticket holder who attended every presentation at Washington's Shakespeare Theater.

We four had been assigned the Falls as our Therapy Dog project. Babette and I were novices, but both Kate and the unlovely Rolf were the team's veterans. I had hoped for a school or library slot, but they were the plum posts that went to those with seniority. As with most endeavors, one had to wait patiently for any promotion.

"Wonder where the brass is," Kate muttered. "Gomer's raring to go."

Before Rolf could take charge, I offered to check things out. Helpfulness is my middle name, but I also relished the opportunity to thwart his macho need to dominate.

Babette followed me, pointing to a discreet sign that directed us toward an office complex. We stopped at the spot marked "Director, Dr. Fergueson," and knocked. Actually, Babette pounded on the door rather than knocked. The trappings of bureaucracy had exhausted her small store of patience. "Not the reception I expected," she huffed. "After all, we're doin' them a favor. What is this place anyway, a ghost town?"

I patted her arm to calm her down. Secretly, I hoped that some snafu would send us packing. Despite the thick carpeting and upscale décor, the Falls had a regimented feel that gave me the creeps. Perhaps it was the silence, overwhelming and almost oppressive, or the fear that I was confronting my own future. Fortunately, our dogs were not fanciful and showed no trepidation. All of them behaved with a dignity and decorum far superior to their human caretakers.

Eventually, a mountainous female wrenched open the door and stared us down. She wore a utilitarian white uniform and a frilly nurse's cap at variance with her no-nonsense manner. Her name tag read, "Carole Ross, RN."

"Yes?" Nurse Ross stared down at our dogs as if her eyes deceived her. For their part, all three canines went on alert, watching her through unwavering eyes.

Babette was either transfixed or ossified. Her bravado of a few seconds before had thoroughly deserted her, and she turned to me in mute appeal. I knew from experience that the way to deal with a bully was to confront her head-on. Nurse Ross might respond to that technique.

"We're here to see Dr. Fergueson," I said firmly but politely, dispensing with social niceties. "We have an appointment. Persephone Morgan and Babette Croy. You know, the Therapy Dog group."

I stand five feet, nine inches tall, but Nurse Ross topped me by at least four inches and fifty pounds. Babette had a mighty spirit but was vertically challenged. She angled away from the door and cowered behind me.

"Oh," grunted the nurse. "Wait here. I'll check."

The anteroom contained several soothing seascapes and a framed diploma certifying that Joan Fergueson had earned a doctorate in Philosophy from Westport University. The name of the institution was unfamiliar, but that was no surprise. With my humble, hard-won bachelor's degree, I was scarcely an expert on graduate education.

"She has some nerve," Babette whispered. "Do we look like kidnappers or somethin'?"

I refused to speculate. Soon enough, the private office door opened and an attractive, middle-aged woman emerged and ushered us inside. She wore a conservative gray business suit and no jewelry save a gold circle pin on her right lapel. Dark, lustrous hair was expertly fashioned into a sensible bob and tamed with a clip. Except for a trace of powder and a hint of lip gloss, her face was unadorned. The overall look was austere but not unpleasing.

"Ladies. Forgive me for not meeting you. I'm Joan Fergueson." She glanced down at our dogs and smiled. "They're lovely. So well mannered. Better than some of our residents, I'm sorry to say."

Babette had finally found her voice. "Where is everyone? Did we pick the wrong day?"

Dr. F. immediately switched into soothing mode. "Not at all. Today is Tuesday and many of our residents catch the bus into town. They shop for groceries, have lunch…you know. Fun stuff."

That made sense. It also came as a relief. These people weren't prisoners after all, and a day away with friends was an antidote to depression. Maybe life at the Falls wasn't so grim after all. I checked my watch. Unlike Babette, I had a business to run and bills to pay. "Charity begins at home" may be trite, but it resonated with me.

Dr. Fergueson sensed my impatience and reacted immediately. "I'm sure your time is valuable. Let's gather the rest of your group and I can answer any questions and discuss how we operate at the Falls. This Therapy Dog program is relatively new for us. Please grab a seat." She buzzed the restaurant and ordered tea. "Fortunately, our food service here is top-shelf. Most residents enjoy it, although they have the option of cooking their own meals."

Kate and Rolf nodded to Dr. F. and joined us around the conference table. When the tea service arrived, Babette's spirits surged. She spooned honey on her plate, bit into a scone, and sighed. "These are terrific! Homemade, I bet."

That pleased the administrator. "It's a specialty. Help yourself."

Unlike my pal, sweets have never tempted me. I can take them or leave them. Still, good manners dictated that I sample the offerings. I nibbled a scone and went back for more. No need to feign enthusiasm. They were delicious.

Joan Fergueson sat at her desk, tapping her computer screen. "Let's see." For a moment she frowned but quickly recovered. "Oh yes. Mrs. Croy has Irene Wilson. A lovely woman. Former teacher and dog breeder." She turned to Kate. "You've met your resident already. Clark Wingate, one of the few males at The Falls." She bit her lip as she faced Rolf Hart. "I'm sorry to tell you, but there's been a change to your assignment. Mrs. Whitman is no longer with us."

A moment of silence was shattered by Babette's question. "Did she leave just this place or the earth entirely?"

Dr. Fergueson winced. Apparently, she preferred to speak euphemistically about the recently departed. "I'm afraid she was quite elderly. Frail. A sad fact of life around here, but we try to celebrate each day."

Rolf shrugged, as if it was immaterial to him. "I wondered when I didn't hear from Sara. She was quite a character, you know. Stayed up on everything and everybody around here. I suppose you've assigned a new partner for me?"

Joan tapped the computer screen once more. "Mr. Jennings, a former developer. One of our younger residents. You'll have much in common."

I waited patiently for her to mention Magdalen Melmoth. Instead, she continued watching the screen and tapping those keys. Joan Fergueson was no ingénue, and her evasive manner puzzled me. After all, what was the big deal about one elderly resident? "We may have to switch your person, Ms. Morgan," she said with a saccharine smile. "Not to worry. Our residents signed up to participate and we have a long list."

"Really? I met Magdalen this morning and she was charming. My dogs liked her immediately. I'd love to work with her."

The good doctor hesitated, weighing the options before her. "Well, if you're sure. Ms. Melmoth can be difficult. Fanciful." She obviously wanted to say more, but discretion won out. That made me probe further.

"Oh? She seemed very lively to me. I took that as a good sign." I folded my arms, as if the issue was settled.

"It's nothing. Just don't believe everything she says about her lineage. Delusions of grandeur, you know. It's this genealogy craze they advertise. So many residents have signed up. Another way to feed illusions, I suspect." Fergueson's dismissive manner annoyed me. Everyone needed some fantasy life, even a pensioner. I could empathize with the need to connect, even if the results were somewhat suspect. Most folks hoped for bragging rights to noble antecedents, but no one welcomed a criminal or castoff swimming in the gene pool. Many families were blessed with both.

"I'm sure you're eager to get started," said Dr. F. "So, if you and Mrs. Croy have the paperwork ready, we'll be all set." I presented our bona fides and flashed what I hoped was an engaging smile her way. Somehow, winning this small battle in the bureaucratic wars pleased me immensely. Our dogs wore badges, proof that they had graduated from basic and intermediate obedience as well as earned their CGC, or Canine Good Citizen certificates. That assured officials that they had both good manners and temperament and had received the necessary insurance. After witnessing Nurse Ross's gruff manner, I wondered if she could meet the same standards.

Dr. Fergueson rose, indicating that our audience had ended. "Very well, then. I'll ask Nurse Ross to introduce you." Her handshake was stiff and unauthentic, but that was fine with me. No sense in lingering. Nurse Carole Ross lumbered into the office and tried herding us out the door at an unseemly pace. Powered by that scone sugar surge, Babette finally showed some spunk, holding her ground and strutting out in front of the pack. I patted Keats and Poe for reinforcement and meekly followed suit. Had I foreseen the danger awaiting us, I would have clutched them for support and galloped out the front door to safety. But because I lacked the gift of second sight, I dismissed Joan Fergueson's churlish behavior and forged ahead.

Our adventure at the Falls had finally begun.

Chapter 2

Babette bonded immediately with Irene Wilson over a shared love of books and dogs. She stepped into the cozy studio apartment, sized up the tasteful furnishings, and beamed at its occupant as if they were old friends. Clara sealed the deal by approaching Irene and licking her hand.

"That's a good sign. She's particular. Doesn't do that with everyone," Babette said. "Clara likes you."

Irene, a woman in her eighties, was a tall, imposing figure with light brown skin, neatly coiled gray hair, and large, expressive eyes. Her years in the classroom and stately bearing lent her an air of authority. She grinned at Babette and chuckled. "Kids and dogs—my specialty. For years I bred springer spaniels. Showed them too, even at Westminster. Shucks. Sometimes I had more luck with canines than my human pupils, but I loved them all. Still do."

I excused myself after explaining that I was seeking Magdalen Melmoth. A momentary frown flashed across Irene's face, but she quickly banished it.

"Be gentle with her. Mags is one of my best friends here. My only friend, actually. I don't want her to get hurt."

I was intrigued. "Anything else you can tell me?"

Babette had little patience for delay and tact was seldom her strong suit. "Come on, Irene. Spill. You can trust Perri. Don't worry."

Irene bit her lip as she framed her words. "We all have our illusions, even as we age—especially as we age. Just let her talk. Mags …she's a sweetheart. Not an ounce of harm in her."

"Good to know she has a friend like you. We've already met." I wagged my finger at them before heading out the door. "Behave, you two, or I'll report you to Nurse Ross."

* * * *

Magdalen Melmoth's flat was a one-bedroom directly down the hall from Irene's. She answered the door and immediately waved us in. To my surprise, her head bowed, as if she was too shy to make eye contact. "Oh, Perri. Ms. Morgan. I was afraid you weren't coming after meeting the powers that be. I made tea." She pointed to a beautifully embossed silver tea set. "Don't often get the chance to use this old relic. It's kind of like me. Put on the shelf. No use to anyone."

Keats and Poe eyed the goodies on the tray but settled into a sit-stay without complaint. Their good manners were a constant rebuke to me when I felt tempted to overreach. Breeding triumphed over baser impulses every time, and all three of us waited before diving in.

The interior of Magdalen's flat was art deco, surprisingly modern and tasteful but austere. Reminiscent of a monk's cell or a convent, it yielded few clues as to the identity of its occupant. The only exception was color: buttercup yellow walls and red lacquered woodwork. One side of the room contained a lovely chinoiserie bookcase filled with red leather-bound volumes.

"You look surprised," she said. "Not exactly what you expected, is it? You probably envisioned relics and family pieces."

I shrugged. "It's obvious you enjoy nice things. I'm fascinated by your library." I walked over and scanned the titles. Most were classics— Shakespeare, Austen, Tolstoy, and Wilde, although to my surprise, three contemporary books by a certain Wing Pruett were also present. I flushed and turned away, hoping Magdalen had missed my reaction. Unfortunately, she had not. I suspected there was very little in life my new friend missed.

She poured tea and passed the tray of sandwiches my way. "Forgive me, dear. That was my little joke. You see, I read about you and Mr. Pruett, and when you volunteered for this assignment, I couldn't believe my luck. Forgive me, won't you?" Before continuing, Magdalen unwrapped two meaty bones, placed each on a Limoges saucer, and shared them with my dogs. "Treats for everyone today," she said brightly. We sipped our tea in silence before my hostess continued. "Now, let me explain myself."

I didn't know what to expect. Why hadn't I heeded Joan Fergueson's warning and found a nice, uncomplicated animal lover with no agenda? Stubbornness and pride were the bane of my existence and always had been. Always would be.

Magdalen reached over and patted my arm. "Don't worry, dear, I'm not a lunatic. Not really. Just a determined woman. At my age, a woman on a mission is either feared or discounted."

I faked a smile. "No problem. Tell me more."

She dabbed daintily at her mouth and began. "How much do you know about Oscar Wilde? His life, not just his magnificent prose."

"Just the basics." I hesitated to mention the sensational legal action that had placed the great man in Reading Gaol. After all, Magdalen was a lady from another generation when such matters were not discussed.

She nibbled a smoked salmon sandwich and watched me closely. "Does genealogy interest you at all, Perri?"

I shook my head.

"You're still young. When you get to be my age, it's comforting to know your heritage." Magdalen chuckled. "After all, I might be meeting some of them fairly soon." She leaned over and stroked Poe's silky coat. "Funny, isn't it? Pedigree dogs like these fine specimens come to us with extensive family trees. Most humans don't."

Against my will, I began to question Magdalen's mental state. The conversation was bizarre as well as confusing, and I wasn't certain what she wanted from me.

"Where do I fit in?" I asked, "not to mention Wing Pruett." Pruett, an acclaimed investigative journalist and my romantic partner, inspired fantasies in many women. Magdalen was way beyond his usual demographic, but anything was possible. I had proof positive that Pruett's physical assets far exceeded anything DC scribes even hinted at. That memory made me smile.

Magdalen suddenly clenched her hands and rose to her feet. "Listen closely, Perri. I want you both to undertake a mission, one of historical significance. A quest of sorts."

The Therapy Dog guidelines never mentioned anything like this. I sought to placate Magdalen while I plotted a quick exit strategy. She was confused. Had to be. Buttonholing a complete stranger made no sense at all. Only the thought of Nurse Carole and Dr. Fergueson kept me glued to my seat. To ward off their sneers, I allotted Magdalen more time to spin her fantasy.

"What is it that you think we can do for you?" I asked.

Her sweet smile told me I had already lost the battle. "Bring him here. You see, I have a secret."

I visualized Pruett's reaction, and it wasn't pretty. When it came to business, he was hard-nosed and data-driven. "Don't be mysterious,

Magdalen. Give me more details." My tone was too harsh, and immediately, guilt welled up in me. After all, I was charged with comforting Magdalen, not confronting her. Suppose she cried or fainted? I would never survive being bounced from the Therapy Dog Program on my maiden voyage for brutalizing a resident.

Fortunately, she was made of sterner stuff. "Research is his specialty, right?" Magdalen was clearly enjoying herself. "Okay, then. Dig into the background of Oscar Wilde before you come back here. That should get your juices flowing."

I tried to hide my disbelief. "The famous writer?"

"Yes, dear. I believe he was my grandfather and left me a valuable legacy."

Gaping like the village idiot was unseemly, but I couldn't help it. "Legacy?"

Magdalen was thoroughly composed, unlike me. "Quite a coup for a hotshot author, don't you think? Mr. Pruett will get full access to everything I own. I'll sign any necessary legal documents."

Keats put his face in Magdalen's lap, looked up, and watched her with sad, soulful eyes. Poe edged closer to me.

"I don't know what to say, Ms. Melmoth."

Once again, her manner floored me. "Don't worry, dear. Tell Mr. Pruett that I have an original, unpublished manuscript written by my grandfather. That should pique his interest." Magdalen placidly sipped her tea as she watched me closely.

"I don't understand."

"Don't worry. You soon will. My health is fine, but after all, I'm no spring chicken. Someone trustworthy. That's what I need. Before it's too late."

I rose slowly, uncertain of what to do. For some reason I fumbled in my bag for a business card and handed it to Magdalen. "You can contact me in case your schedule changes or something."

"Thank you, dear. Nicely done. That's important for a businessperson, especially a woman." Magdalen placed it in a lovely bronze box with elaborate engraving on it. "Perhaps we could meet here next week," she said. "That will give you time to do some research. I understand Mr. Pruett is very thorough." Magdalen smiled, as if she was sharing a secret joke. "Time, you know, makes slaves of us all. No need to prolong things. As the Bard said, 'Delays have dangerous ends.'"

Chapter 3

"Sounds like she's nuts," Babette said. "Maybe ole starchy drawers Fergueson was right about Magdalen after all. Too bad. I really liked her. Magdalen, I mean, not the dragon lady."

Buoyed by the success of our dogs and their program, we left the Falls in high spirits. A round of musical chairs, tricks, and meet and greets received a warm welcome from the residents. Once again, I was awed by the power of the canine-human connection. Outwardly timid ladies hugged and kissed our dogs with a zeal they never would have shown to strangers. A few reminisced about beloved dogs and cats that had shared their own lives. In the face of that reaction, my prior reluctance to participate felt petty and mean-spirited. I was now a true believer. Even the songs Kate had shared with the group gave me a warm, family feeling that, as an orphan, I had missed out on.

Babette and I sat in my living room, sipping cider and awaiting the arrival of Wing Pruett. I'd phoned and sketched out the basics for him, and to my surprise, he was intrigued enough to change his plans and pop on over. That inspired Babette to order pizzas from her favorite gourmet spot and brew barn burners, a lethal mixture of cider, brandy, and whiskey that tasted harmless and kicked like an entire mule team.

"How are things going between you two?" Babette asked. When it came to romances, particularly mine, no area was out of bounds for my pal. Privacy was an overrated barrier in Croyland. She ignored my frown and plunged in immediately. "Any hint of wedding bells? I'll need to make arrangements, you know. Give me plenty of notice."

I chose to ignore my ill-mannered but well-intentioned pal. "Things are fine between us. Don't you dare mention wedding bells when he gets here. He'll think I put you up to it." Actually, that topic was verboten in my household. I'm a self-sufficient, single woman, thirty-two years of age, with eyes firmly fixed on my future. Whether that future included a certain investigative hottie and his darling daughter remained an open question, one that I was reluctant to broach. Three years ago, when my fiancé, Dr. Pip Hahn, succumbed to cancer, I banished all thoughts of romance. The pain of that loss still haunted me, and the wound was remarkably raw. No sense in mentioning it to Babette, the ultimate pragmatist. Her response—which she frequently voiced—was simple: get over it. Pip's gone, so live your life. What she couldn't or wouldn't understand was my refusal to obliterate him from my heart. His memory sustained me and kept Wing Pruett's less-desirable habits at bay. It was a complicated and occasionally painful dilemma.

"Phooey," Babette said. "That man adores you. He's obsessed with you. Trust me on that. I can tell. All he needs is a little push." Her smug smile raised all sorts of danger signs.

"Back off," I said as forcefully as I could. "Focus on your own love life for a change. Last time I looked you were still single." It was a low blow, but an effective one. Since her divorce from the perfidious Carleton Croy, Babette had lived the single life. It was not to her liking. Carleton, Babette's husband number four, was no prize package, but she frequently bemoaned the loss of marital benefits and his abundant physical assets. Whenever she launched a paean to his manly parts, I used every trick in the book to block it out. Selective memory was a tricky thing. From her three elderly spouses, Babette had derived material comfort and big bucks. She was fond of saying that they died smiling all the way to eternity. Not so with Carleton, a faithless wretch who shared his splendor with most of her friends, berated her, and had no money at all.

"I know you mean well," I said, "but Pruett and I understand each other. Don't push it. You'll spoil everything."

Tenacity was one of Babette's strengths and she didn't yield easily. Fortunately, an unearthly screech from the barn distracted her and announced our visitor's arrival. Zeke, an irascible pygmy goat, had very few virtues, but he rivaled a particularly piercing air raid siren as a noise alert. I always suspected that his vigilance had more to do with sheer selfishness than any protective instinct, but it served a useful purpose. Zeke was another rescue project who had absolutely no allegiance to me. Fortunately, since adding Raza, an Arabian mare, to my little brood, Zeke's boorish behavior had improved. Maybe loneliness had caused his antics and exasperating refusal to act civilized. It was a reason, but not an excuse. Luckily for that shaggy pygmy, I overlooked his misdeeds in Pip's honor. Like it or not, Zeke was mine for the duration.

After a perfunctory rap on the door, Wing Pruett bounded into my home. No doubt about it, he had an aura that intimidated men and captivated any sentient female within a fifty-mile radius. It wasn't just his physical presence, although that was considerable. Not many men possessed the body beautiful, perfectly molded features, and mounds of thick black hair, especially in our nation's capital, where power, not sex appeal, was the ultimate aphrodisiac. Some wag had termed Washington, DC, "Hollywood for ugly people," but a man like Wing Pruett could hold his own any place in any crowd. Why else would the *Washingtonian* dub him the sexiest man in Washington? As soon as I saw him, I deliberately powered down to neutral. Truth was tricky, my feelings for Wing Pruett complicated. When he said that he loved me, I wanted desperately to believe him, but common sense dictated that such a sultry superstar would probably move on to greener pastures someday. No need obsessing about that. Long ago I'd resolved to live in the moment and enjoy every second of his company. I maintained a cool, slightly bemused façade when our eyes locked. No sense in feeding that aura of entitlement that immersed Pruett.

"Hey, ladies." Pruett neatly evaded my dogs, planted a kiss on my cheek, and squeezed Babette's hand. He was a work in progress when it came to animals, but with my help and the able assistance of his daughter Ella, Pruett had made great strides. You've got to love a man who acknowledged and conquered his worst fears.

"I come bearing gifts. Got dessert for you," he said, presenting a neatly wrapped box of treats from Georgetown Cupcakes. Immediately, Babette's eyes widened. Sweets placed second only to sex in her personal pantheon. In view of her previous escapades it made sense to me. Sugar was much more accessible and less problematic than many of her romantic partners. Cupcakes never cheated on her, demanded alimony payments, or required a prenup. My pal swore that although the ecstasy of a sugar high was short-lived, it was well worth the glucose slump that followed. With Pruett around, I preferred to save the calories and go for the real thing.

Babette immediately leaped up to play hostess. It was an automatic reflex even when she was in someone else's home. "How about a barn burner, Wing? They're my specialty, you know."

Pruett slid next to me on the couch, close enough for our arms to touch. I tried to forestall a full body flush by sipping cider, but it didn't work. He pretended not to notice, although I was positive he had.

"Sounds great," he said. "I'll just help Ms. Perri relax a bit." His fingers nimbly unfastened the pins in my hair, causing it to cascade down my back. "Much better," he murmured. "Your crowning glory unleashed."

Who could argue with a move like that? My hair was the one point of vanity I allowed myself. His touch didn't transform me from a stodgy professional to a wanton woman, but I relished the contact. Somehow that relatively innocent act elevated my senses more than anything else he could manage in public view. I caught the satisfied glint in Babette's eyes and looked away. Knowing her, she was already planning our honeymoon itinerary.

Before getting down to business, we spent a few moments in companionable silence sipping our barn burners. I had to admit that the potent liquid warmed the cockles of my heart and several other spaces too personal to mention. Finally, Pruett put down his mug and retrieved his notebook. Even in the age of electronic gadgets, he preferred to go old-school when pursuing a story.

"Okay," he said. "Give me your take on Magdalen Melmoth. Delusional or merely complex?"

I hesitated, but Babette plunged right into the fray. "My lady, Irene Wilson, vouches for her. They're best friends and Magdalen confides in her. She didn't know the specifics of this manuscript business, but she said it was something big."

Pruett donned his mask of inscrutability as he listened. That was de rigueur for him during interviews. I'd also used that technique during my military days because people often searched for facial clues and tailored their account to suit perceived biases. Wing Pruett's face was impossible to read. After Babette finished, he made notes and turned my way.

"Tell me everything Magdalen said, verbatim if you can. We'll discuss impressions afterward."

There wasn't much to tell. I repeated Magdalen's story, particularly her advice to research Oscar Wilde before our next meeting, and the sense I got that she might be in peril.

"She didn't say that outright. Just spoke of the urgency of time."

"She's fairly old, isn't she?" Pruett asked. "Maybe she was just being practical."

Babette refilled her mug and edged into the conversation. "Hell, Wing, they're all in that eternal waiting room. Every one of them." She snapped her fingers. "Magdalen could pop off just like that and no one would be the wiser."

I couldn't dispute her logic, but some inner voice told me there was more to it. Much more. "Let's assume Magdalen told the truth," I said. "An unpublished manuscript by Oscar Wilde would be worth millions. Just think of it. People have killed for far less."

Pruett looked up. "I managed to do some research on this, and it was quite enlightening."

"Wow," Babette said. "That was quick. I'm surprised you had the time."

His lips twitched in a semi-smile. That in itself was a dead giveaway. Pruett typically delegated research chores to one of the many eager interns who swarmed his office. They tended to be young, J-school graduates with stars in their eyes. The overwhelmingly female gaggle also boasted good looks and an unsettling hero worship of one Wing Pruett.

"What did you find?" I said. "The suspense is killing us."

He bent over his briefcase, playing for time. After retrieving his glasses, Pruett tapped the screen of his iPad and shared the news.

"Okay. Bear in mind that all this is purely speculative. Oscar Wilde died young, as you know. Only forty-six." He shook his head. "What a waste. Anyway, he did marry at least once and produced several offspring, but there's a catch."

Babette clutched Clara's collar so tightly the poor dog yelped. "Come on," Babette said. "Spit it out. We're dying here."

Pruett and I locked eyes. I knew what he was going to say because I too had done some research. Any reasonably intelligent being with a computer could gather rudimentary information on an historical figure. Wilde's fame had grown in the past few years as new generations learned to appreciate his genius and old taboos were discarded.

Pruett adjusted his glasses. "First the bad news. No record of Oscar Wilde having any progeny outside of marriage. It's surprising that he had any at all. As you probably know, he wasn't inclined that way."

Babette leaped up. "You mean she lied? All that hooey about being his granddaughter was a lie?"

Pruett held up his hand. "There was something else. Something that requires more investigation. In his last years in France, Wilde used the pseudonym Sebastian Melmoth on occasion."

My pal's mouth dropped. The optics weren't flattering; she bore an uncanny resemblance to a gaffed fish hanging on the docks. "Don't assume anything from that," Pruett said. "Again, I repeat, there was no mention of any other offspring."

Words of caution failed to dampen Babette's spirits. Now that she had a ray of hope, she plunged headlong into the breach while I considered the pros and cons of the issue. Magdalen probably was misguided. That was far kinder than the other terms—delusional, senile, or lying. Still... Wilde's passions swayed with the wind, especially during his final years. He even pursued religious conversion, which might argue for a return to a more conventional relationship with a woman. Suppose he produced a child along with an undiscovered manuscript? Stranger things have happened.

"Where do we go from here?" Babette asked. "I can't face those ladies if we don't do something. Anything."

They both looked my way, waiting for me to weigh in. After all, Magdalen Melmoth was my project. Mine and my dogs'. I refused to abandon or dismiss her without listening to the rest of her story. Pruett might beg off, but I would not.

"We're scheduled to go back next week." I turned toward Pruett. "Will you join us?"

The gleam in his eyes said it all. "Just try to keep me away."

Chapter 4

I spent the balance of the week working hard, filling orders for customers and toying with some new designs. My mother-daughter belts were big sellers at the various dog and horse shows and were even stocked in a number of high-end boutiques. Booming sales were a balm to my soul, but I couldn't dispel my anxiety over Magdalen Melmoth. I simply couldn't. Research only heightened my concern. The Internet teemed with sites dedicated to Oscar Wilde, but none of them hinted at any Melmoth offspring or rumors of undiscovered manuscripts. I chuckled every time I recalled one of Wilde's bon mots: *Be yourself. Everyone else is already taken.* Had my new friend decided to claim her heritage, or was she merely living a dream?

Pruett joined me that next Wednesday on our trek to the Falls. He insisted on driving his Porsche Macan, even though it was a tight fit with two large dogs stuffed into the back seat. I didn't even try to resist. Better to fire up his luxury SUV for that journey than my Suburban. That old soldier had crossed the 200,000-mile mark some time ago, and I dreaded the expense and bother of ever replacing it. Pruett, on the other hand, tired of his vehicles after a year or two and automatically discarded them. It was probably a cautionary tale for other aspects of his personal life as well. I knew for a fact that he never remained in a relationship longer than two years, so my option would soon be up for renewal.

"You look nifty, Persephone." He twirled me around, admiring my choice of garb. I am certainly no fashion plate, but on occasion I can up my game. A cashmere twinset, new jeans, and freshly polished boots were my idea of haute couture. Not exactly *Vogue*, but apparently, he approved. Pruett had a keen sense of fashion. He wore a handsome tweed blazer, a white turtleneck, and khaki cords that raised all manner of licentious thoughts in my mind. With sublime effort I restrained myself from losing control and jumping his bones.

"I did a bit more digging," he said. "Spoke to a professor at GW who specializes in Wilde. Wrote a book about him too."

"What did she say?"

He neatly evaded the trap and tweaked my chin in the bargain. "Just so happens this professor is male, Ms. Smarty-Pants. Bruce Douglas, professor of English literature at George Washington University. We were roommates at Johns Hopkins a hundred years ago."

Pruett enjoyed flaunting his age and superior wisdom. In actuality, he was only thirty-six, four years my senior, and as for wisdom—I could match him every time with life experience.

"So, what did your old roomie have to say?" I asked.

"I had to be cagey," Pruett said. "Couldn't let him get on the scent or we'd have a howling mob of academics storming the old age home."

I nodded, awaiting the bombshell I knew was coming.

"Okay, the Goose said...

"Goose?"

"Goosey Brucey—his nickname. Anyway, he said that, if verified, an undiscovered manuscript by Oscar Wilde would fetch seven figures at least, especially if it was a novel."

That made sense. Wilde was a prolific writer of poems, essays, and plays, but he had produced only one novel, *The Picture of Dorian Gray.* Any addition to that legacy would ignite the literary world. I tried to tamp down the excitement building within me. After all, the musings of an elderly lady might be no more than wishful thinking. My task was to join Poe and Keats in supporting Magdalen. Therapy Dog guidelines specified that spreading comfort and joy was our primary objective. I resolved to do just that.

"Earth to Perri. Wake up!" Pruett gently nudged me as we neared the gates of the Falls. "Dreaming about me, were you?"

I lowered my sunglasses and stared at him. "Not likely. Why dream when you're sitting right next to me?"

Pruett shook his head and chuckled. "Always one up on me, aren't you? You keep me on my toes." He pulled into a visitors' spot and scanned the area. I could tell that, like me, he was pleasantly surprised. On the surface, the Falls was everything an upscale housing complex should be.

"Not bad," he said. "I expected something from "The Fall of the House of Usher," or *Bleak House.*"

"Feeling literary, are you? I adore Poe, gloomy as he was, but Charles Dickens bores me silly. Very overrated in my opinion. Right down there with Melville and Thomas Hardy."

Pruett stared at me for a moment before responding. "You are really something, Ms. Perri. So very practical and self-sufficient, but amazingly well versed in the classics. Wow!"

How typical of him to assume that only an Ivy League graduate could be erudite. Pruett was an alumnus of Columbia's graduate program while I scraped and saved to make it through state universities. That didn't make me a second-class citizen or automatically make him a scholar. I was saved from embarrassment by the timely arrival of Babette and Clara.

"Hey, you two," my pal sang out. "No hanky-panky in front of the old folks."

Pruett sprang out of his Porsche and opened the back hatch for my dogs. "Wouldn't think of it, ma'am. Best behavior."

I assumed we needed some special permission to bring in a guest, but when that guest was famous the rules apparently didn't apply. Nurse Carole Ross was absent, but we were immediately greeted by Dr. Fergueson and a distinguished-looking man wearing a stethoscope whose name plate read "Jethro Tully, MD."

"What a treat," the administrator said, extending her hand. "You are Wing Pruett, are you not?"

"Guilty," Pruett said.

Dr. Tully moved closer and stood toe to toe with Pruett. They were similar in size, age, and build, although the good doctor wore his light brown hair in an almost military cut. His features were regular with the exception of slightly protuberant green eyes. The overall affect was not unpleasant.

"Not doing an exposé, I hope," he said. His manner was jocular but guarded.

Pruett did his innocent act. "Absolutely not. My fiancée invited me to watch therapy dogs in action and I couldn't resist."

I heard Babette gasp and felt myself flush. Fiancée indeed! Why delude myself—it meant nothing. Pruett used any tactic necessary when he was on the scent of a story. He'd thrown me under the bus before, so this was nothing new.

Meanwhile, Babette sidled up to Dr. Tully and gave him the big-eyed look. "Are you here all the time, Doctor?" She had a particular fascination for medical men, although in a pinch any presentable male was fair game.

Tully smiled down at her. "My specialty is gerontology, so I'm sort of the go-to doctor here."

"Ooh. Lucky patients." Babette had once been a cheerleader and still incorporated some of those moves into her everyday life. Thankfully, she no longer used pom-poms, although it wouldn't have surprised me if they reappeared. Age was no barrier to Babette's romantic adventures. She looked far younger than her years and maintained a strict regimen of facials, diet, and exercise to stay that way.

Jethro Tully lowered his voice when several of the residents appeared. Each of the ladies waved at him, some behaving more coquettishly than others. He favored them with a rakish grin in return. "I understand you'll be visiting Magdalen Melmoth today," he said.

I decided to play innocent. "Yes. Such a lovely woman."

Tully exchanged glances with Joan Fergueson but merely nodded. "Just so. Like many of our guests, she sometimes retreats into fantasy. Part of the aging process, I assure you. Nothing to get alarmed about."

"Anything in particular we should watch out for?" Pruett stayed low-key. "I suppose a bit of fantasy is useful for all of us, don't you think? Otherwise how would we make it through the dreary days."

Dr. Ferguson nodded. "We're quite accustomed to that at the Falls. Some years ago, a resident swore she was the daughter of Czar Nicholas. Insisted on calling herself Anastasia, if you can believe it. We humored her, of course."

"Harmless fantasies for the most part." Jethro Tully bent down and patted my dogs. "Beautiful. I understand they served in Afghanistan."

"Perri always says they're smarter than most humans," Babette said. "I believe it. Of course, my Clara is no slouch either."

As we chatted, Pruett's eyes wandered. He scanned the reception area, missing nothing at all. When several of the residents asked to pet our dogs, he gallantly stepped aside and introduced our canine caravan. Frankly, I believed that the more audacious ladies in question were more interested in mauling Wing Pruett than learning about the therapy dog program. They hooked arms with my guy and soon guided him to one of the sofas, amid a flurry of dimpled smiles and eyelash batting.

"I'll join you later," Pruett told me. "These ladies have captured me."

Babette and I exchanged looks and headed for the elevators, where we joined Kate Thayer and Rolf Hart. Doctors Fergueson and Tully shrugged, excused themselves, and exited the building.

"What's he up to?" Babette asked in a stage whisper, pointing to Pruett.

I pressed the second-floor button and yawned. "No telling."

Rolf gave me one of his semi-smiles. "Well, Perri. I had no idea you were friends with a celebrity. I recognized Wing Pruett immediately. Quite the catch."

I recognized the subtext of his comment: What does a guy like Pruett see in a nobody like Perri Morgan? No surprise. I'd often asked myself that same question.

Kate intervened quickly. "Who wouldn't recognize him? He's even better looking in person! Wow. Lucky you, Perri."

"What's he doing here?" Rolf asked. "Not much material for an investigative hotshot at the Falls."

This time Babette was prepared. I knew by the gleam in her eye that she was locked and loaded. "Are you kidding? That man is crazy about Perri. Follows her everywhere she goes. It's almost embarrassin'."

Rolf harrumphed and said no more, but Kate winked at me.

We parted in the hallway, when Babette headed toward Irene Wilson's studio. I moved slowly as I approached Magdalen's apartment, unable to shake a feeling of impending doom. Keats and Poe stayed close to my side, faithful sentries and protectors.

Magdalen answered the doorbell immediately, looking pert and quite exuberant. Her smile never wavered as she scanned the hallway for any other visitors. "Welcome, Persephone," she said, "and of course my doggy dears as well. I have tea ready."

I quickly explained that Pruett would be joining us once he disengaged from his claque of groupies. Magdalen chuckled and whisked me into her parlor. "I'm not surprised. Elaine and her reading group somehow got wind of Mr. Pruett's visit. They're terrible flirts, but I can't really blame them. We don't often see handsome men here. Actually, men of any type are fairly scarce."

I envisioned Babette in thirty years still scoping out presentable male visitors regardless of age. No judgments. It made sense. We chatted about inconsequential things, awaiting the arrival of the guest of honor. I was curious about her assessment of Dr. Jethro Tully and his role at the Falls.

Initially, she hesitated. "I want to be fair. He's very professional. Impersonal but not unfriendly. Apparently knows his stuff too. I looked him up on the Internet. Googled him."

I sensed a mile-wide caveat. Magdalen's generation was raised to revere physicians and speak no evil or anything even mildly critical. She bit her lip and finally stammered a reply.

"It's nothing concrete. He's always been perfectly civil, but I just don't trust him. My mother had two terms for a man like Dr. Tully: smarmy and oleaginous." Magdalen chuckled. "They mean much the same thing, but I love the expressions. Unfortunately, people today tend to use so few of the words in our vast language. He just acts so entitled. So much swagger. I guess that's it. Insists on special bottled water from Italy and imported espresso. You know the type, Perri. Underneath the charm I sense something else. He patronizes the residents." Magdalen curled her lip. "We may be old, but most of us still have our wits about us."

I wanted to probe for specifics, but at that moment, Pruett knocked on her door and was ushered into the room with great ceremony. Magdalen took his hands, looked him up and down, and nodded her approval. "Well, Mr. Pruett. I see that for once the press buildup was totally justified."

This was nothing new for Wing Pruett, but to my surprise, he flushed. "You've been on my mind, Ms. Melmoth, ever since Perri told me about you. I'm fascinated by your story."

Magdalen motioned us toward the dining table, poured tea, and shared a plate of sandwiches and lemon tarts. "Eat, please. I know that men need sustenance, and a hearty appetite is a compliment to the hostess. As for my heritage, you must think I'm senile, Mr. Pruett. The doctor called it 'fanciful,' as if the meaning was all that different." She stared at both of us, eyes blazing. "He's wrong. It happens to be true. All of it. I am the granddaughter of Oscar Wilde and I can prove it."

Chapter 5

No one spoke for a moment. As tension built, the silence was deafening. It took the soothing presence of Keats and Poe to break the logjam and restore order. Poe sidled up to Magdalen and placed his paw on her knee. That freed her to bend down and hug him. As she stroked his shiny coat, Magdalen Melmoth told her story.

"My parents never said much about our heritage. Father died during the Second World War, like so many other fine young men. My mother was hesitant to tell me much about his family. I grew up surrounded by a large, boisterous Irish group, my mother's family, the Kingsburys. It was a comfortable life, filled with fun, horses, and every type of pet." She paused, as if recalling those halcyon days. "Why, I did all the things a farm child enjoys—even operated machinery and bailed hay. I was quite a tomboy in those days."

That gave Pruett the opening he sought. "No one mentioned Oscar Wilde or hinted at your connections?"

She shook her head. "Only on her deathbed did my mother speak of Sebastian Melmoth, my grandfather. That was the name she used. Never the other one. It simply wasn't done in those days, you see, particularly when something scandalous was involved."

Pruett leaned forward, his shoulders tense as he surreptitiously took notes. He knew that by letting Magdalen tell her story her way, he would ultimately get the information he needed. Patience was a virtue he often lacked, except in pursuit of his professional goals. "Perhaps your first name was a clue. If I'm not mistaken, a beautiful poem called 'Magdalen Walks' was one of Wilde's big successes."

Her cheeks turned a delicate shade of pink. "How perceptive of you, Mr. Pruett. Of course, that poem was about Magdalen College, Oxford, but still..."

"What was your father's name?" I asked, praying that this family saga wouldn't go on forever.

"Fingal. A common family name in Ireland, I understand, although not here. We immigrated to America when my mother remarried. Mama always caught the eye of the men around her, you see. Declan Farraday was a good man, quite a prosperous builder in his day. He offered to adopt me, but Mother refused. She said it would be tantamount to renouncing my father." Magdalen shook her head. "We simply couldn't do that."

Pruett was growing restless. I knew his moods and could read him perfectly. To his credit, he gritted his teeth, turned up the charm machine, and stayed the course. "What did your mother tell you? Did she offer any proof or documents?"

Magdalen's gentle smile reproved him. "Of course not. Mother said that my grandfather was a noted literary genius whose reputation had been tarnished in England." Magdalen's cheeks colored again. "Naturally she never specified what caused his downfall. In her day it simply wasn't done. 'The love that dare not speak its name'—that was the closest she came. Of course, later as I read more about him, I understood."

Pruett furrowed his brow. "What about your father? Any diaries or letters about his parents?"

Once again Magdalen chuckled. "None that I know of. Just oral tradition. My father was a brilliant man. He took two firsts at Oxford. I recall Mother said that he followed in his father's footsteps. Sebastian Fingal Melmoth was his full name."

I tried not to sigh. Memories were therapeutic, but essentially unhelpful. They got us no closer to Oscar Wilde and the manuscript.

Pruett's manner was gentle but firm. He held Magdalen's hand and looked directly into her eyes. "Tell us about the manuscript. It's important, Magdalen."

There was something refreshingly girlish in her manner, a throwback from another more modest age. A photo on her mantel showed teenaged Magdalen clad in jodhpurs and formal riding regalia holding a palomino's bridle. Wow! She was quite a stunner in her youth. Made me wonder why Magdalen had remained single.

"I've never actually seen it," Magdalen admitted, "not the entire manuscript at least. But I've read fragments. and Mother said it was the best thing my grandpa ever wrote."

Pruett gritted his teeth. His frustration was understandable because he was a gung ho, carpe diem kind of gonzo journalist. I decided that strategic intervention was in order to save the day.

"Oscar Wilde only wrote one novel. Is this a novel, Magdalen? If so that's big news."

Once again, she hesitated. The silence was broken by a rap on the door and the entrance of Babette and Clara. After preliminary small talk, Babette cut to the chase. "What did I miss? Tell me everything about that manuscript, Magdalen. I barely slept last night just thinkin' of it."

Magdalen fluttered and flushed, but after taking a mighty sip of tea, she continued her story. "To answer your question, Persephone, the work is a novel. The title sounds somewhat odd, but then, by all accounts, my grandfather was known as an eccentric."

Talk about your understatements of the year. If indeed Magdalen's grandpa was the celebrity in question, he was called many things of which "eccentric" might have been the kindest. Oscar Wilde's brilliance stretched to so many areas that some considered him a dilettante. I called him a genius. I checked my watch. Our session was scheduled to end soon, followed by a general seminar for all residents involved in the Therapy Dog program. I bit my lip in frustration, but once again Babette rode to the rescue.

"What's the title, Magdalen? You must know that much at least. You're killing us here." Babette framed her question with a sweet smile that tempered her pointed words.

Magdalen tilted her head toward the ceiling. "Oh yes, dear. Forgive an old lady for woolgathering. You mentioned *Dorian Gray*, Perri. Well, Sebastian Melmoth used a character in that novel for his final work. He called it *Sybil Vane.*"

Babette leaned forward. "I don't get it. Why is that such a big deal?"

Pruett smiled. "As I recall, Sybil was the young actress who almost saved Dorian Gray. Right, Ms. Magdalen?"

She clapped her hands in delight. "How perceptive you are. That's absolutely true. After the dogs perform, I'll explain how to find it. I'm counting on you—all of you—to preserve my grandfather's legacy." Magdalen reached into her pocket and pulled out an antique gold pocket watch. "I see that our time here is up. Persephone, if you will do the honors." She reached into the drawer of her escritoire and withdrew a manila envelope. "Keep this safe until we get back here."

* * * *

The house was packed for our presentation, although the stars of the show were canine, not human. Keats, Poe, and Clara, joined by Gomer and Portia, gave a formal demonstration that included several dance routines and a formal explanation of the Therapy Dog program. Several familiar faces surfaced in the crowd, including Doctors Fergueson and Tully. Nurse Carole Ross stood guard at the back of the room wearing the grim visage of a prison matron. I wasn't intimidated, but I confess she puzzled me. Her manner was at variance with the genial, relaxed attitude of the rest of the staff and residents. It was hardly conducive to a homey atmosphere. The audience was overwhelmingly female, a reflection of the longevity of women over men. Perhaps that explained why Wing Pruett garnered the attention of virtually everyone in the audience. He was ensconced on a sofa between two ladies of a certain age who shamelessly doted on him. Magdalen and her pal Irene Wilson snagged a front row seat. They slyly waved at us as we finished our performance and clapped for our dogs. We were expected to mingle with the residents afterward and allow them to greet our pets. Although the results were gratifying, the program took far longer than I'd anticipated. Of course, my mind was preoccupied by thoughts of that manila envelope and dreams of a literary bombshell. I couldn't really gauge how much time had elapsed and suspected Pruett felt the same way.

Kate Thayer shooed Gomer away from some low-hanging treats and sighed. "I have to duck out early today. That old jalopy of mine broke down again and every time the mechanic gives me a progress report I almost faint."

"For crying out loud, Kate, get a reliable vehicle. It's not safe." Rolf sniffed as he adjusted Portia's collar. "Ride back with me and I'll loan you one of mine."

It was a kind gesture and yet...I couldn't help thinking it was but another self-aggrandizing move by Rolf. The man's enormous ego was constantly on display. Don't get me wrong. I admired initiative, but most of the truly successful people I knew didn't tout their accomplishments. No one ever suggested that educators, particularly retired ones, could afford expensive cars. Most chose the same route Kate had—nurse the old one as long as possible. I understood that all too well. Fortunately, despite a few dings and dents, my aged Suburban was battered but unbowed. Even the thought of buying a replacement made me blanch.

A faint blush rose on Kate's cheeks. His allusion to her finances had obviously embarrassed her. "Thanks, Rolf, but I'll manage. That old Jeep seems like part of the family by now. Kind of an elderly uncle who is still lovable despite his quirks."

Rolf snorted. "Don't let pride be your downfall, Kate. As it is, you pay a boatload of property taxes in DC. Must be hard to manage on a teacher's pension. My portfolio takes a hit every time the assessor waves his pen." He consulted his watch, an outsize gold Rolex, and grasped Portia's lead. "I've got to meet an important client this afternoon," he said. "Finally have a chance to wrap up that land deal in Shenandoah County if the old codgers who own it don't get sentimental. Let's leave as soon as we can."

By the time the social hour concluded Magdalen had vanished. Irene Wilson told us not to worry. Magdalen was fatigued and had slipped away to take a nap. She asked that we call her later on that evening. Pruett was miffed, I was disappointed, and Babette was livid.

"We came all the way out here to see her," she fumed. "Naptime just doesn't cut it. I don't care how old she is either."

Irene made excuses for her friend and dithered about it to the point of tears. "Mags has been under such stress lately," she said, "and then there were all those peculiar goings-on. They really spooked her."

Pruett immediately sensed a story. "Peculiar?" he asked with his most winsome smile. "Come on. Give us a hint."

Irene looked around and lowered her voice. "First there was a mix-up with her heart pills. Mags noticed that they were a different color and kicked up quite a fuss."

"Understandable," Pruett said. "I'd react the same way. Probably an error by the nursing staff, I bet."

Irene beamed at him. "Exactly, Mr. Pruett. Nurse Ross got quite testy about it, and Dr. Tully had to calm everyone down. One of the residents passed recently, you know, and that leaves all of us a bit shaky. Sara Whitman was only in her early seventies and livelier than most." She lowered her eyes as if hesitant to continue.

Pruett put his arm on her shoulder. "Pardon me for saying this, but death can't be a stranger at the Falls. What made this so unusual?"

Irene raised her head, as if she'd had a renewal of energy. "We're realists here, Mr. Pruett. At least most of us are. But Sara just completed a full physical. Top to bottom. No problems. She wasn't happy here and planned to leave. Come to think of it, she was thick as thieves with that real estate man. You know, the one with the borzoi. I think he egged her on."

Both Babette and I spoke as one. "Rolf Hart?"

Irene nodded. "There was a bit of a bother about that, and Nurse Ross gave Sara what for. Said she didn't appreciate anything and didn't deserve to live here."

"Anything else?" Pruett asked. "Don't be shy, now. Not if you want to help Magdalen."

Irene dithered again but finally relented. "Mags and Sara weren't friendly."

That could mean virtually anything. Who would expect everyone living in close quarters to bond? I certainly didn't. If properly channeled, some level of conflict was probably even healthy. Magdalen was a feisty woman who refused to hold back her opinions. Sounded like Sara Whitman was the same.

"They got into it, did they?" Babette wasted no time in clarifying things.

Irene gave a half-hearted grin. "Threats flew and I thought for a moment that things might get physical. Sara liked to snoop, you see. Magdalen accused her of prowling around in her things. Papers and the like. We're all sensitive about privacy around here, as you can imagine. Sara denied touching anything, but Mags didn't believe her, and it's true that someone had been riffling through her belongings."

"What kind of threats were made, Irene?" I felt like covering my ears in a hear no evil pose.

"Just the usual." Irene brightened. "Like on television. All the police shows have someone threatening to kill someone else."

Babette yawned. "Big deal. I say that at least once a week, especially about my spineless ex-husband." Her lip curled as she recalled Carleton Croy.

"Then there was the prowler. At least Mags thought that was what he was. She caught someone jiggling the door handle in her room and screamed bloody murder."

Alarm bells were clanging in my mind. Either Magdalen was delusional or she was quite right to be concerned about her safety. Prowlers, pills, and premature deaths didn't bode well for anyone, let alone a vulnerable elderly spinster.

"I bet it's part of this manuscript stuff," Babette said, turning to Irene. "How many people know about it?"

For a moment, Irene hesitated. "Manuscript?"

Delicacy was never my pal's strong suit. "Don't be coy," she said. "You're her best friend after all. I tell Perri everything and I'll bet you share too."

Irene nodded. "Mags did mention something, but frankly I thought she might be …"

"Lying?" Babette said.

"Oh no! Nothing like that. Exaggerating maybe. Life here is pretty dull, you know." Irene bit her lip and once again appeared close to tears.

I prized loyalty in my friends and empathized with her dilemma. "Tell you what," I said. "We'll call Magdalen later and make sure she's okay." Babette grunted and Pruett gave Irene a little hug that elevated her spirits much more than anything I could offer. We exchanged pleasantries and took our leave. I clutched the manila envelope as tightly if it were a living thing, positive that the contents would go a long way toward unlocking the key to Sebastian Melmoth's literary legacy. If it existed, that is.

The suspense was prolonged by Pruett's insistence that we stop for dinner at his favorite French bistro in Leesburg. Babette concurred. She seldom refused a chance to chow down à la française, particularly when a man was footing the bill. Over an exquisite meal of crepes, we shared our hopes and reservations about this latest quest. Most of our discussion centered around mysterious Magdalen Melmoth. Pruett had mixed feelings, Babette termed her a kook, and I was undecided. Until we scrutinized the contents of that envelope, speculation was counterproductive and useless. I planned to give my new friend the benefit of the doubt.

After reaching Great Marsh, I tended to my pets while Pruett and Babette sipped bourbon and swapped theories. Feeding and grooming one cantankerous goat, a lively Arabian, an entitled feline, and two large dogs took considerable time and effort. By mutual agreement the envelope remained sealed until all three of us were present.

"Okay, gang," I said when I finally joined them. "Let the games begin."

I did the honors, using an antique letter opener to carefully pry apart the flap of the envelope. As the contents spilled on to my farmhouse table, we held our collective breaths and stared. Nothing earthshaking emerged; simply several handwritten pages with the legend *Sybil Vane*, and a packet of yellowed sheets of what looked like correspondence fastened by a pink ribbon.

"Wow," Babette grumbled. "Is this the big reveal? Looks like a bunch of junk to me."

"Hold on." Pruett's long, slender fingers carefully untied the letters. He remained focused on the task at hand, blissfully unaware of my impatience.

"This might be something after all," he said. "Remember. no email, texts, or cell phones in those days. People communicated the old-fashioned way."

As I reached for the *Sybil Vane* pages, Babette snatched them from me. "Wait a minute, girlfriend. We're partners, remember? Heck. We might be making history— touching a masterpiece." She fumbled in her purse for the reading glasses she abhorred and perched them on the tip of her nose.

I kept my doubts to myself. No need to shatter Magdalen's dreams prematurely. Time enough for that later. I soon realized we had in our possession the prologue to a novel. The full title read *Sybil Vane, a novel by Sebastian Melmoth.* It appeared to be a first-person narrative of the title character's life and tragic death at her own hand. The language was formal, much more typical of the nineteenth century than our own. Nevertheless, it was compelling. I scanned the first paragraph, unable to avert my eyes.

"I never sought to end my life—not until HE who was my sole reason for existence cast me aside. He dismissed any claim I had to beauty or talent as wanting. Like Hamlet, I reviled self-slaughter, but life was bereft of meaning without him and I succumbed."

Babette gasped and clutched my arm. "Good Lord! This is excitin'."

Before I could respond, my iPhone buzzed. I considered ignoring it but reached for it from sheer force of habit. The lure of potential customers outweighed personal convenience every time. The voice on the other end was faint, barely audible.

"Who's speaking please?" I asked.

"It's Irene. Irene Wilson."

Alarm bells clanged in my head, but I kept my voice calm and unemotional. "Yes, Mrs. Wilson. How can I help you? Is Magdalen okay?"

Irene Wilson sobbed loudly into the phone. "That's just it, Ms. Morgan. Mags has disappeared." She gulped. "And something else. Nurse Ross— she's been murdered."

Chapter 6

By unspoken agreement we three leashed the dogs, bundled up, and trekked to my old Suburban, the only vehicle large enough to accommodate our entire crew. For once Pruett was too engrossed in reading Magdalen's correspondence to grouse about who would drive. The rules were simple—my car, my choice. I also happened to be a better driver than Pruett, although neither one of us discussed that issue. Because her night vision was impaired, Babette was content to curl up in the back seat with Clara and doze. She was untroubled by the driving question; she honored the old Southern tradition of letting males take the lead whenever possible unless her own wishes were thwarted.

"Anything interestin' in those letters?" she asked Pruett. Naptime ended and Babette was ready to rock. "You're a million miles away."

He pushed down his horn-rimmed glasses and grinned. "Can't tell yet. Murder and kidnapping tend to distract me. For all we know, Nurse Ross may have died from natural causes and Magdalen simply fled the scene. Too soon to know. Mrs. Wilson might have exaggerated."

I hoped he was right, but I doubted it. The sound of Irene's panicked voice reverberated in my ear. Obviously, some type of incident had spooked her and sent the entire facility into a tailspin. Nurse Carole Ross appeared indestructible, a true iron maiden. My few interactions with her had not been pleasant, but surely the woman had done nothing to warrant a violent death. As for Magdalen, the isolated location of the Falls argued against an escape plan for an octogenarian on the run. Public transportation was limited and to my knowledge, Magdalen did not own or drive a car. More than likely she had fled to the porch or another part of the residence. I consoled myself with that thought even though I didn't quite believe it.

"Bet ya Mags was kidnapped," Babette said. "Good thing she gave you that envelope, Perri. There might be clues inside."

I hadn't considered my obligation to turn everything over to the authorities. After all, we might be in possession of evidence in a murder case. Apparently, Pruett had already thought of that. As we approached our friendly Staples store, he barked a command and scooped the evidence back into the manila envelope. "Stop. This won't take long." He loped out of the car, leaving Babette and me to marvel at his fast thinking.

Babette teased, "Gotta say, Perri, you are one lucky girl, my friend. Got a man who's smart and sexy."

I ignored the comment and reminded my pal that at thirty-two years of age, my girlhood was far behind me. Naturally Babette pooh-poohed everything I said.

"Don't go all feminist on me," she said. "Men like him are in short supply. Ask around. Women over forty don't exist for a lot of fellows, even ugly guys with no future."

Babette's analysis rang true. Pruett often said that in the nation's capital, power meant more than pretty especially for males.

"Mission accomplished?" I asked when he jumped back into the Suburban.

"Yep. Now we can turn this over to the cops with a clear conscience." The sentiment was admirable but not at all like him because Pruett often skirted the boundaries of law and propriety when pursuing a story. I threw a skeptical look his way, then focused on driving. Rural roads in Virginia were poorly lit and quite treacherous for the unwary motorist. Hills, holes, and sudden curves abounded. Deer sightings were frequent and often deadly. Pruett managed to distract both Babette and me by sharing the latest exploits of his daughter, Ella, and her prize pointer, Lady Guinevere. It didn't take much to captivate me because I savored every scrap of information and silly anecdote about that child. I loved Ella as if she were my own, even though she was the natural offspring of Pruett and photojournalist Monique Allaire. Maternal instincts had surfaced late in life for me, but they were in full bloom where Ella was concerned. Go figure.

Despite the hour, the Falls was ablaze with lights. The entrance was packed with police vehicles, ambulances, and the discreet but ominous coroner's van. I shivered as I recalled our previous brushes with sudden death. Surely this would end up being a case of natural causes. With her age and blocky physique, Nurse Ross appeared to be a prime candidate for heart ailments. Plus, according to Babette the woman smoked. She'd detected the odor of tobacco when they first met and trumpeted it to

Pruett and me. My dear pal never met a grudge worth relinquishing and she resented our shabby treatment by Carole Ross.

"Downright unmannerly," she fumed, as if this was the ultimate social sin. "Not a nice woman at all."

"Surely not a death penalty offense," Pruett teased. "You'd eviscerate the ranks of Congress if that were so."

Babette knew when she was being teased. Fortunately, Pruett got a hall pass no matter how many times he taunted her.

Initially the deputy on guard waved us off the premises, but once again Wing Pruett came through. "We have information for Sheriff Page," he said with a specious smile. I doubted if that was true, but sure enough, after furnishing his name to the deputy, Pruett was ushered into the facility with Babette and me trailing in his wake. When I met the sheriff, everything became clear.

Aleita Page was a sheriff from central casting, assuming your territory was Hollywood, not rural Virginia. Everything about her was shipshape, from neatly braided locks and trim waist to her hourglass figure. Pruett greeted her with a familiarity that suggested a close, perhaps even intimate knowledge. They exchanged hugs and lingered just a tad longer than necessary.

"She's gorgeous," Babette stage-whispered. "Watcha wanta bet she and Wing had something going on?"

Sometimes I forgot that Babette was my best pal. In this instance rhapsodizing about Pruett and another woman hardly qualified her for sainthood or friend of the year. I clutched the manila envelope, squared my shoulders, and soldiered on toward the large conference room in the office complex, reminding myself yet again that both Pruett and I were free agents.

Joan Fergueson was already seated with Dr. Jethro Tully hovering behind her. Both physicians were composed but solemn. Fergueson's complexion was devoid of color, almost bloodless, and her hands were clenched so tightly, I feared she might break a bone. Tully was another matter entirely. His manner was cold, clinical, and dare I say indifferent. He appeared to shrug off his colleague's death without wrinkling his brow or tailored suit.

"What's this, Sheriff?" he said. "Hardly the time for visitors, I would think."

Dr. Fergueson raised red-rimmed eyes and looked our way. "Ms. Morgan? Is Magdalen with you?"

I shook my head but said nothing, waiting for Sheriff Aleita Page to speak. When she did so, it was with confidence and authority.

"One of your residents called Ms. Morgan. She, Mr. Pruett, and Mrs. Croy were kind enough to respond. Maybe if we pool our resources, we can find our missing person." She consulted her notes. "Miss Melmoth, is it?"

"Magdalen." Tully took charge and quickly supplied his patient's basic statistics: age, physical description, and personality profile. Without explicitly saying so, he hinted that Magdalen was delusional and close to dotty.

Sheriff Page gave him a level stare. "Are you suggesting that she's violent? Pending an autopsy, we're treating Nurse Ross's death as suspicious and Ms. Melmoth as a missing person."

I gave Tully a hard stare. "We met with her and her mental state was clear as a bell." I nodded toward Pruett and Babette. "Ask my friends if you don't believe me."

Babette was never one to mince words, especially in the cause of justice. "How did Nurse Ross die? We heard she was murdered."

Joan Fergueson coughed. "We don't know that. If the press gets wind of it..." A look of horror eclipsed her face as she recalled that Wing Pruett was a distinguished member of the Fourth Estate. Once again, Aleita Page intervened. "Nothing's certain yet, so I think we can count on Mr. Pruett's discretion. Right, Wing?"

Pruett said nothing, his cherubic expression a total charade. I knew from sad experience that if a hot story sprang up, all bets were off, and no person or institution would be spared. I suppressed Babette's derisive snort by administering a sharp elbow to her ribs. Let them keep their illusions as long as possible. My concern was finding Magdalen before any harm befell her. To do that, I needed to speak with Irene Wilson as soon as possible to find out what she knew. After all, she was on the scene and was the one who had summoned us.

"Excuse me," I said. "My dogs are locked up in the car and need to stretch their legs." As excuses went, that was pretty feeble, but given the high drama surrounding us, it passed unchallenged. Pruett raised his eyebrows, but Babette got the message and joined me.

"Lookin' for Irene?" she whispered.

I nodded and headed for the stairwell, figuring the elevators were probably locked down to secure the building. Luck was with us and we managed to evade the deputies on patrol and reach Irene Wilson's studio.

She cautiously opened the door and waved us in. "Oh, thank the Lord. I prayed you'd come. They shut down the switchboard, but of course I have my cell phone." Her hands trembled and her voice shook with emotion. "Please help Mags. I'm afraid for her."

Babette, who personified Southern hospitality, settled Irene into a wing chair and prepared tea. In times of stress, her impeccable manners and nurturing instincts came in handy.

"Tell us what happened," I said. "We don't have much time."

Irene nodded. "I was with Mags at her place when Nurse Ross brought up a parcel. Naturally we opened it. Who could refuse a treat, especially one that was wrapped so beautifully?"

"Brown paper wrapping or fun stuff?" Babette asked. It was a good question, one I wished I had thought of.

Irene hesitated. "Why, now that I think of it, there was no outer wrapping. Just really pretty foil with a ribbon." She took a deep breath and continued. "Turns out it was candy. Belgian. An entire pound. Well, Magdalen doesn't care for sweets, and I'm a diabetic so I can't partake. We gave it to Nurse Ross instead—for the floor staff, you know. Lots of people do that. It's a fairly common practice."

I knew where this tale was going, and the picture wasn't pretty. Judging by her sturdy build, Nurse Ross liked candy. A lot.

"I don't suppose a card was enclosed?" I asked. A poisoner would hardly sign his own name, but every clue was important.

Irene shook her head. "No. Just one of those computer messages saying, 'Best Wishes.' No name. We joked that Magdalen had a secret admirer."

"I bet you probably get a lot of parcels," Babette said slyly. "Amazon delivers everything. Amazin', isn't it?"

I saw where she was headed and applauded her. At times my friend was sneaky enough for both of us.

Irene frowned. "Mail and parcels are delivered every day at noon. Right before lunch. It makes a special treat, don't you see. That way everyone can ooh and ah about it at our tables. Nurse Ross never brought things to our door before." She backtracked, as if afraid she was maligning the departed. "Not that we'd expect her to. The staff is very busy, and Nurse Ross had other things on her mind."

"Like what?" Babette cut to the chase per usual

"Mags thought Carole—Nurse Ross—had a beau. Someone she met here, I think. Maybe a relative of one of the residents."

I hated to be unkind, but Carole Ross hardly seemed a figure of romance. Still, I was glad her final days had been joyful. Romance nourished the soul of everyone, man or woman.

I poured each of us another cup of chamomile tea, hoping to calm Irene and continue the narrative. Any minute either Pruett or the sexy sheriff would probably interrupt us and spoil everything. "When did Magdalen disappear?"

Irene's eyes filled as she recalled her friend. "I went out to the elevator and found her—Nurse Ross. She was on the floor, with the candy spilled all around her. I'm afraid I screamed bloody murder." She flushed. "That's really not like me, you see. Mags and several other residents came right out. When she saw what happened Mags didn't faint, but she got so pale, I thought she might. She has a dicey heart, you know."

I recalled that recently there had been some mix-up with Magdalen's heart medication, a mix-up that had involved Nurse Ross. "When did Magdalen disappear?" I asked.

Irene put her head in her hands. "I can't say for certain. You see, more people crowded around—seemed like every resident in the building came out—and between that and all the wailing and chattering, I lost track of Mags." As she raised her head, Irene's eyes filled again. "Some friend I am. I let her down."

I had to think quickly. No doubt Sheriff Page's troops were conducting a thorough search of the entire facility. They would find Magdalen if she was still there. If—a small word with a world of meaning. "Think hard, Irene. Does Magdalen have any friends who live nearby or places she likes to visit?"

Irene shrugged helplessly. "I can't think of any. None of us even has a car. We rely on public transportation or the staff."

Staff? That gave me an idea. Babette would call it an inspiration. "What type of car did Nurse Ross drive? Do you recall?"

Another shrug from Irene. "Some kind of sedan. Black, I think. Nothing that stood out."

Babette rolled her eyes, but I stayed steady. "Great. Anything else strike you? What about her cell phone? I presume Magdalen had one."

That brought a smile to Irene's face. "Oh yes. Mags is technically savvy. A computer whiz too. Wouldn't think it to look at her, but anyone with a problem went to Mags for help, even some of the staff. Nurse Ross got her to do several things."

Hmm. A new and somewhat surprising side of Magdalen Melmoth had emerged. My own prejudices made me assume that a woman in her eighties would fear or reject technology. What other aspects of her character had I overlooked?

The sound of footsteps in the hallway announced the arrival of company and a temporary end to our inquiry. I answered the door and admitted Dr. Fergueson and Sheriff Aleita Page. The lithe form of Wing Pruett lurked behind them, beckoning me. I nudged Babette and made what I hoped was a graceful exit.

"You get some rest, Irene, and we'll speak with you tomorrow."

"Yeah," Babette said. "I'm sure Magdalen is just fine." Whenever Babette fibs about anything she bites her lip. She didn't fool me and I'm fairly certain Irene saw through her as well. "You call me if you need anything," Babette said as we hastily ducked out and joined Pruett. Better to beat a hasty retreat before the sheriff or Dr. Fergueson barred the door.

"Keep walking and don't say a word." Pruett's benign smile was an obvious ruse. He pressed the elevator button and waved us in before him. "According to the ladies downstairs, they monitor these elevators. Guess nothing is sacred anymore."

We walked single file through the front door, into the parking lot, and to my car. Fortunately, Pruett and I weren't competitive. Still I couldn't wait to steal the march on him by sharing what we had learned. The needs of my dogs came first, of course. I opened the rear hatch and released them, giving them the Schutzhund command for go. They immediately streaked off into the backfield and freedom. Pruett wrapped his arms around me as we watched them, admiring their grace and beauty.

"What did Irene say?" he asked. "I figured you two were up to something, so I tried to distract Aleita as long as I could."

I looked up into dancing eyes, striving mightily and unsuccessfully to look innocent. "I'm pretty sure you did a good job of distracting the sheriff. More than enough."

He shrugged. "Always was an overachiever," he said trying hard to sound modest. "She's a sharp cookie, though. Wasted in this Podunk place, if you ask me."

I forced myself to forgo the foolishness and focus on the only thing that mattered: Magdalen Melmoth. "They suspect poison, I suppose. That candy was meant for Magdalen." I recited a faithful account of Irene Wilson's testimony.

Pruett played it cool at first. "They won't be sure until the autopsy is finished. Could be natural causes, you know. Apparently, Nurse Ross had some health concerns of her own."

I gave him my sweetest smile. "Just goes to show you. Stuffing candy into your mouth is hazardous even if it's fine Belgian chocolate. According to Irene, the box was open, the contents scattered all over the floor."

"Hmm. Most untidy." He was baiting me, or trying to. I squeezed his hand and called to my dogs. Pruett immediately backed up. He had made giant strides toward conquering his demons, but charging dogs still unnerved him.

After we settled into my Suburban I leaned back on the headrest and closed my eyes—to think, not to sleep. That was my story, but before I knew it, Pruett was gently awakening me in my own driveway.

"Come on, sleepyhead. Babette will beat us into the house." He kissed my forehead in a gesture so loving that my heart and several other more visceral organs reacted. Maybe he did love me after all. The thought warmed me from head to toe and sustained me as I faced a sobering reality. In my driveway, in front of Babette's Mercedes, was a dark, nondescript sedan I'd never seen before.

"Hmm," Pruett said. "Looks like you have company. Should I be jealous?"

If only it were that simple. I'm not blessed with second sight, but somehow I knew what I would find in that vehicle. As we approached the driver's side door, it opened, and the fragile frame of Magdalen Melmoth emerged.

Chapter 7

"Perri—I hope I haven't disturbed you. I didn't know where else to go."
Despite the horrendous circumstances of the day, Magdalen was perfectly
composed. Oddly so.

I was too shocked to speak but, fortunately, Babette was not. She flung
open her side door, leapt from my car and confronted Magdalen. "How in
the world did you get here?" she asked. "They've got half the state searching
for you."

Magdalen bowed her head, acknowledging the problem. "I drove, of
course. Fortunately, my night vision is still excellent. Perri gave me her
business card the first time we met, so I looked up her address on the Internet.
Thank heaven for GPS."

Before we continued our discussion, Pruett nudged us toward the house.
The weather had gotten chilly, and despite her obvious spunk, Ms. Melmoth
was, in her own words, no spring chicken. Sounded like a good idea.

"We all need a hot toddy," Babette said as she bustled about my kitchen.
"I'll make them." We made ourselves comfortable in the family room, while
Pruett lit a fire. Thatcher, my irascible Maine coon, sized up our guest and
immediately plopped in her lap, purring loudly. Clara the border collie,
wrapped herself around Magdalen's feet.

"You're quite a hit with animals," Pruett said.

Magdalen stretched out her arms and sighed. "True. I love them and they
seem to reciprocate." After Babette served our hot toddies Magdalen took
a sip and stared directly into his eyes. "I know you have some questions for
me, so ask away. Please. Don't feel shy."

"Is that Nurse Ross's car?" I asked.

"Oh yes. All the staff leave their keys in the ignitions, you know, so that
made it easy. Luckily her sedan is older. Keys, not those newfangled fob

things. I had no trouble at all and, quite obviously, she wasn't going to need it." Magdalen saw the look of shock on our faces and reacted immediately. "Forgive me, dears. That sounded so callous."

Pruett, who holds an advanced degree in mendacity, brushed away her apology. "You did what you had to do. I presume you felt threatened."

She nodded. "This is so selfish of me. I don't want to endanger you by staying. I'll find some other shelter. A hotel."

The toddy, combined with my recent nap, helped to settle me down. "Don't even think of it. My guest room is always ready for visitors. What else can we do for you?" My head spun with thoughts of police reaction and the agony suffered by Irene Wilson.

Magdalen, on the other hand, seemed composed and clearheaded. "I know I need to go back there, but first I must speak with an attorney. Do you know one who might help me?"

I knew Babette employed a battery of lawyers, but Pruett spoke up first. "My attorney is one of the best. I'll set up an appointment with him first thing tomorrow if you like." He pulled out his cell phone, dialed, and stepped out of the room.

"Such a nice young man," Magdalen trilled. "You are one lucky girl, Perri."

I am way too old to blush and well beyond girlhood, but nevertheless that's what happened. Magdalen tut-tutted and Babette laughed out loud.

"That's just what I tell her, Magdalen. Pruett adores Perri. Anyone can see that."

I quickly changed course from my personal life to Magdalen's. "How many people know about the manuscript? Irene does, but have you mentioned it to anyone else?"

"No."

"What about your doctor?" Babette asked. "He hinted that you made stuff up. That tells me he knows or suspects somethin' fishy."

Before she answered, Pruett glided back into the room, sat next to Magdalen on the sofa, and squeezed her hand. "Everything's all set. Bright and early tomorrow at nine thirty. Micah Briggs is one of the good guys, plus he's tops in his field. You'll like him."

Magdalen closed her eyes with fatigue or relief, I couldn't say which. That was my cue to lead her to the guest room and make her comfortable.

"Everything will work out," I told her. "You're safe here. We've got dogs, a security system, and a big, strong man to protect us." I felt hypocritical about the big, strong man remark, but for women of Magdalen's generation it seemed appropriate and comforting.

"I feel better already," she said wryly, "although I'd bet you're quite adept at protecting yourself. Army training, you know." Before I left the room, she tugged at my sleeve. "Perhaps Mr. Pruett should move Nurse Ross's car into your garage. No sense in advertising that you have a guest." Magdalen winked at me, as if it were our little secret, emphasizing anew that despite her genteel ways, this woman was no pushover.

* * * *

Sleep eluded me that night. Every creaking board and shifting wind caused me to bolt upright and peer into the darkness. Images of the seemingly indestructible Nurse Carole Ross covered in chocolate haunted my dreams. At dawn I surrendered, tiptoed to the kitchen, and fired up my Nespresso machine. A pet parade immediately surrounded me, demanding tribute. After attending to their needs, I eased back into my wing chair, closed my eyes, and sipped the magic brew.

"Mind if I join you?" Pruett asked. Despite the early hour, he had already showered, shaved, and spruced up. He seldom wore a suit and when he did the results were spectacular. I tucked the throw under my chin and drank in the sight, mindful of the ragtag outfit I wore.

"Hope I didn't wake you," I said. "Good thing you left that suit here. Let me get you some espresso."

He waved me away. "Not to worry, my liege. Even a humble bachelor can master a coffee capsule, you know. It's my specialty."

I must have dozed off because when I awakened Pruett was busily tapping his iPhone. As for my other guests, stentorian snores from above confirmed that Babette, who had elected to bunk in with Magdalen rather than return to her empty house, was still fast asleep. Magdalen had yet to make an appearance. After last evening's shock, that was hardly surprising. Not a problem. I subscribed to the more the merrier philosophy and was pleased to host a full house.

"I'll freshen up and fix breakfast," I told Pruett.

"You look plenty fresh right now," he teased. "Flannel always turns me on."

In the dark, I had grabbed Pip's old robe by mistake. There was nothing Freudian about that gesture. Pip and everything about him still comforted me like nothing else ever could. He was and always would be a vital part of my life. Pruett knew and respected that. I think.

"It won't take long," I said. "Natural beauty, you know."

He ignored my joke and turned serious. "Right you are. 'She walks in beauty, like the night…' Lord Byron might have been describing you, my love."

We locked eyes, and for a moment I considered leaping into his arms. The sudden appearance of Magdalen Melmoth saved me from perdition.

She had apparently pressed her clothing from yesterday and applied a touch of lipstick. The term "fresh as a daisy" fit perfectly.

"Pardon me, children," she said. "Am I interrupting anything?"

Pruett and I both assured her that she was not. "Just give me a few minutes. I'll get dressed and make breakfast," I said. For some unknown reason I felt guilty, as if I were a child caught in an indiscretion. I sped upstairs and did my best to revive myself. The results pleased me, although I fell far below Byron's illusion of romance.

I emerged, tempted by the scent of eggs, bacon, and pancakes courtesy of that dazzling duo, Melmoth and Pruett. Apparently, a hint of the feast had wafted up to the guest room as well. Babette was busily setting the dining room table with my best china and a few added touches from the back garden.

She reached greedily for espresso, stifling a yawn as she did so. "Well, missy," she said, "about time you put in an appearance. Now we can finally eat. I'm starvin'." My pal was a woman with many appetites, all of them lusty. I couldn't argue with the sentiment, though. Death and danger made me ravenously hungry too. Strange as it seemed, there was something life affirming about a plate filled with scrambled eggs.

"I'll drive Magdalen into the city," Pruett said. "That way she can meet Micah and get comfortable. Pick her up afterward at my place if you want."

Magdalen removed her apron and dried her hands. "Nonsense. You're not running a taxi service for me. Perri has a business to maintain. I'll just call an Uber."

Once again, Magdalen gobsmacked all three of us. Who would have expected the Uber phenomenon to penetrate all the way to the Falls?

"Are you sure?"

"I insist," Magdalen said quite firmly. The issue was closed as far as she was concerned.

Fortunately, Babette proposed an alternative. "Well, I don't run any business, and it's no big deal to drive into Georgetown. Besides, Magdalen and I can have lunch afterward. It'll be fun!"

Magdalen was either too kind or too polite to disappoint Babette. She agreed, and after breakfast the trio made their exit. When he kissed me goodbye, Pruett whispered that he would notify the sheriff about Magdalen's whereabouts. "Don't worry," he said. "Everything will be fine."

Famous last words.

Chapter 8

After neglecting my business for several days, I finally paid the piper. A stack of invoices awaited me, and several customers inquired about pending orders they had yet to receive. No sole proprietor can afford such lapses if she expects to remain solvent. It was crunch time, nose to the grindstone at Creature Comforts. My absorption with leads, collars, and belts caused me to forget Magdalen Melmoth and her problems for a few hours at least. When Pruett called, I realized it was almost five p.m.

"Hey, leather lady," he said. "Got some time for an update?"

Hearing his sultry tones warmed my soul. "For you, sure. I always have time."

"Glad to hear it." Pruett provided a concise summary of Magdalen's conference with Micah Briggs, minus any specific details that might compromise her privacy.

"I bet she liked him," I said. Most women did. Micah was a fortyish, sturdy fireplug of a man with curly red hair and twinkling blue eyes that radiated compassion. Sort of a modern-day Perry Mason crossed with Paul Bunyan.

Pruett chuckled. "I can't say for certain, but Babette sure took a shine to him. It was hard prying her out of his office while he conferred with Magdalen."

That sounded true to form. My ebullient pal developed instant crushes on any available male, and a few who were already spoken for. If I recalled correctly, Micah was a bachelor, so the field was clear for an all-out Croy assault. Suddenly I sensed a hesitation in Pruett's voice, one that concerned me.

"Anything go wrong?" I asked.

He sighed. "Not wrong exactly. Micah called Babette and me back into his office to witness Magdalen's will. Naturally we couldn't see the provisions, but I did glimpse your name."

I forced myself to take a deep breath. No sense in panicking or imagining things. "Okay."

"Wait 'til she tells you herself. She and Babette should be back soon. By the way, I spoke with Aleita and she needs to take a statement from Magdalen. No big deal and no lab findings yet on those chocolates. Autopsy results on Nurse Ross should be finalized tomorrow."

I wanted to ask where he would stay that evening, but pride and a sense of restraint ruled the day. Like many of us, Pruett needed his space. Besides, with daughter Ella on a European jaunt with her mother, his residence was empty. I closed my eyes, picturing a bacchanalia at the elegant Chez Pruett in Georgetown.

"Perri—you still there?"

"Sure."

"Call me after you speak with Magdalen. I have things to do here, but I already miss you like crazy. You've gotten under my skin, lady."

To stave off awkwardness, I resorted to flippancy. "They have medication to cure that, you know."

Pruett had his own brand of medicine. "Nope. I'm a hopeless case. Terminal. Head over heels." He blew a kiss into the receiver.

As I hung up, a tingling caused me to shiver. Talk about your hopeless cases!

Chapter 9

Babette, Clara, and Magdalen clambered into the house soon after that. All three women clutched bulging shopping bags from Babette's mother ship—Neiman Marcus.

"Shopping?" I asked. "Sounds like trouble."

"Mags needed a bunch of supplies," Babette said, "so we had to stock up. It was fun. A spot of retail therapy works wonders."

I had limited experience with that, and frankly I found shopping tedious. Still, I tried always to be a good sport. Perhaps I was the oddball after all. Magdalen's cheeks were pink and her spirits seemed very high from the excursion.

"Hot toddy time," Babette trilled, brandishing a bottle of whiskey and all the fixings. "Takes the chill right off."

I looked pointedly at my watch. It was barely six p.m., although I supposed one could arguably call it cocktail time. Who was I to put the damper on another's happiness? Until they made diet whiskey I would never worry about her predilections. Fear of fat kept Babette firmly in the social drinker lane.

"Everything went well?" I asked.

"Wonderful." Magdalen's smile was luminous. "Mr. Briggs took care of everything. Such a sympathetic man."

Babette sighed. As I suspected she was perilously close to another all-consuming, potentially catastrophic crush. Four marriages had done nothing to dampen her enthusiasm for love and romance.

"I'd heard of him before, but for some reason we'd never met. Quite a charmer, Perri, and gracious as well." I really hated it when Babette gushed over a man even when it was justified. Typically, such behavior preceded a rush of emotion and ended in disaster. "Pruett said he's single. Micah, I mean, not Pruett." Babette turned toward Magdalen and smirked. "We all know Pruett is taken."

Magdalen played along. "Indeed we do." She patted Poe's silky head and asked, "Could I possibly meet this cantankerous goat of yours before the light fades?"

"Zeke?" Few people cared to confront an actively hostile pygmy goat, and most avoided him whenever possible. "Of course, Magdalen. I need to feed him anyway before he gets angry."

"Count me out," Babette said. "I'm comfy right here on the couch."

We grabbed our wraps and headed toward the barn. Zeke was wild-eyed until he spotted his boon companions, Keats and Poe. He had bonded with my dogs early on and considered them siblings, or at least partners in crime.

While I cleaned his stall and forked hay into his feed bowl, Magdalen spoke. "Forgive me for the ruse, dear, but I had to speak with you alone."

I stayed silent as she continued. "You know I completed my will today, I suppose."

"Yes."

"I wanted you to know that I willed my few possessions to you and made you executor of my grandfather's literary estate. Sebastian Melmoth, of course, not Oscar Wilde."

"I don't know what to say, Magdalen. Isn't there someone—some relative or old friend—who would be a better fit?"

Her smile was sad. "None. I need someone I can trust to do the right thing, and I know that's you. When you get to my age, friendships fade, and most family members have departed."

I still hadn't processed the enormity of her bequest. "But Magdalen, a newly validated work by Oscar Wilde would be priceless."

"Yes. I only ask that you credit my mother and her family in the preface. They deserve that recognition. I have some additional information at the house that you and Mr. Pruett will find useful."

"I don't know what to say."

"Sometimes, my dear, silence is indeed golden."

* * * *

That evening we enjoyed what in prior times would have been termed a hen party. Soft jazz filled the room, a companionable fire burned, and we supped on one of my few signature dishes—spinach quiche. Magdalen entertained us with tales of life in rural Ireland, I talked about dog shows, and Babette contributed her share of slightly scandalous asides about her wealthy friends and neighbors in Great Marsh.

"I hope I'm not shockin' you, Magdalen," Babette said after one especially lurid tidbit.

Magdalen adjusted her cushion and laughed. "Oh no, dear. Sex is and has always been part of life. My grandfather certainly partook. He paid the price for it, of course."

I shivered, thinking of the majestic piece, *The Ballad of Reading Gaol,* and the tag line, "each man kills the thing he loves." Magdalen might be thinking the same thing, but she seemed untroubled by it. When Pruett texted me an hour later, I broke the news to her.

"Sheriff Page will be here at ten a.m. tomorrow to interview you. Are you okay with that?"

"Certainly. I don't plan to mention the manuscript, though. Why complicate things?" Thatcher jumped into her lap at that moment in a gesture of solidarity. "I think I will go home with the sheriff tomorrow. I spoke with Irene today," Magdalen said. "She misses me and frankly, I've imposed on your hospitality long enough."

Alarm bells clanged in my head. "No. You can't. Please don't leave yet. It may not be safe."

Babette joined me in urging Magdalen to stay, but she was implacable. "Remember, ladies, the Bible says there is a time for every purpose under Heaven. At my age, that time may be drawing near, but I don't fear it." She gently displaced Thatcher and rose. "Forgive me if I make an early night of it. Big day for all of us tomorrow."

Babette left shortly thereafter, and for the first time in a long while I was alone with only my thoughts and my pets for company.

* * * *

I slept so soundly that it took shards of sunlight and the gentle urging of my dogs to awaken me. I leaped up, guilt ridden. The Puritan work ethic was alive and well in Persephone Morgan, and lolling about in bed aroused guilt in every pore of my skin.

After attending to my pets, I devoted a goodly amount of time to my hair, makeup, and wardrobe. Call me frivolous, but I'd seen the look that passed between Aleita Page and Wing Pruett. I intended to up my game as best I could before the sultry sheriff made her appearance. No need to give aid and comfort to potential competition.

Magdalen joined me in a modest repast of oatmeal, fruit, and toast, but her attention wandered as her appetite waned. "Sure you feel up to this interview?" I asked. "I can contact the sheriff and cancel."

She closed her eyes and smiled. "No, dear. Forgive me for woolgathering. I left some more information on the bed for you and Mr. Pruett. It's a burden, I know, but your help is nothing short of a blessing. Finding the manuscript is my final crusade, a quest worthy of Don Quixote himself."

That knight errant tilted at windmills, so Magdalen's imagery did not comfort me. Perhaps Doctors Fergueson and Tully had correctly diagnosed the situation after all. A sudden cacophony of sounds swept those thoughts from my mind. Zeke's braying and the barking of my dogs announced the arrival of Sheriff Aleita Page and her deputy.

If anything, the sheriff was even more attractive than I remembered her. Her shiny black braid, flawless skin, and trim figure combined in a most felicitous mixture, one that any man, especially Wing Pruett, would appreciate.

After accepting a cup of espresso, Aleita Page looked around the room. "Will Wing be joining us today?"

I bit my tongue before answering. No need to be snarky. She was probably a very nice person in addition to being a competent professional. Probably.

"He's in DC today. Some big exposé among the lobbyists." Pruett had won two Pulitzers and numerous other awards for his investigative reporting. From her reaction, I surmised that Sheriff Page had probably been closely following his progress.

Magdalen asked me to stay during her interview and the sheriff agreed. Her manner was low-key, probing but not hostile. A method designed to elicit information without alarming the subject.

"Why did you leave the Falls so hastily?" she asked. "Did something frighten you?"

Magdalen explained about the incidents with her pills and the ransacking of her belongings. "Packages are never delivered that late," she said. "When I heard the commotion, I panicked."

Aleita Page shook her head. "Understood. But taking Nurse Ross's car caused us a spot of bother. Chain of evidence, you know. I wish you had come to me instead."

"Sheriff, the doctors at the Falls think I'm senile. For all I know they think I'm homicidal as well. Nurse Ross was the only one who took me seriously. We weren't friends exactly, but we understood each other. Her death grieves me."

That was my cue. I asked Aleita Page about the autopsy results on Nurse Ross and the analysis of the chocolate. She demurred initially, but I persisted. "Nurse Ross officially died of a heart attack," she said.

There was more to that story and I intended to get it. "Did anything in that candy cause her death? I understand she had heart problems."

Aleita hesitated. "Forensic analysis isn't complete yet, but it looks like poison was injected into those sweets. Apparently, the victim ate five or six pieces, enough to disrupt her heart rhythm."

Magdalen folded her arms and nodded. "I wondered about that. My friend heard her complain about her tricky heart, but frankly we thought it was a sympathy ploy. She was greedy for sweets, you see. Probably wanted to eat her fill before she shared them with the other nurses. Never eat sweets myself, but some people can't resist."

Aleita spread her arms wide. "I'm not a physician, so don't quote me. One thing is certain, though. Someone tampered with that candy, perhaps someone who didn't know your habits."

Most people would dive into an elegant box of chocolates. I shuddered picturing Babette doing that very thing. Meanwhile Sheriff Page moved on. "Tell me, Ms. Melmoth, why would someone wish to harm you? Have you offended anyone? Made any enemies?"

Magdalen's composure was sublime. I suddenly realized that for a sweet old lady, she wasn't all that sweet.

"Your friend Irene Wilson mentioned a manuscript. Anything to that?"

I stared straight ahead as Magdalen responded. "My grandfather, Sebastian Melmoth, was a literary genius. He wrote a wonderful novel that I've asked Perri and Mr. Pruett to help me find."

Aleita Page took a note and looked up. "Hmm. Melmoth—don't think I've heard of him." Her tone was slightly patronizing, bordering on dismissive.

My admiration for Magdalen swelled yet again. By telling the absolute truth, she had totally disarmed the sheriff. Well played, Magdalen! After a few mundane inquiries, the interview ended. Magdalen agreed to ride with the sheriff while her deputy drove Carole Ross's car back to the Falls. After hugging my pets and me, Magdalen Melmoth gathered her things and took her journey back to western Virginia.

Chapter 10

I considered waiting for Pruett, but curiosity consumed me. *Tidy up the guest room*, I told myself without much conviction. Who knew what might be in there? Truth was, I was drawn to that spot as ineluctably as a fly to honey. Through sheer force of will I finished my chores and made tea before creeping upstairs into the guest room. As Magdalen's potential heir, I had certain responsibilities that I simply could not shirk, and finding that manuscript was priority number one. She was counting on me.

Everything was as I expected, neat and tidy. Used sheets were carefully folded and the bedspread was draped over the pillows. True to her word, Magdalen had left a thick manila envelope with my name on it in the center of the bed. Before tearing into it, I experienced a brief period of self-doubt. Should I wait for Pruett or Babette? They were my partners after all, and deserved to share in the excitement. I debated the pros and cons and rather quickly decided on action over apathy. For all we knew, something in that folder might be time sensitive and require my immediate attention. On the other hand, why waste their time if the information was useless?

Thatcher sealed the deal by leaping on the bed and kneading the envelope. That seemed like an auspicious sign, an implied permission to proceed. I carefully pried open the flap and slid out the contents. The first items were unspectacular and a trifle mundane: the birth certificates of Magdalen and her parents, and the wedding documents of Sebastian Fingal Melmoth and Henrietta Kingsbury. A sad missive from the war office announced Sebastian's death, in service to king and country. A subsequent record listed the marriage of Henrietta Melmoth to one Declan Farraday. I hesitated, then sifted through the documents back to Magdalen's father's birth certificate. It listed his parents as Sebastian Wills Melmoth and

Jennifer O'Flahertie, and the year was 1899, twelve months before Oscar Wilde's death. the following November. Was it possible? Was Magdalen's father truly the offspring of the literary great?

I shivered with anticipation as I continued riffling through the documents. Unfortunately, it appeared there was no smoking gun, no absolute clue pointing to the manuscript. Then a packet of letters festooned with elaborate ribbons caught my eye. They were handwritten in a highly decorative cursive style that had almost vanished with the computer age. A slight hint of lavender wafted from the thin, wrinkled sheets, adding to the mystique. Reading another's correspondence always seemed like an invasion of privacy to me, even when the parties involved had long since departed from the earth. I salved my conscience, curled up in the corner wing chair, and snuggled under a mohair throw.

The letters dated from the years 1939 to 1940. To avoid the horrors of the blitz, Magdalen and her mother had taken refuge on the Kingsbury family estate in Ireland while their husband and father languished on the front lines. The letters contained intimate portraits of a young family, filled with anecdotes about Magdalen and hopes for the future. Those hopes were dashed in 1940, when Fingal Melmoth was killed in battle. Only in his final missive did Magdalen's father refer to his own parents and what he termed their "legacy."

I took a deep breath before reading further. Would this provide a vital clue? The young father and husband fondly recalled his childhood, his father's brilliance at Oxford, and his mother's active participation in women's suffrage. One line was of particular interest: *"Mother praised Father's success in the classics. She cherished his many writings, especially the novel* Sybil Vane, *a sequel to his previous fiction. I never knew my father, but her portrayal of him was so vivid that his presence was ever with me. I trust you will preserve it for Magdalen as part of her heritage."*

Talk about feeling gobsmacked! There, in a few words, a young soldier expressed his fondest hopes for his child's future and established a possible link to literary history.

The impact of those words made my head spin. I leaned back in the chair, closed my eyes, and considered my options. Pruett was probably unavailable, haring off after some political scandal or other. I seldom called him during working hours unless it was a true emergency. No need to appear possessive or tiresome, or to risk rejection. Babette, on the other hand, would abandon whatever she was doing and immediately hightail it over to my house. She would descend on me, demand instant access to the material, and propound a dozen courses of action, most of which were impractical. Just thinking of it left me weary and indecisive.

Fortunately, fate intervened before I made any decision. The sound of Zeke's braying sparked a noisy reaction from the Malinois, and alerted me that a visitor had arrived. I parted the drapes and peered out. The figure of a man laden with files emerged from an unfamiliar black Cadillac sedan. I was uneasy until I spied a blaze of red hair under his fedora. Who else could it be but the sturdy figure of Micah Briggs, an infrequent but always welcome visitor? Before greeting him, I hastily texted Babette. Despite having confronted danger and almost certain death at times, I was unwilling to face the explosive reaction of Babette Croy if she was excluded from Micah's visit.

"Perri," Micah said, kissing my hand. "Forgive me for invading your privacy. I had paperwork for Magdalen and couldn't reach her. I tried phoning you, but you didn't answer. Wing said it was okay to drop this stuff off."

I blushed, picturing my cell phone resting comfortably in my office most of the day while I delved into Magdalen's treasures. An unintelligent choice for a business owner, or anyone else for that matter.

"Come on in," I said. "Obviously you aren't deterred by my ferocious guard dogs." In a shocking loss of dignity, both Keats and Poe hovered around Micah, begging for attention.

"They know me," he said. "Probably those liver treats I always carry."

I cleared a space for his folders on the kitchen table and fired up the Nespresso machine. "I'm glad you're here. For several reasons. Besides the chance to catch up with you, I could use some lawyerly advice."

Micah blushed. It was a strange reaction from the attorney dubbed "DC's legal pit bull," although I'd always suspected that beneath the gruff exterior lurked a shy and solitary man.

He gave a courtly half bow and said, "At your service, ma'am. Anything to oblige." After I explained the situation Micah frowned. "Wow! Give me a minute to think. Magdalen is my client, so things could get tricky."

We sipped our espresso in silence as Micah pondered. Finally he took the simplest, most direct approach. He phoned Magdalen and got her permission to join the hunt for the manuscript.

"That was painless," Micah said. "Magdalen was thrilled." He hesitated. "She sounded tired, though. I suppose at her age all this excitement takes its toll."

I heard the crunch of tires on gravel and the joyful barking of my dogs. Soon enough Babette Croy rapped on my door, full of exuberance and primed for action. Her flawless appearance confirmed all my suspicions: Babette had brought out the big guns to impress Micah. His reaction was priceless but not unexpected. Once again he seemed less pit bull than golden retriever, disarmed and made slightly shy by the apparition that confronted him.

"Glad I caught y'all," Babette said. "This is all so thrillin'. I'm devoted to Oscar Wilde, you know. Can't get enough."

Micah didn't know that, and neither did I. Despite her many virtues, Babette was scarcely a literary scholar and I doubted she had read much if any of Wilde's work. I shrugged it off. It didn't really matter anyway. To aid Magdalen we needed a laserlike focus on the main prize, if it actually existed: the novel *Sybil Vane*.

Micah adjusted his reading glasses as he and Babette pored over the material. They sat close together, although it might have been more by necessity than choice on his part. I had absolutely no doubt what Babette's motives were.

When they finished Micah cleared his throat and finally spoke. "Very interesting," he said. "Suggestive, although not conclusive."

Babette shook her finger at him in frustration. "Stop with the lawyer talk. Are we on the right track or what?"

He spread out his hands wide. "Maybe. These documents definitely lean that way. Of course, we have no idea if they are genuine or not. What if the author was delusional or just misinformed?"

I could tell by the way her cheeks puffed out that my pal was smack in the middle of a major snit. Babette lived her life by a simple credo: things should conform to her wishes rather than reality. "It must be true," she said. "It just has to be. Magdalen seemed so sure."

Micah and I exchanged looks. Perhaps the fantasies of an elderly lady were just another case of wish fulfillment gone awry. No. Even considering that felt disloyal and roused every guilty bone in my body. Magdalen was not fanciful. Right or wrong, she had reason to believe her family's heritage. The birth certificates validated that Sebastian Melmoth was indeed her father, and research confirmed that Oscar Wilde had adopted that surname name during his final years in France. Moreover, someone else apparently believed in the manuscript as well. How else could one explain the clumsy attempts to silence her and the reality of Nurse Ross's murder?

"Penny for your thoughts?" Micah said.

I grimaced. "Probably overpriced at that. I was thinking strategy, trying to plan our next move." Before I explained, the ringtone on my cell phone jolted me back to reality and Pruett's mellifluous voice brought me to attention.

"Miss me?" he asked in a tone that assured me he already knew the answer. In the background, Babette chortled loudly enough to be heard. "You have company, I see. Am I disturbing anything?"

"Nope. Micah and Babette are here and we're puzzling over those documents Magdalen left."

Pruett changed immediately to a no-nonsense, newshawk mode. "Be right over. Don't do anything until I get there. I have some stuff you'll want to hear."

Eavesdropping was among Babette's major skills, so she had gotten the gist of the conversation. "That boy reminds me of a bird dog my daddy used to keep. No stopping him when he got the scent of something big."

Pruett reminded me of a panther rather than a bird dog, but nevertheless I took her point. "If we're having a strategy session, I'd better call for provisions. Okay with you two?"

Babette leaped into the breach. "What's your favorite food, Micah? We love that Peruvian chicken place, right, Perri? Come on, Micah. We'll buzz over there and pick some up before Pruett gets here." She grabbed his arm and hustled him out the door before he had time to object. Meanwhile I fed my pets, turned Raza out to graze, and tended to one ornery pygmy goat named Zeke, who had very pronounced methods for getting his way. By the time Pruett's Macan sailed into view, I felt presentable enough to meet even his high standards. A touch of lipstick, a wisp of blush, and a quick flick of my hairbrush saw to that.

He stepped warily around Keats and Poe and held out his arms to me. "You are some sight, Ms. Perri. I really missed you." The gleam in his deep brown eyes was enough to melt even the most resilient woman's defenses. I wasn't all that strong, so I immediately succumbed and folded into his embrace. Sometimes Babette got it right. She always exhorted me to loosen up and accept Pruett's love without reservations. When it came to romance she knew every move before anyone else did. I was a willing pupil but still in need of work.

"Where's the rest of the crew?" Pruett asked. "Don't tell me I scared them off."

I explained about their food run and pointed to Magdalen's papers. "That's what we were debating. Read up if you have time before they get back."

"Got something for you," he said. Pruett reached into his briefcase and presented me with a bottle of scotch. It was Johnnie Walker Blue, a favorite of Babette's and, apparently, Micah's as well. Call me a party pooper, but I detested the vile stuff. I could tell by his snarky grin that he knew darn well how I felt. He bent down and kissed my forehead. "Don't worry. I didn't forget you. Ella baked these before she left." He produced a packet of misshapen sugar cookies festooned with a big red bow. Despite their unusual appearance, those sweets looked perfect to me. Anything from seven-year-old Ella Pruett touched my heart and soul.

"Delicious," I said, biting into one. "I won't share even a crumb with you. Besides, you have work to do." I handed him the Melmoth papers and shooed him away.

Pruett finally got serious. He sat in my leather wing chair, put on his reading glasses, and perused the material. By the time Babette and Micah returned, he had read and reread everything, especially Sebastian Melmoth's letters.

The scent of roasted chicken temporarily distracted all of us, including our dogs. Keats, Poe, and Clara sat respectfully behind the table, waiting their turn. Cats behave differently. Thatcher simply jumped into my lap, speared a hunk of chicken, and calmly consumed it. When all of us were satiated the hard work began.

Not surprisingly, Babette started first. "I knew Magdalen wasn't addled," she said. "This proves it."

Pruett bit his lip. "Not necessarily. It only proves that her father, Sebastian Melmoth, believed his own father was a genius. No names were ever mentioned, and anyone could have written a novel based on the Dorian Gray opus."

Micah nodded. "That's right. The book was a big sensation in Europe. It's possible that Melmoth Senior knew Oscar Wilde and admired him. Maybe he penned an homage to him."

Babette grimaced. "Maybe, maybe, maybe. This gets us nowhere. We're spinning our wheels while Magdalen sits in that place with a target on her back."

She was right, of course. Whatever the fate of the novel, Magdalen Melmoth posed a threat to someone who was willing to kill for it.

"I say we visit Magdalen tomorrow. Sort of a wellness check. The dogs are due for a Therapy Dog visit anyway." I turned to Pruett. "I'm sure Sheriff Aleita would love to swap theories with you, Wing."

Pruett ignored the sarcasm and checked his phone. "Okay. Tomorrow's Saturday anyway. How about it, Micah?"

The lawyer gave us a thumbs-up, as did Babette. Meanwhile I had a brainstorm of sorts.

"Here's another suggestion. We need to track down the Farraday clan if that's possible. Who knows what their story may be?"

"Such a smart woman," Pruett said. "Don't you just love brainy broads, Micah?"

Sarcasm aside, he was right. Intelligence had always been one thing I could count on and I was proud of it. That emboldened me to suggest yet another line of inquiry. "If Babette and I trace the domestic side, perhaps you and Micah can research the Kingsbury family in Ireland. They had quite a large brood from what Magdalen said. Someone might still be around."

We agreed on tactics and went about our separate tasks. Babette grabbed her laptop and followed me into my office while I fired up my search engines. We hadn't gone far before she wrinkled her brow and stopped. "Perri, where's your phone book?"

Nobody used a phone book anymore. As far as I was concerned, those enormous tomes of old merely consumed space and yielded nothing a search of Google couldn't give. Frankly I saw them as just as archaic as telephone booths.

I shrugged. "No clue. I doubt I even have one. You have to request them these days, you know." One look at Babette's face aroused my suspicions. "Why?"

She shot me one of her mysterious looks, dialed her cell phone, and left the room. "I'll just have Dora check something out for us." Dora was her personal assistant, a pleasant woman of middle years with the patience of a saint and the maturity of a PTA president. Her job description required her to be on call twenty-four/seven and she did so cheerfully and without complaint. When Babette called Dora a treasure, she was merely stating the truth. My pal had learned the value of extreme vetting the hard way after her previous assistant came to an untimely end. Now she welcomed into her inner sanctum only those with an unblemished record and a capacity for tolerating the unusual.

When Babette bustled off I busied myself by crossing my fingers and typing the name Farraday into PeopleFinder. Unfortunately, the results exceeded my wildest hopes. Farraday was a popular surname, with over five hundred entries in the continental United States alone. Some occupations stayed in the family and the building trade was among them. The list narrowed when I linked the name to construction companies, although the numbers were still daunting. I printed a directory containing sixty-eight names from Maine to Missouri and began the arduous process of matching phone numbers to each. None of those listed were named Declan Farraday, but that didn't concern me. Magdalen's stepfather would have departed long ago. Perhaps his offspring chose more contemporary names. I focused on listings in rural rather than urban settings; Magdalen had reminisced about living on a large homestead.

The work was tedious, and despite my diligence I had little to show for my efforts. Poe and Keats displayed solidarity by surrounding me in a warm, furry embrace, but even that failed to lift my spirits. I banished every thought of my neglected customers and the orders unfilled, telling myself that I was serving a higher purpose. An hour later, when Babette sashayed into the room wearing a saucy grin, I knew I was doomed.

"Made any progress?" she asked. Her tone was arch. That really irked me, but I gritted my teeth and stayed silent. That was one game I always won over Babette.

Finally, she relented. "Gee Perri, you're such a grump. No fun at all."

I painted a smile on my face that would shame a saint. Babette thrust a sheet of paper into my hand with a flourish and sighed. Actually, she harrumphed, but why quibble?

"Here it is. The address we were searching for. Best of all, it's close by. Right over in Shenandoah County, not fifty miles away." She made absolutely no attempt to hide the smirk that covered her face and brought out the mean girl in me.

"How do you know that? Did you speak with someone?"

She averted her eyes. "Sort of."

I raised an eyebrow and said nothing. During my army days I'd perfected that quizzical look when questioning recruits. It always paid dividends.

Babette's shoulders fell. "Okay. If you must be a stickler, Dora tracked her down, but I heard everything. It was my idea."

Just then Pruett and Micah joined us. Pruett walked over to me and massaged my aching neck muscles. The feeling was so heavenly, I hoped he would never stop. "What's up, ladies?" he asked. "Sounds like you hit the jackpot."

My guilt-o-meter hit the limit and I immediately caved. "Babette gets all the credit. Come on. Tell them."

My pal beamed with a delight that was almost childlike. She waved the printout in the air and launched into her tale.

"Magdalen's stepfather was one Declan Farraday, a prosperous builder. The old man's long gone, of course, but I contacted his son, a guy named Carrick Farraday." She batted her lashes. "Quite the charmer he is. A retired gentleman living in Strasburg, and get this: He remembers Magdalen and her mother!"

Micah flashed her a look of pure admiration. "Wow! You did great!"

Pruett was less interested in flattery. He focused laserlike on the practicalities. "When can we see him? You didn't mention the novel or Oscar Wilde, I hope."

Babette folded her arms and pouted. "Of course not. What kind of ninny do you take me for? I merely mentioned that we were friends tryin' to reconnect someone with her past. Actually, I hinted that Perri was helping a client who was searching for her roots. Everyone does it these days."

Pruett nodded. "Good. Good. When can he see us? We need to strike while the iron is hot."

The smirk returned as Babette gave us the news. "Carrick expects us right after dinner. Tonight."

Chapter 11

In the end we formed a caravan consisting of two vehicles, four adults, and three canines. Micah and Babette paired up and, accompanied by Clara, piled into his Cadillac. Pruett drove the lead car with me, Keats, and Poe as his wingmen. I was at once tense and excited at the prospect of meeting one of Magdalen's relatives even though my expectations were low. Pruett said very little during that eighty-mile drive, but I studied his perfect profile, knowing how those mental gears were grinding. We formulated a loose plan, one that allowed us to explain our interest while probing for any evidence of the manuscript.

"I'm puzzled by one thing," I said. "Why in the world didn't Magdalen mention that Carrick Farraday lived so close to her? She must have known. That woman is a demon when it comes to manipulating Internet search engines."

Pruett considered the question before responding. "Maybe they were estranged or lost touch. You know how families are. All kinds of crazy things can cause a rift."

Actually I had no personal experience with family rifts or solidarity. I was an orphan who had always longed for contact with any sibling, cousin, or step relation. As Magdalen's putative heir, I had another ethical conflict that gnawed at me. Carrick Farraday and Lord only knows how many relatives might come out of the woodwork if the Oscar Wilde novel was found and validated. Money sets the proverbial cat among the pigeons, and *Sybil Vane* was a potential blockbuster.

I turned to Pruett. "We have to see Magdalen as soon as possible. I phoned her this afternoon, but she didn't answer her cell. I was reluctant to go through the switchboard at the Falls."

Pruett raised an eyebrow. "That bad, huh?"

I sounded paranoid even to myself. Had I been co-opted by a fanciful tale or was Magdalen in real danger?

Pruett reached over and squeezed my arm. "It's hard sometimes to sort out fact from fantasy, but Nurse Carole Ross was definitely murdered. That's not speculation."

"Heard that from Sheriff Aleita, did you?"

In his profession there were very few boundaries, and Pruett never apologized for pushing the envelope as far as he legally could. He patted my arm once more and said with attitude, "I never divulge my sources, but I can say that the chocolate contained enough strychnine to gag an entire herd of goats. Someone Magdalen's age wouldn't stand a chance."

My anxiety level rose exponentially as I pictured the scene. Magdalen was the equivalent of a tethered goat awaiting her fate. I blamed myself for getting involved in this foolish quest rather than immediately dampening her hopes. I would never forgive myself if anything happened to Magdalen Melmoth.

Pruett must have read my mind. He put his arm around me and spoke softly. "Hey. Stop second-guessing yourself. She asked for your help and you gave it. Simple as that. QED. You can't control every bad thing in life, Perri. Don't even try. Believe me, I know."

He was right, of course, but that didn't lessen my anxiety or quell the rising tide of panic I felt. No doubt about it—Magdalen touched my emotions. Her bravery, ingenuity, and refusal to back down were emblematic of a senior superhero. I felt connected to her in ways too obscure to explain even to myself. I didn't understand it, but I made a firm decision: If Carrick had any viable information, I planned to turn it over to Sheriff Aleita and her minions. That was the only way to protect Magdalen Melmoth and stay true to my pledge.

Babette had fabricated a plausible cover story, saying that our group was doing genealogical research on Sebastian Melmoth and trying to trace any descendants. Initially we intended to focus on my situation and desire for information, but I was uncomfortable with stressing my orphan status. We agreed to link our work to antecedents of the Irish Kingsburys and not to mention that we had found Magdalen. If questioned, Pruett would pretend to be writing a piece on the personal toll of tracking lost ancestors. With his talent for duplicity, I knew that boy would be convincing. His skill bordered on the pathological at times and gave me pause for thought.

As we exited the freeway, he turned up the GPS. Rural areas were often a tricky proposition in the evening and directions were crucial. I'd never been to Strasburg, although I'd met several dog breeders who lived in the area. The north central Shenandoah Valley had the advantage of mountains, rivers, verdant fields, and a small but growing population with roots dating back to the Revolutionary War. Apparently the burgeoning suburban sprawl from the DC area had infected even this idyllic setting. Signs announcing the imminent arrival of both single-family homes and town houses dotted the landscape. Builders called that progress, but it saddened me. Surely some corners of rural America should remain pristine, particularly when so much history was involved. I wondered what the reaction had been to this incursion. Local residents were proud of their heritage and touted it whenever possible. I'd seen too much carnage up front and personal to romanticize battles from any conflict, but for many in Virginia reenactments— particularly Civil War ones—were both a passion and a profitable sideline. Tourists flocked to them and adored the faux action. Pruett had no use for that either. He had covered several bloody conflicts—most recently in Syria—and confronted the toll of actual wars. He also had no need to indulge in macho fantasies to bolster his ego; every day he got more than his share of adulation.

"Kind of a nice country feel to the place," he mused as he surveyed the terrain, "although that may not last long. Wonder if Ella would like it?"

Wing Pruett's devotion to Ella was one of the things I cherished most about him. That didn't mean I couldn't rib him about it, of course.

"Lots of acreage around here," I said. "Better grab some while you still can. Think how many more dogs Ella could have. Horses too."

That ended further speculation about the wonders of the bucolic life. Pruett's introduction to animals had come rather late in life and was still a work in progress. For the sake of his daughter and me, he tried valiantly to adjust to the four-footed set and had made great strides. Currently Ella had one dog, a champion pointer. I knew, however, that the little girl was eyeing another dog to add to the mix, a Leonberger, a gentle breed of considerable size. Pruett had temporarily fended off those overtures, but in the long run my money was on Ella.

After easing through the main thoroughfare, we turned abruptly and reached a bumpy rural road.

"There go the springs on this heap," Pruett groused. He cherished his snazzy SUV almost as much as he did me, and perhaps a bit more. Props to Micah—he powered his Cadillac over those same roads without flinching.

A mile or so later, a large farmhouse emerged in the clearing. Nothing fancy, just a weathered, two-story structure that looked solid and homey, the way Carrick himself might be. I visualized a flock of chickens, geese, and several cows and horses, a living embodiment of Old MacDonald's farm. To counteract the fading sunlight, our host had thoughtfully illuminated the driveway with floodlights. As we pulled in, a deep, soulful bark sounded a warning. Pruett's eyes widened, but I knew better. It must have been kismet or something very much like it. To my delight the canine in question was actually Ella's dream dog—a Leonberger. The giant German working breed frequently topped 150 pounds and looked daunting to a nervous Nellie like Pruett. An enthusiast would see only a furry bundle of love that was cute and cuddly. Instead of charging us, the dog lost interest, heaved a gigantic sigh, and immediately collapsed back on the porch.

"Good thing Ella isn't here." Pruett shuddered. "Seeing that dog would start her off again."

I gave Keats and Poe the "bleib" command, Schutzhund for stay, and eased out of the Porsche. As the front door of the house creaked a welcome, we got our first glimpse of Carrick Farraday.

His height surprised me. Despite his age, Carrick was lean and stood a good six feet six inches tall. He extended his hand and grinned. "At last. Don't get many visitors out here, so Paddy and I are out of practice. We've been on pins and needles waiting for you."

"Paddy?"

He pointed to his dog as I introduced our quartet. "That's a fine-looking vehicle you've got," he said to Pruett, pointing to the Porsche. "'Course the Caddie's not too shabby either."

Babette instantly went into Southern mode. "You're so kind to see us, Mr. Farraday. I'm sure you were surprised."

Carrick motioned us inside. "Nonsense. When does a geezer my age get to entertain two beautiful ladies? By the way, bring your dogs in too. No need to leave those beauties outside. I'm a breeder myself, you see."

My eyes widened. "Don't tell me you breed Leonbergers? I saw Paddy when we came in. He's fantastic."

That established an instant rapport between us, dog person to dog person. Those of us who love animals are kindred spirits, easy prey for anyone who praises our pets. Pruett blanched as he looked around. "Where are they? The rest of them, I mean."

Carrick chuckled. "Don't worry. My kennel is in the back. Daisy just had a litter and she's not keen on any involvement by Paddy, even though the big lug is the da." He gestured toward the room surrounding a gigantic hearth. "Please. Sit down and make yourselves comfortable. I made tea."

He winked at the men. "Combined with a slug of Irish whiskey, it really hits the spot."

Pruett brightened. "Now you're speaking my language. We won't keep you too long, sir. Just a few questions." He introduced us, stressing my quest to help a friend seeking family roots. That was my cue and, recalling Magdalen's plight, I poured emotion into it.

"I was raised in foster homes," I said. "Didn't think much about that until recently, but with all the advertisements about DNA testing and tracing one's ancestry, I decided to give it a try. Professor Douglas at GWU suggested I help trace someone as an experiment of sorts."

Babette plowed headlong into the conversation. "Perri joined the army, graduated from college, and has her own business in Great Marsh. Kinda like Wonder Woman, but without the cape and lasso."

Another chuckle from Carrick. "Admirable," he said. "You may not recall, Ms. Morgan, but I bought several of your dog collars online. Fantastic quality. It's tough finding durable products for the big breeds, you know."

The unexpected praise warmed me, especially coming from a professional breeder. "Before we start, perhaps you'll show us Daisy and her pups. Pruett's daughter goes gaga over Leonbergers and I love the breed myself." Naturally that led to similar praise from Carrick for my Malinois, and Clara, Babette's border collie. Micah seemed content, but I knew by the tapping of Pruett's fingers that he was impatient. Too much doggy love by half for that boy.

"Come on, then," Carrick said. "We can just take a peek. Daisy outdid herself this time. Nine pups, can you believe it?" He led us back to a separate kennel structure the size of a small barn where Daisy and her brood were resting.

"No problem touching them. They're five weeks now and love to play. Daisy would probably appreciate a bit of rest."

Needless to say, Babette and I immediately made fools of ourselves by petting and cuddling the pups. Micah joined in, but Pruett stood back and watched.

"Are they all promised?" I asked.

"All but one." Carrick pointed to a large male with a wide splash of white on his chest. "That's Prospero," he said. "Probably not show quality with that white hair, but a lovable cuss if I do say so myself."

I lectured myself on all the reasons why another pet was simply not in the cards but remained unconvinced. If Pruett hadn't nudged me back to the house, I might never have left the whelping room.

"Easy does it," he said. "Keats and Poe don't want another dog in the mix."

"Ella would love him," I said. "Hope she doesn't find out."

"Don't worry," Babette said. "I snapped a picture of Prospero to send to her." Pruett gave her a horrified look and she laughed. "Just kidding."

"This is an ideal setting for a kennel," Micah remarked. "Although I see by those highway signs that may change."

A sudden scowl darkened Carrick's face. "Developers! Vultures I call them. Damn pests have been plaguing all the property owners around here. Planning 'country estates'—their words, not mine. I threatened to sic Paddy on them and they scattered." He shrugged. "'Course that was an idle threat. Paddy'd lick them to death, but they didn't know that."

Micah shook his head. "Did they have any luck?"

"Yeah. Couple of my neighbors sold up." Carrick's lips tightened. "Can't say as I blame them, though. They were getting old and couldn't turn down a couple of million bucks. Not that I could either, but I did."

"Understandable," Pruett said. "It's your home."

Carrick slapped him on his back. "Exactly. Born and raised here and hope to end my days here too. Besides, my deed restricts ownership to the Farraday family. Da locked things up good and tight in some kind of family trust. Don't know the particulars, but I know that much." He chuckled. "That cooled off most of them right away. They went for easier pickings."

He led the way back into the living room and the real test of our visit began. I mentioned the Kingsbury family and a possible connection between them and the Melmoths. That's where Micah joined in. As an attorney, he lent an official air to the proceedings and was able to cite the specific information that led us to Carrick.

"The trail grew cold with Henrietta Farraday," Micah said. "We hoped to find some linkage to your family, sir. I found a number of Kingsburys in Ireland—almost an overwhelming number. Quite a prolific clan, if I may say so."

Carrick nodded. "Yes indeed. They took that go-forth-and-multiply line as a direct command." He reached down and patted Poe's head as he spoke. "Henrietta was my stepmother, you see. Fine woman. She married my da in 1949, when I was a wee lad of six months. My own ma died in childbirth." His face crumpled for a moment as he said that. "Not unusual in those times, of course, and a boy needs a mother."

My next task was a delicate one. How to mention Magdalen without appearing too eager? Fortunately, Pruett had me covered.

"The immigration papers listed Henrietta's daughter. Did she live with you?"

Carrick's face lit up. "My, yes! Magdalen, my feisty big sis. We were a tag team, don't you know. Oh Mags. How I loved her."

"Did you two keep in touch?" Micah asked. "Sounds like you were close."

A shadow eclipsed the grin on Carrick's face. "Ah now, that's a shame, it is. You know how families can be. Da went first and then Henrietta passed in 1969. After that our family started unraveling."

"Magdalen?" I asked tentatively.

"Don't you know, that girl was always strong-willed. No rules for her, you see. My da—well, he was an old-time Irishman, ruler of the house, king of the castle. No chit of a girl was going to disobey him. When Mags finished college, she had dreams—big plans. She wanted to be a writer, like her own father. Da wanted her to stay home with her family and keep house. He ran a construction business and Mags was clever with figures." The tale was so riveting and the family drama so vivid that I lost track of time and place.

"It was the 1960s, you see, and the old ways were out the door." He grimaced. "There was a big dustup—oh, I can still see their faces. Mags packed her bags, squared her shoulders, and walked straight out that door with Da shouting that he never wanted to see her again."

Tears coursed down Babette's face. "And…?"

"That was the last I saw of my sister. She kept in touch with Henrietta, at least I think she did. Mags's name was never spoken aloud again in this house." He poured a generous slug of whiskey into his teacup. "Sounds harsh, I know, but those old fellows were like absolute monarchs. Don't get me wrong. Declan Farraday was a good man but very much a product of his generation."

Time for Pruett to edge into the conversation. "You never tried to trace your sister?"

Carrick sighed. "Not really. Things weren't so easy before the Internet, and by now, if she were alive, Mags would be in her mid-eighties. I Googled her name several times but got nothing. Probably should have hired a private investigator, but frankly I was afraid of what I might find."

Micah raised his eyebrows.

"I mean, I guess I wanted to picture Mags roaming Europe, writing salacious novels. You know. It would have broken my heart to know for certain that she had passed."

I slowly digested the information, visualizing young Magdalen Melmoth asserting herself under difficult circumstances. Losing one's family was heartbreaking, a huge price to pay for independence. I knew that all too well.

"Did you have any other siblings?" I asked. "I always yearned for a big family myself."

He sighed. "No siblings, just my Uncle John, Da's younger brother. He's long gone, of course, but his daughter lived somewhere around here for a while, and her daughter went on to have the career Mags could only dream of." He grinned. "Never married myself. I'm sure no lady would have an old codger like me."

Pruett drained his cup of tea and said, "How so?"

"Like most bachelors I'm set in my ways," Carrick said.

"Pruett understands that." Babette smirked. "Just ask him."

Something Carrick said sent a warning flash in my mind. "Was Mags's father a writer, Mr. Farraday?"

"That depends on who you believe. Harriet said so, and Mags was sure that her da was a genius. My own father didn't take kindly to such talk, though. Felt it fed Mags's fantasies, you see." He grimaced. "Might've been a tad jealous as well."

Pruett nodded. "I know that feeling. My daughter is only seven, but I feel so helpless sometimes when she gets the bit between her teeth. I don't suppose Henrietta left any papers around the house? Some links to the Melmoth family?"

Babette launched into a long digression about her own family and how she'd squirreled away keepsakes in her attic.

My mind wandered as they spoke, and I wondered if my own parents were watching from afar, and if they felt proud of me.

"I might have some things piled up around here," Carrick said. "After Da and Henrietta passed, I kind of lost track of things. Didn't have the heart to relive those memories."

Micah saw his cue and asked if Carrick would permit him to sort through any papers on behalf of his client. "Under your supervision, of course, sir, and at your convenience."

We agreed to reconvene in a week, after Carrick had time to consider the offer and to locate the information.

The bombshell of the evening occurred as Carrick and Babette continued their chat. I was so far down memory lane that I nearly missed the entire exchange.

"Well, at least your uncle's granddaughter did okay," Babette said. "I bet that makes you feel proud."

Carrick nodded. "She's a doctor. Not a physician but a PhD. Lovely girl, Joan is."

The room was toasty warm, but a sudden chill enveloped my body. "Joan?" I felt duplicitous until I pictured Magdalen, helpless at the hands of potential killers.

"Ah yes. Her married name is Fergueson. Dr. Joan Fergueson. She lives not too far away from here."

Chapter 12

Pruett looked away, Micah stiffened, and Babette gasped.

"Something wrong?" Carrick asked.

This time Pruett's duplicity came in handy. "It's so weird," he said, "but I believe we've met her, or at least someone with a similar name."

Carrick's blue-eyed gaze sharpened. "No kidding."

I explained that Babette and I did Therapy Dog work at the Falls, and that the staff director was a Dr. Joan Fergueson. "She's a woman in her middle thirties," I said.

Carrick paused. "Might be my Joanie. She kept her own name at first but finally changed to his." He folded his arms and stared at us. "What's really going on here? I've tried to answer your questions and I deserve the truth from you."

I kicked Babette in the shin before she began blubbering and allowed Micah to take the lead.

"My client asked us to help find any trace of the Melmoth family, especially any close connections." He shrugged. "We had no idea that Dr. Fergueson was related to your family."

Carrick clenched his hands. "Who is this client?"

Lawyers are trained to dissemble, and Micah immediately illustrated why he was the pride of Georgetown Law School. "I'm sorry. Until I contact my client, I can't reveal any more information. Ms. Morgan and Mrs. Croy were only trying to help. Mr. Pruett is a respected journalist who is writing a feature about tracing one's roots. Believe me, we were not trying to deceive you." Those words appeased Carrick somewhat, although he still remained wary.

"May I call you tomorrow after I confer with my client?" Micah's wording was stiff and lawyerly, but it served its purpose. Legalese was an ointment that deliberately obscured meaning and reduced inflammation.

We rose as one and prepared to decamp. The warmth of the room and our meeting had vanished, leaving in its wake a decided chill.

I pressed Carrick's hand and said, "Thank you for your kindness and for sharing your beautiful dogs with us."

He nodded stiffly, ever the old-school gentleman. At that point I doubted whether he would honor his pledge to share family data or any other information with us again. Fortunately, Babette had no inhibitions whatsoever. She flung herself into Carrick's arms and sniffled noisily. "You can't dismiss us so easily, Carrick Farraday. I'll be back. Don't you let Prospero go without callin' me. Ya hear?"

On that surprising note, we sped back to northern Virginia to plot our next move.

* * * *

Pruett was stone-faced as we navigated the back roads, but I was no chatterbox either. Betrayal was foreign to me and I felt sickened by our attempt to deceive a fine man like Carrick Farraday. When we reached route 66 East, I turned to Pruett. "What next? I can't face Carrick again unless we fess up."

He brushed a strand of hair from my eyes, a tender gesture that thoroughly captivated me. "Look, Perri. We had no idea how Carrick would be, and we didn't lie. Not really." I rolled my eyes when he said that. No amount of rationalizing would convince me otherwise. Intent to deceive was the same as a deliberate lie. I'd learned that in my catechism days, and nothing had changed since.

Pruett was undeterred. After all, his stock in trade involved luring the unsuspecting into revealing information. Behavior I considered shameful was merely a tool of his trade.

"Remember," he said, "we had no idea that Dr. Joan Fergueson and Carrick Farraday were related. How could we possibly know? It does raise some interesting questions, though."

"Like what?"

His eyes gleamed. Frankly they recalled the line from Poe's masterpiece *The Raven*, about fiery eyes that burned into my bosom's core. A touch dramatic perhaps, but with his slick black hair and sharp profile, Wing Pruett resembled a bird of prey.

"Tomorrow we'll see Magdalen and have it out with her," he said. "Enough posturing and dissembling. Being old doesn't necessarily make her trustworthy. She's been playing us from the start, parceling out just enough information to keep our attention."

He was right, of course. I'm usually a shrewd judge of character, but Magdalen Melmoth had captured an empty space in my heart and probably had done so deliberately. What had Irene Wilson said about her? Magdalen was a demon with computers and social media. Surely a woman with mad technical skills could have found the same information we had. After all, Carrick Farraday practically lived in her neighborhood and, unlike us, Magdalen knew his first name. I leaned back and rested my head on the buttery leather seat of the Macan. Exhaustion and, yes, disappointment overwhelmed me. I resented being used as a stalking horse by a person with a hidden agenda, especially someone I had liked and trusted. Overall our foray had been successful, but at what cost? We'd gotten insights into Magdalen's childhood, rebellious teen years, and family, and also confirmed that her father was a writer. Nothing definite about Oscar Wilde. Not one bit.

"Wake up, sleepyhead." Pruett touched my shoulder as we swung into the driveway of my home. "Need me to carry you inside?"

I bounced up immediately. "Hardly. I was just thinking. Resting my eyes." For some reason I hated to be caught napping. It heightened my sense of vulnerability, particularly around Pruett, whose constant state of hyperactivity was almost superhuman.

"Sure. Must have been mistaken." I knew he was laughing at me, but I refused to yield. No need to play the fragile vessel around him when there were plenty of women vying for that role. I gritted my teeth and stayed strong.

He checked his watch. "I think we have time for a strategy session if Micah and Babette are up to it. How about if I warm some brandy and light up the fireplace?"

That offer was just too good to refuse. Before long, four adults, three dogs, and one surly coon cat were gathered about the fireplace, inhaling the comforting scent of fragrant oak logs. Fortunately Zeke the pygmy goat stayed in his shed, with beautiful Raza to keep him company.

We quickly summarized our impressions of Carrick and the bombshell revelation about Dr. Joan Fergueson.

"I knew that heifer was up to no good," Babette said. "Told you that, Perri, the first time we met her. Old starchy drawers." She paused. "In fairness, those croissants they served were the best I've ever eaten. Heavenly."

Micah glanced up from his iPhone and said, "It's puzzling. Surely Dr. Fergueson knows the background of her residents. Magdalen's name would stand out a mile to someone with her family history." He shrugged. "Why hide it? Maybe she's playing a double game."

My mind was awash with answers to that very question. Had Mags revealed her supposed ancestry to either the staff or the other residents? Irene Wilson knew and might have quite innocently mentioned it. If the lost Oscar Wilde manuscript actually existed, Joan Fergueson may have coveted it and acted accordingly. Murders had been committed for far less.

Pruett added his perspectives to the mix. "I watched Carrick closely the whole time and I don't believe he was lying. He truly didn't know Magdalen's whereabouts unless he gave an award-caliber performance."

The consensus about Carrick was easy to reach; we all liked him. Babette was also gaga over his dogs, especially the pup Prospero. I'd seen that air of determination before and knew what it presaged. When the Croy express started rolling—watch out.

"We need to speak with Magdalen," I said. "Tomorrow."

Micah and Pruett had prior commitments, but I was undeterred. "No problem. Babette and I will swing by the Falls first thing. Don't worry. We'll keep you updated."

They didn't like it, but they bowed to the inevitable. Tomorrow would be a day of reckoning for us, Magdalen Melmoth, and Oscar Wilde as well.

* * * *

Before leaving the next morning, Pruett gave me plenty of unsolicited advice. Based on my army training, I knew how to protect myself, although Babette's skills were questionable. We joked that if faced with danger, her only option was to talk her adversary into a stupor. There was more than a grain of truth to that; martial arts had not been on the debutante menu when Babette came of age. Pruett mentioned that and continued to dither over me until I finally called a halt to it.

"We'll be in full view of dozens of people," I said. "Besides, I'm eager to chat with Dr. Fergueson before she hears from Carrick first. Tomorrow's our regular Therapy Dog day anyhow, so it won't look suspicious."

Pruett nervously ran his fingers through that thick crop of hair. His morning interview was with a congressman, so he was formally garbed in the DC uniform of a navy suit, a starched white shirt, and a tie. The effect was dazzling, but I kept my hormones in check. No time for nonsense today. No sir!

"Don't try anything cute with those people," he warned. "Remember, there's a murderer running loose around there."

"What does Sheriff Aleita say?" I teased. "Surely you have some inside info on the case."

His normal good humor deserted him and Pruett was not amused. "Funny, Perri. We're talking homicide here." He looked down—a dead giveaway that he was trying to avoid something. "Besides, Aleita hasn't gotten much farther than we have. Do you know how many outlets sell Belgian chocolates these days? Impossible!"

I pinched his cheek. "Come on, Golden Boy. Fess up. Who's their chief suspect?"

Pruett straightened his tie and adjusted his jacket. "I have no idea. Besides, they're wondering if Nurse Ross was the intended target all along. Guess who that puts in the bull's-eye?"

I got the uncomfortable feeling I already knew the answer.

"One Magdalen Melmoth, that's who." Pruett gave me a superior smirk. "Seems that Magdalen had a big blowout with Ross that very week. Something about medication or lost items. Very explosive."

I realized how absurd that was, but in a rural police force anything was possible. Magdalen might be railroaded into a jail cell if she wasn't careful.

"Does Micah know?" I asked, trying to quell panic in my voice. As a major fangirl of Perry Mason, I knew what he would tell his client: keep your mouth shut.

"He knows. Believe me, Ms. Melmoth is in good hands. Just be careful what you do at that place." He shuddered. "The Falls. Even the name gives me the creeps. Like something out of a horror movie."

Luckily for the sake of my nerves, Babette drove up at that point and tooted her horn. I kissed Pruett's forehead, gathered my dogs and gear, and decamped as fast as I decently could. My pal was a ray of sunshine, garbed in shades of yellow with a pinch of orange. Naturally everything was perfectly coordinated, from her parka to her thigh-high boots. In contrast, I wore my peacoat, plaid flannel shirt, and perfectly pressed jeans with ankle boots. Both of us wore makeup, although I had to admit that hers was more skillfully applied. Our vehicle of choice that day was Babette's new Range Rover, a snazzy ride with every possible premium feature and a fantastic red exterior. Fortunately I never envied my pal's wealth or judged her conspicuous consumption. Both were aspects of her character that combined nicely with a loving heart and generous soul. As we clambered into the beast and sped off toward the Falls, I noted a telltale flush on Babette's face that meant only one thing. Sex, love, or the prospect of both had once again entered her life.

"Did Micah get home all right?" I asked.

My friend was uncharacteristically closemouthed. "Yep."

"He's a good guy," I said. "A keeper for sure."

Whatever had gone on between the two of them remained a mystery, and I could only assume that things went well. No need to press. Sooner or later Babette would share every detail, even the most intimate ones. She simply couldn't help herself.

"Let's check in with Dr. Fergueson first thing," I said. "We'll know right away if she spoke with her uncle. What's your bet?"

"Carrick seemed like a straight shooter to me. If he contacted her, she'll probably tell us. Safer that way." She grimaced. "Dr. Starchy Pants is one cautious critter, trust me on that. Won't give away anything unless she has to."

We pulled into the driveway, unloaded our gear, and queued up behind the other Therapy Dog participants. I waved to Kate Thayer but didn't stop to chat. The oleaginous Rolf Hart stood behind her, surrounded by a gaggle of admirers. He virtually ignored his lovely borzoi, who he seemed to regard as a fashion accessory rather than a beloved pet.

Today's group included two golden retrievers, one rambunctious Lab, and several miniature poodles. Blending in seemed the better part of valor and the crowd made it easy. Pruett would approve of a cautious approach and I hoped to assess the climate at the facility before acting. Right on cue, Dr. Joan Fergueson entered the lobby and welcomed us with a specious smile. To my surprise, she was accompanied by someone new in medical garb. It seemed early and a tad disrespectful to have replaced Nurse Ross so soon after her death. Dr. Fergueson addressed that by noting that increased staffing at the Falls had been planned weeks before. The newcomer was introduced as Edgar Williamson, a burly man of middle years who looked like he meant business. His shaved head and perpetual scowl added to the dampening effect. Babette elbowed me as we stood in a semicircle around him.

"Hope we don't have to tangle with that guy, Perri. He looks mean."

"Be cool and watch out for Irene and Magdalen." Babette was task oriented; give her a job and she forgot everything else. As I scanned the audience, I saw several residents who had mobbed Pruett last week, as well as a number of less mobile people in wheelchairs and walkers. No sign of either Irene or Magdalen. Babette clutched Clara in a death grip and twisted her own long locks into a ponytail. "Let's get this show on the road," she muttered. "Time's a wasting."

Most Therapy Dog programs followed an established pattern: a general introduction to the residents, a nod to each dog and handler duo, and an interactive session with plenty of laughter and a few prizes. The warm reaction by our audience was genuine, and because of their size, both Keats and Poe were tasked with opening and closing the session with a formal bow. I was so consumed by the explosion of love and awe for the dogs, I zoned out and forgot our true purpose. Fortunately Babette applied a sharp elbow to my side, bringing me painfully back to my senses.

"For heaven's sake, Perri, stay on task. Stop mooning around." Babette the Enforcer was in the house and I couldn't argue with her.

"You slip out and find Magdalen," I said, "while I chat up Dr. Fergueson. She glared at us the minute she came into the room." It was probably paranoia on my part, although the look on Joan Fergueson's face was far from friendly. Her greetings to the volunteers were artificial and good cheer was noticeably absent from her prepared remarks. Then again, I'd never noticed much warmth radiating from her before, so nothing had really changed.

"Hope that mean nurse doesn't catch me," Babette whispered. "He looks like a thug. Too bad Dr. Tully didn't show up. I know how to handle his kind of hottie."

After a few false starts she finally sidled toward the elevators, while I edged closer to Joan Fergueson. This morning the administrator had traded her somber attire for a flattering cherry dress whose vibrant color suited her well. Somehow I'd never noticed before that deprived of her drab uniform Dr. F was an attractive woman. Her jewelry was expensive but understated: an intricate gold necklace and a ruby ring that highlighted the color of her dress. Did she deliberately understate her sex appeal by shielding herself with the bland mask of bureaucracy? Some women equated drab, shapeless clothing with authority. Nonsense, of course, but not unusual.

"May I speak with you for a moment?" I asked. My smile was nonthreatening and letter perfect. "I met a friend of yours last evening."

She swiveled her head wildly, as if looking for salvation. "Yes. Yes. Of course, Ms. Morgan. Just give me a chance to close the program out."

I pondered her reaction, then shrugged it off. Clearly the woman was unsettled by my request, although she might have other pressing matters on her plate as well. Better not to read too much into it. Before long, she waved me into one of the more secluded conversation areas, adjusted the hem of her dress, and gave me a nervous smile.

"You mentioned a friend of mine," said Joan Fergueson. "Who might that be?"

I'd had plenty of time to practice deception, a skill that had grown appreciably since I met Wing Pruett. Some day—in the future— I needed to evaluate that character flaw and make amends.

"We met your uncle last evening," I said. "What a wonderful man!"

At first Joan looked puzzled, making me wonder how many relatives she had.

"You know, Carrick Farraday."

Light finally dawned on the woman. "Oh. Uncle Carr. Yes, he is a real charmer. How did you happen to meet him?"

I gave an expurgated and slightly untrue account of our actions. "I'm a leather smith, you know, and turns out we've actually done business before. His Leonbergers were simply majestic!"

Joan coughed faintly. "Yes. Yes. Overwhelming. I haven't seen him in quite a while, of course. The demands of everything here keep me so busy."

Our conversation faltered, leading me to up the ante. "I had no idea you were related to Magdalen too. Strange how things turn out, isn't it? That old six-degrees-of-separation theory at work."

Dr. Fergueson turned aside and coughed once more. "You'll have to excuse me. I can't seem to shake this cold."

"No problem," I said. "Most everyone has some kind of bug this time of the year."

That pause allowed Dr. F to regroup. She gave me a vague, minimally polite stare, as if I had made some glaring faux pas. "I'm afraid I don't understand. What makes you think Ms. Melmoth and I are related?"

That took me aback. "Magdalen's mother was Carrick's stepmother. Magdalen lived with the Farradays until she finished school. I just assumed you knew all about it."

Despite the warmth of the room's central heating, Joan Fergueson radiated pure frost. "Family history never interested me much. I assure you there's been some type of mistake." Her features were set in an impenetrable mask that epitomized the term "stone-faced." Had I stared at the monuments on Mount Rushmore I would have been more likely to spark a reaction. Joan Fergueson was one tough cookie who was unlikely to crumble easily.

Most people call me plucky, although Pruett says I'm hardheaded. Faced with Joan's resistance I tried another tack. "By the way, how is Magdalen? I didn't see her at today's program and it kind of worried me. She's so keen on the Therapy Dog program. She's not ill, I hope."

Joan gave me a steely glance designed to quell incipient rebellion by the masses. "You must understand that even if what you say is accurate, Ms. Melmoth and I are very remote connections at best. I try to discourage favoritism here, and frankly I screen out most of the residents' chatter. I can assure you that Magdalen has never suggested such a thing to me. I'm surprised Uncle Carrick even mentioned the matter."

I considered my options and decided to seize the moment. I have always been an impulsive kind of gal anyway. "I was surprised myself. We had no idea you were related. As it turns out, Magdalen was concerned about some missing family papers and I promised to help find them." I shrugged. "It seemed like such a small favor and Wing thought it might make for an interesting piece."

Her eyes widened. "Wing Pruett was part of this charade? Haven't we had enough bad publicity?" She clutched the top of the sofa as if it were a lifeline. "Since Nurse Ross died our residents haven't stopped chattering. You can't believe how many calls I've gotten from their relatives, and the local press has simply hounded me." For once the seemingly imperturbable Dr. F seemed surprisingly human and ready to crack.

Normally I loathe rubbing salt in a wound, but in this instance… "Murder tends to upset folks, I guess. The residents here are so vulnerable."

A low sound from Keats alerted me to a possible problem. When I turned around Edgar Williamson was right behind me. For a large man he moved quickly, and his steps were surprisingly quiet. Stealthy.

"Something wrong, Dr. Fergueson?" His voice was guttural, more growl than gruff. Had I been alone I would have felt threatened.

She shook her head. "Everything's fine, Edgar. Ms. Morgan was just leaving."

I summoned my great big Brownie smile. "Of course. By the way, are there any storage facilities on-site for the residents? Might as well sift through Magdalen's belongings while I'm here."

Joan Fergueson puffed up like an affronted cobra. "Impossible! I can't allow a stranger to pillage her belongings. I have a fiduciary responsibility here."

I enjoyed administering the coup de grâce to this uptight bureaucrat. Maybe Pruett wasn't such a bad influence after all. Puncturing the balloons of the self-important provided instant gratification. "Oh. You probably didn't know that Magdalen designated me as her heir. Power of attorney and all that legal stuff. I can have her lawyer fax you the information."

Joan Fergueson showed admirable self-control. The information obviously floored her, but she recovered quickly. She squared her shoulders and assumed the mantle of authority once more. "Please do that. Each resident has a locker in the lower level. I keep a key and so do they. We don't want them prowling about alone. Injuries, you see. Insurance liability."

Magdalen had neglected to share that bit of information with me. I fumed inwardly but maintained my composure. Sangfroid, they called it in composition classes. The French have such a way with words. "Terrific. Mrs. Croy and I will check with you first." I shook Joan's hand and made my escape before Nurse Edgar could intervene.

Chapter 13

I found Babette, Magdalen, and Irene Wilson huddled together in Irene's suite sipping chamomile tea and munching biscuits. Guilt was spread over their faces like strawberry jam.

"Okay you three, fess up." I resurrected my sergeant self, hands on hips and serious frown. All I needed was a uniform and a nightstick. First, I tackled Babette. She was the youngest and most likely to yield under pressure. "What kind of trouble have you been brewing?"

My pal lacked the gene for lying. Her downcast eyes and swaying movement proved that.

"Stow it, will you, Perri? We've just been talkin' about things."

Magdalen coolly intervened. "Have some tea, dear. You must be parched." She lowered a plate of chicken gizzards to the floor for my dogs, and those stalwart guardians quickly succumbed to the bribe.

"So, you met Carrick Farraday," Magdalen said. "Sounds like he hasn't lost his charm over the years. He was always such a scamp."

Control yourself, I thought. *Remember, she's an old lady, not some fresh recruit.* "Why didn't you tell us where he lived, Magdalen? It would have saved so much time."

Nothing fazed this woman. She was made of pure steel. "I had faith in your group, dear. I knew you'd get there without my help." Magdalen lowered her eyes. "And quite frankly I worried that after all this time, Carrick might have forgotten me, or worse still that he might not be compos mentis anymore." She and Irene exchanged looks. "We see that all the time around here. Of course, Carrick is considerably younger than our residents."

Babette immediately applied a liberal dose of soft soap. "We understand, Magdalen. Don't we, Irene? After all, there's no real harm done. We've been cookin' up plans for a big ole family reunion. Wait 'til you see those dogs of his!"

I took several deep breaths. Self-control was critical in situations like this. "Carrick has some of your family papers. He even invited us to sort through them."

Magdalen clapped her hands. "Perfect! How dear of him to keep my mother's things after all these years."

"Speaking of mementos, Dr. Fergueson said each resident has a storage area. Any chance that the manuscript might be there?" I spoke through gritted teeth, trying mightily not to upset her.

Irene Wilson gasped. "My, oh my. I forgot all about those old lockers. Mine is chock full of stuff and I bet yours is too, Mags."

Magdalen leaned her head against the sofa back. "Of course. It's so taxing to traipse down there that I've totally put it out of my mind." She hesitated. "The last person I spoke to about that was Nurse Ross. She offered to sort through it for me and I gave her my key."

I shuddered, fearing the worst. "When was that?"

Magdalen sighed. "The day before she was murdered. She never did return that key."

My mind was going nonstop and my thoughts weren't pretty. Had Nurse Carole Ross found something in Magdalen's papers that cost her her life? That didn't make any sense. The murderer had no guarantee that the nurse and not Magdalen would consume the sweets. I made a mental note to self to have Pruett check with his pal Sheriff Aleita about that key. If it were missing, one had to suppose that anything of value in that locker would be long gone. Either way, before we left I would ask Dr. Fergueson to change the locks.

"When would you like to meet Carrick?" I asked Magdalen. "Pruett and Micah will join us, of course."

Babette rubbed her hands together. "We need to get this show on the road PDQ. What's your weekend lookin' like, Magdalen?"

Irene's smile was a mile wide. "Oh, this is so exciting. Like a treasure hunt or one of those PBS mysteries." She put her arm around Magdalen's shoulders and gently squeezed them.

"I suppose Saturday would be alright if it's convenient for Carrick." She bit her lip. "Truth be told, I dread the whole thing. Maybe we should leave the past alone. My parents were fine people no matter what their lineage was."

This was a different side of the intrepid Magdalen Melmoth I had come to know and admire. I understood her fear, but it still disappointed me. Perhaps even superheroes have their limitations.

"It's totally up to you, of course. We never mentioned your name to Carrick, or your whereabouts."

Magdalen rose and plucked her copy of *Dorian Gray* from the bookcase. The connection appeared to strengthen her, and when she turned to face us, her hands were steady. "Go ahead and make the arrangements, Perri. The Good Book says that the truth will set us free. I guess it's about time I faced facts."

* * * *

Joan Fergueson was absent when we went to find her, but to Babette's delight, Dr. Tully had taken her place. I had to admit that my pal was right about one thing: Tully not only looked good, he also possessed the rare gift of staring into a woman's eyes and actually listening to her, or appearing to do so. He beckoned us over to a sofa and immediately embarked upon a fulsome display of praise for our efforts.

"Your kindness overwhelms me," he said in his plummy voice. "The residents live for these sessions with your therapy dogs."

Babette beamed as if he had proffered a priceless gem. "It's nothin'," she lisped, fluttering those long lashes of hers. "We love comin' here, don't we, Perri?"

Tully made me recall something Magdalen had said. He really was smarmy! Scrape off the good looks and glamorous veneer and you might well find the soul of a confidence man, or even a killer.

I steered Babette back into safe harbor. "Sharing our dogs enriches us too, Dr. Tully. While we're on the subject, I need the key to Magdalen Melmoth's carrel. She lent hers to Nurse Ross on the sad night she passed away."

His reaction was so flawless, I had no idea whether it was genuine or manufactured. "Unfortunate," he said. "We frown on staff members doing special favors for our residents. Erodes morale, you see."

I matched his smile with one of my own. "I totally understand. Dr. Fergueson said that you keep a copy of each resident's key. Mrs. Croy and I will take a quick peak at the locker and return the key to you before we leave." I raised my hand. "Promise."

I had to admit his smile was captivating. Babette must have agreed because she loudly sighed as Tully headed toward his office.

"Give me a second while I find it," he said. When he returned, he held two keys in his hand. "Funny thing. Carole must have returned the key to our office. Well, no matter." He handed me the numbered key. "I'll be at lunch, so just drop it in this envelope when you're done."

Babette started to protest until I stomped on her toe—hard. She gave me a puzzled look, but stayed silent until Tully left the area. "What's the big deal, Perri? That hurt!"

I herded her toward the elevator and pushed the Down button. "Wait 'til the guys hear this. Carole Ross got that key the day she died. She returned it to Dr. F sometime that same evening. Why didn't Magdalen mention that?"

"Sounds fishy to me," Babette said. "Or maybe she forgot. She's no teenager, for heaven's sake. Maybe old Mags lost a step or two."

The elevator door opened noisily into a darkened corridor faintly illuminated by those unsightly, utilitarian light bulbs that supposedly help to save the planet. In typical fashion, Babette shrank back, allowing me to precede her. I fervently hoped that no rodent would make an appearance while we were there; my pal had an almost pathological fear of them. I'd seen Babette totally lose control and a bout of hysteria was not on my agenda for today. To be sure, I was no fan of rodents either, but during my stint in the army I'd learned to endure them and a number of other unpleasant things I hoped to never again see.

The lockers were large, padlocked spaces separated by numbered signs. We had no trouble at all locating Magdalen's. Like her, it was neat, almost prim, with labeled wire baskets arrayed on each shelf.

"Look for the one that says 'documents,'" I said. "According to Magdalen, it has all her papers. Too bad the light isn't better in this place."

Babette reached into her capacious handbag and produced a SureFire flashlight. "Here we go. I never leave home without this baby. That ribbed surface is designed to bop an attacker right where it hurts."

"What?"

"On the nose, Perri. The nose. For heaven's sake, woman, get your mind out of the gutter."

If I'd thought about it, I would have blushed. Fortunately I was so focused that her ribald comment sailed right over my head. "Here. Check out these photo albums." I handed several of the elaborate, hand-tooled leather books to Babette, while I sorted through a pile of folders. Most contained utilitarian items such as tax returns, receipts, recipes, and deeds. Suddenly one document with an official seal caught my eye. My hand shook a bit as I unfolded it.

"Hey," I shouted to Babette. "Check this out."

Her response was less than enthusiastic. Babette was nose deep in those photo albums from yesteryear and had no desire to return to the present. I called to her again, more urgently this time.

"For Pete's sake, I'm not deaf. What's so darn important?" she snarled as she snapped the album shut. "Can't a body get any peace around here?"

"We found it, at least I think we did. The smoking gun!"

"What?"

I brandished the document just beyond her reach. "What we have here is the last will and testament of Magdalen's father, Sebastian Fingal Melmoth."

Chapter 14

Babette was seldom speechless, but this was one of those times. She stared at me with her mouth agape and said nothing for at least two minutes. When she recovered, she leaped toward me and grabbed the corner of the will.

"Hey! Watch it. You'll destroy evidence." I pried her fingers from the document and held it aloft just out of her grip. Oh, the advantages of six extra inches of height! "Here. Calm down and we can both read it."

Fingal's will was concise. He endowed his bride with all his earthly goods, including his literary estate and that of his father, Sebastian Melmoth of Paris, France. In the event of Henrietta's death, he decreed that all remaining items were the sole property of his daughter, Magdalen Melmoth. The legacy included stocks, cash on hand, and "all papers, manuscripts, and notes related to the literary product of the Melmoths, *père et fils*."

Babette curled her lip. Pouting was one of my pal's few faults and she had mastered the art. "Big deal. How does that even help us? Seems like a big mess to me."

I held up my hand. "Hold on. This establishes that there is a body of work somewhere relating to Sebastian and Fingal Melmoth. It may amount to nothing, but it's a start." I tucked the document into my bag after checking my watch. "Grab those photo albums too. You never know what we might find. We had better make tracks or Dr. Dreamy will hunt us down."

Babette grinned. "That doesn't sound so bad to me. In fact, it might be fun."

"I thought you were fixated on Micah. Don't be greedy."

She shrugged. "Never too much of a good thing, especially when it comes to men. Besides, every woman needs a doctor in the house."

There was no reasoning with her when romance was in the offing. Despite four marriages and a few close calls, Babette remained the eternal optimist, ready and far too willing to love again. I ignored the banter and focused instead on the matter at hand. Sorting through Carrick Farraday's papers now seemed more important than ever. One way or another it might bring closure to the issue of Sebastian Melmoth, Oscar Wilde, and the elusive *Sybil Vane*.

After depositing the key on the good doctor's desk, we sped back to Magdalen's room. She and Irene were engrossed in watching a mystery on PBS but were too polite to ignore us. Magdalen switched off the television and both ladies gave us their full attention. The albums captivated them. Although a number of the photos had faded with age, enough remained to properly set the scene. Magdalen winced as she viewed a formal portrait of her parents in full wedding regalia. They were posed in the severe fashion of the day, although her mother's costume featured a short skirt, flapper style, and bobbed hair. Henrietta was quite a beauty, and judging by her saucy grin, I could see where Magdalen got her spunk. Fingal Melmoth was a tall, lanky youth with dark, dancing eyes and a shock of dark hair. The photo was dated 1928. Fingal would have been in his late twenties at that time, full of promise and high spirits. I racked my brain for memories of Oscar Wilde in the few photos I had seen. Was the resemblance real or perceived? I knew I was as susceptible to a romantic tale as anyone else in that room and the power of suggestion was stronger than I cared to admit.

Magdalen's hand trembled as she caressed the photo. I imagined that her thoughts were far away, with the father she had known for far too short a time.

"I was born five years later," she said. "Scandalous in those days, you see. Babies were expected within the first year. But my mother didn't care. Other people's opinions never bothered her one bit." She sighed as she flipped through pages of the young couple, joined later by a baby in her pram, and a menagerie of pets including dogs, cats, and horses.

"Your dad could have skipped his war service, couldn't he? He was forty or so when the Second World War broke out." Irene squeezed her friend's hand. "I had plenty of uncles in that fracas, but my father had a bad heart and was rejected."

They spent some sharing memories of those days when any man who was physically able insisted on joining up. It was a world that was both foreign and familiar to me and I soaked up every particle of information.

With typical candor, Babette brought us back to reality. "No sign of your dad's parents in there, Magdalen. Too bad. That would have cinched things for us. What a couple!" Babette cried. "Your parents were so good lookin,' Magdalen. You sure favor your Mom."

She agreed that her mother was considered a great beauty. "Dad wooed her so ardently that she simply couldn't resist even though he was penniless." She sighed. "He wrote her all manner of love poems too. People did in those days, you know."

Irene signed. "Too bad they stopped doing that. Emails just don't do it for me."

Poems! I recalled the love letters in the first batch of documents— fastened with ribbons and lovingly preserved. Were folks more sentimental in those times? Perhaps not. Today's lovers hoarded emails and texts with the same devotion. Different times, different methods, similar goals. If Henrietta Melmoth Farraday saved those mementos, as I felt certain she did, they might provide important links to the past. My fingertips tingled with anticipation. Perhaps the answers we sought were slumbering undisturbed in Carrick Farraday's attic. My sense of urgency increased. All the more reason to arrange that reunion as soon as possible. Time was our enemy in this duel with the past.

I knew that Carrick would enjoy sharing memories with Magdalen, and I suggested that she bring the albums with her. After she agreed, Babette and I said our goodbyes and sped back to Great Marsh with our mission partially accomplished.

                                   * * * *

Micah acted as our liaison with Carrick Farraday. The arrangement worked well because attorneys were accustomed to delays and impervious to any slights real or perceived. Magdalen was his client, which conferred upon him the necessary imprimatur to deal on her behalf. Pruett rescheduled everything on his agenda in order to accompany us. When that boy smelled a big story nothing and no one would keep him from his appointed rounds. Sort of like the postal service without the uniform or federal benefits. With masterful self-control I resisted the temptation to picture Pruett in the summer shorts workers wore in the DC area. After all, we had a mission to accomplish.

Babette had her own agenda. When we assembled at my place on Saturday morning, I spied a giant dog crate wedged in the back of her Range Rover and a smug expression on her face.

"Where's Clara?" I asked, although I already knew the answer. Babette intended to lay claim to the pup Prospero and didn't want to frighten him by immediately introducing another dog into the mix. "He's not old enough to leave yet," I objected. "They like pups to be at least seven weeks before they leave their mothers. Some breeders say eight or nine weeks."

Babette gave me a poisonous look. "I know that, Perri. You're not the only one who understands dogs, you know. Carrick and I have already discussed the issue. The crate will help familiarize Prospero with my scent and Clara's too."

Nothing about my BFF surprised me anymore. When Babette got a notion in her head, she was a force to be reckoned with. I'd learned to get out of her way or prepare to be mowed down. Why hadn't she mentioned her negotiations with Carrick about the pup? I wondered what other information they might have exchanged.

Micah and Pruett agreed to swing by the Falls to pick up Magdalen, an arrangement she had readily agreed to. Few women would protest having two handsome guys as their escort and Magdalen was at heart a bit of a flirt.

When we reached Carrick's compound, it was deserted except for a battered pickup truck and his dog van. Like most show people, Carrick had a conversion vehicle modified to accommodate dogs, drains, and crates. It wasn't fancy like Steady Eddie, Babette's behemoth, but it was functional. Carrick had adapted a traditional box truck into a practical model for his giant canines. It reminded me of the man himself: sturdy, no frills, and dependable.

As soon as we exited the car, Paddy issued his mournful, warning bark and ambled over to greet us. This time I didn't hesitate. I bent down and gave the furry giant a big hug and a nose kiss.

"He's one lucky lad, that boy." Carrick appeared from the side of the house and greeted us. He helped Babette wrestle the crate from her Rover without mentioning Prospero or their arrangement. We begged for a chance to see the pups again while we waited for the others to arrive. In the ten days since we first met them, the brood had transformed from furry bundles to assertive babies too cute to resist. Babette immediately scooped Prospero into her arms and cradled his head. "Isn't he special?" she asked. "I feel so lucky to have him."

Carrick tried unsuccessfully to hide his pride, but a big grin spread all over his face. "A gift from the Almighty, that's what they are. Makes a man feel just a little bit closer to heaven. I know this lad will have a good life with you, Mrs. Croy."

He didn't know the half of it! We adjourned to the house for tea while awaiting the rest of our crew and I explained Magdalen's excitement and angst at meeting him again. "Her heritage is so important to Magdalen, especially her father's side of the family." I deliberately chose not to mention the manuscript or that Irish genius of another age. That was Magdalen's prerogative.

"We found some scrapbooks that might interest you, though. It was fun seeing Henrietta's photo and Magdalen as a child."

Carrick watched me with his piercing blue eyes. "My niece called me yesterday. Magdalen is still a handful, according to her." He chuckled. "I would expect no less." He closed his eyes. "As the Bard said, 'Age cannot wither her, nor custom stale her infinite variety.'"

I recognized the quote from *Antony and Cleopatra,* but Babette frowned. She was no fan of obscure language and preferred some of the more risqué contemporary romance novels. *Say what you mean* was her frequent plaint.

"Forgive an old Irishman," Carrick said. "It's almost a congenital problem. Poetry, literature, and high drama—we love it all."

He shared a pot of tea, brewed strong and dark like the eyes of my lover. I bowed my head in shame, thankful that no one could read my mind. Prurient thoughts were quite unlike staid and sensible Perri Morgan. If I didn't put a stop to it, I'd be worse than Babette!

Fortunately, my pal had more practical thoughts in mind. "Great tea," Babette said. She supplied individual spinach quiches and homemade scones to add to our feast.

"Harney's Irish Breakfast. Pure Assam," Carrick said. "Wakes a body up good and proper."

I angled my head to the side, trying to check my watch without appearing obvious. Where in the world were the guys? Surely Magdalen hadn't changed her mind. I shuddered as I considered other alternatives: accidents, illness—the list was endless. Fortunately, Carrick came to my rescue by suggesting that we review the materials while we waited.

Babette clapped her hands in glee. "Oh goody! I love a treasure hunt." Once again, I wondered how many grown women could act that way without appearing addled. In this instance her emotion was genuine, and it worked. Carrick gazed fondly at my friend and brought out the goods.

They were layered inside a trunk, the type of item formerly called a hope chest. That custom had basically bitten the dust when a wave of independent women wondered why their hopes were confined to linen, silver, and marriage proposals. I supported the cultural shift, but occasionally wished that at least a few of the more harmless traditions had survived. This ornate piece of furniture was quite lovely, carved in rosewood with a highly polished sheen. "Henrietta brought this with her from Europe," Carrick said. "I recall on rainy days how she let me and

Magdalen sort through the contents. We called it her treasure chest and were ever so careful not to ruin anything."

He removed several vintage garments that emitted a whiff of mothballs. Babette immediately swooped down on them, caressing the fine fabric and holding them up to her body. The workmanship was beautiful, but, unfortunately, they were made for a generation of much smaller women. Magdalen might fit in them quite nicely, but both Babette and I were out of luck.

The real treasure lay on the bottom of the chest, a sheaf of documents, letters, and what appeared to be a manuscript. My pulse quickened. Had we finally reached the end of our quest? I reached down, but before claiming the prize, my cell phone interrupted me.

Wing Pruett's somber voice echoed like a prophet of doom. "We won't be joining you today, Perri."

"What's wrong?" I whispered, hoping against hope for the good news I knew would not come.

"Magdalen's been detained by the police. Aleita was vague about it, but I suspect they plan to charge her with the murder of Carole Ross."

I sputtered something unintelligible. Pruett responded, but whatever he said barely registered. Did Aleita Page really believe that an eighty-five-year-old woman could plan and execute such a heinous murder? It was too monstrous to even contemplate, and I feared that Magdalen might not survive the ordeal.

* * * *

"Murder! Impossible." Carrick Farraday blanched as he said the words. "Mags never had a mean bone in her body. Not then, not now. People don't change that much. Who was the victim anyway?"

Babette took a giant gulp of air before answering. "A nurse at the Falls. Big and kinda grim-lookin'. How in the world can they blame Magdalen for that? It's a miracle she wasn't killed herself."

The rest of Pruett's message finally hit me. Just when things couldn't be worse, they suddenly were. I steeled myself for high drama when my audience heard the rest of the story.

"Luckily Micah's there with her. That way they can't bully Magdalen." I stalled, taking the coward's way out. Unfortunately I couldn't fool Babette. She stood before me—hands on hips—and glared.

"What are you hidin', Persephone Morgan? Come on. Spill."

Carrick gripped the arms of his chair in a vise. He stayed silent but watchful as the scene played itself out.

I kept my voice calm and low. No sense in fueling hysteria. "There's another complication he mentioned. Just a possibility, not a certainty."

I could tell that any minute Babette might spring at my throat and throttle me. If that happened, even my Malinois wouldn't protect me from their beloved Auntie B.

"Remember the talk about that other resident who passed? Irene mentioned her yesterday."

Babette nodded. "Yeah. Sara Whitman. The one who popped off unexpectedly." She blinked twice before continuing. "Now wait just a darn minute. You can't be serious. They're not blaming Magdalen for that other woman's death too?"

I spread my hands in a gesture of futility. "Sheriff Price ordered an autopsy. I don't know the particulars yet, but Pruett will fill us in. He said to meet him back at my place."

The silence in the room was oppressive, so thick that a wave of nausea almost assailed me. I rose, signaling to Keats and Poe. "We'd better get going or they'll be waiting for us. You know how impatient Pruett gets."

Carrick's reaction was strong but understated. "How can I help?" he asked.

We agreed that after Micah sorted things out, Carrick might visit his step sister. As we headed toward the door, something else occurred to me.

"Any chance we could borrow those documents? I promise to take good care of them and return them promptly."

He looked uncertain for a moment but recovered quickly. "Of course. Take whatever you want. Maybe they'll cheer Mags up if she gets to see them."

Nothing deters Babette when she has a question. "Just what's in those papers anyway, Carrick?"

He scratched his head. "I have no idea. It's been years since I sifted through these things. Truth is, I didn't even remember them until you brought it up."

I've become a pretty good judge of character over the years. During my stint in the army, I spent time in Psych Ops, learning how to gauge and influence behavior. Our model, to Persuade, Change, and Influence, had many civilian applications, chief among which was the ability to discern truth from lies. I carefully watched Carrick's expression as he spoke, and my training told me that he was telling the truth. It also suggested that he was hiding something.

"If you want to help, there's one thing you might try," I said. "Find out what your niece knows about all this. She might share things with you but not with us." I shrugged. "It's worth a try anyhow."

Carrick agreed, and after promising to call him as soon as we had any more information we left and headed back to Great Marsh.

Chapter 15

"I just can't understand it," Babette moaned. "Kind of late in life for Magdalen to turn into a serial killer isn't it? Pruett's old flame must be an idiot!"

I ignored the reference to Aleita Page and focused on the problem at hand. No sense in speculating until we heard the facts. Besides, Aleita was both brainy and beautiful according to Pruett, connoisseur of the fair sex. I racked my own brain trying to think what information could possibly have surfaced.

Babette riffled through the sack of documents Carrick had given us. I realized she was restless and desperate for something to do, but as my foster mom had constantly stressed, haste makes waste.

"Will you stop that before you ruin something?" I said. "You can't see in the dark anyway. Besides, Oscar Wilde and his progeny are irrelevant to Magdalen's current situation."

My pal mumbled something distinctly unladylike. It was a rare display of poor manners by a Southern belle raised to flourish in polite society. Compared with army expletives, however, Babette was a rank amateur totally outgunned in any slanging match.

"What were you talkin' about?" she asked. "The manuscript triggered this whole mess."

She sobered up as I stated the obvious. The murder of one, possibly two people had far more impact than any literary find. In addition, we couldn't prove any linkage between the deaths and the manuscript.

I puzzled over a larger question as well. How would an elderly woman gain access to a lethal substance like strychnine? Several years ago some of my neighbors recommended it for eliminating gophers and other pests.

Pip had refused outright. Neither one of us could bear the thought of killing another creature, even one as annoying and destructive as a gopher. Unnecessary suffering by either humans or animals was contrary to our belief system. I'd already seen enough of it to last me for the rest of my life, thank you very much.

"Are you listening to me, Perri?" When Babette was on the warpath, watch out. "Dreamin' again, aren't you? I swear, Wing Pruett has his hands full with you."

I smiled at the thought of Pruett using his very talented digits. Fortunately Babette missed my reaction and continued her rant about the manuscript, Magdalen, and our obligation to aid her. Before long we reached my little bit of heaven in Great Marsh and found Pruett and Micah waiting patiently at the door.

Their faces were somber and they said very little until we were nestled around the fireplace sipping hot chocolate spiked with brandy. Keats, Poe, and Clara joined our circle as the guys updated us.

Micah took center stage because Magdalen was his client. Apparently she had been formally questioned about the murder of Nurse Carole Ross and, due to a lack of evidence, had been released without being charged. Aleita suggested an evaluation of Magdalen's mental fitness, but Micah staved that off.

"We were lucky," Micah said. "The magistrate was no spring chicken himself and I think he resented the sheriff's actions. Fortunately I'm guardian ad litem for mentally incapacitated adults and that expedited things. Appointed me to represent Magdalen's legal and medical interests."

Magdalen—incapacitated? That must have infuriated her.

"Phooey," Babette said. "There's nothin' crazy about that woman. Why, she's as sane as I am. Just because she's old doesn't mean she's a murderer or crazy."

None of us was unwise enough to comment on Babette's sanity, or Magdalen's either for that matter. Micah mentioned, however, that by having her evaluated Mags might be spared the indignity of a jail cell. Temporarily at least. It therefore remained a viable option.

"Surprisingly enough Magdalen didn't resist meeting with a therapist. Her only stipulation was that it not be Dr. Jethro Tully." Micah raised his eyebrows. "I guess he's the resident gerontologist at the Falls and she questioned his objectivity."

Babette snorted loudly. "Perri called him smarmy just like Mags did. Personally, I found him very appealing."

I learned my head back against the couch and closed my eyes. "Why did they arrest her?"

Pruett squeezed my hand as he explained. "They didn't actually arrest her. Just brought her in for questioning. Aleita didn't want to, but she had no choice." He sounded evasive, which meant that he knew more than he was willing to share.

Leave it to Babette to surface the proverbial elephant in the room. "What changed? Why single her out now?" She pounded the table. "Stop pussyfootin' around and tell us."

Pruett and Micah exchanged looks. "What do you want to know?"

"Everything." I dove headlong into the morass. "Okay. How in the world would Magdalen get strychnine? It's a controlled substance, for heaven's sake."

Micah rubbed his hands together. "Gophers."

"What?" Babette and I spoke as one.

Apparently my neighbors were correct. One can still obtain pesticides containing strychnine online. In addition to eliminating a host of outdoor pests, they presumably could serve up human pests on that endangered species list. I fired up my computer, and sure enough several vendors sold the stuff at a reasonable price.

"Did Magdalen Melmoth order that stuff?" Babette's voice dripped sarcasm. "Somehow I just can't feature that."

"Nope. But the gardener at the Falls kept a supply of it in the shed. He said Mags was a keen gardener eager to help him with his chores." Pruett sighed. "Apparently she quizzed him about pesticide use in the name of ecology. Or so she said."

The evidence was scarcely compelling. After all, as a farm girl, Mags knew plenty about herbicides and their uses. Her interest seemed natural to me.

Every once in a while, Babette astounded me. This was one of those times. "I suppose he keeps that shed locked up good and tight."

Both guys shrugged.

"Aha! That means anyone on the place had access to the same stuff." Babette had a smug expression on her face. "I rest my case."

Micah flashed her a look of open admiration. He had just learned what the rest of us already knew: Babette Croy was far more than just a pretty face. "Good point," he said, "but there's one other thing."

I dreaded the answer that was forthcoming.

"No one else had a blazing row with Nurse Ross before she was murdered. Magdalen certainly did. She admitted it. Apparently accused her of all sorts of chicanery."

Considering the victim's sour disposition, I was positive other residents may also have nursed grudges against her. A contained environment like the Falls was a petri dish for breeding grievances of all sorts.

Questions were still percolating in Babette's brain. She poured herself another drink and swirled the liquid around in the glass. "How would a body get strychnine into chocolates anyway? Seems like someone would notice."

Neither Pruett nor Micah responded, but I had my own thoughts. High-end candy was often handmade, so it was irregularly shaped. No one was likely to notice or complain about any imperfections, especially in a facility where many residents suffered from failing eyesight. What better way to conceal the bitter taste of strychnine than to inject it directly into the candy? The Falls was a place with plenty of residents suffering from diabetes and other ailments. Finding a syringe would be no problem, and disposing of it would be even easier. I assumed that strychnine had been introduced into the candy via a needle. That rich milk chocolate would easily mask the bitter taste of the poison. The candy! Had Sheriff Aleita traced the purchase to anyone in particular? I waited for that particular pump to drop, praying that my new friend's name would not be mentioned.

Babette was unaccustomed to being ignored. "I'm still waitin'," she said, stamping her foot for emphasis.

Pruett threw back his head and laughed—a big hearty guffaw. "Who could ignore you, my lady? As it happens, someone injected poison into the candy—not every piece— just the soft centers. Not so hard to do when you think about it."

I closed my eyes and envisioned the scene. How clever to inject poison into the soft-center candy. Many of the residents probably avoided chewy caramels that might compromise bridgework or dentures. Someone with brains had expended time and effort planning this caper. It required stealth and discipline, two qualities Magdalen had in abundance. The one element she lacked was cruelty. No way would the literate, charming woman I had come to know do such an evil thing, whatever the provocation. Nothing could convince me otherwise.

Micah hadn't said much since he arrived. Perhaps he was busy considering his client's dilemma and the consequences to come. More likely he felt constrained by his attorney-client relationship with Magdalen. He cleared his throat and captured our attention. "You probably don't know this, but

Magdalen has a secret admirer—at least that's what she says. Seems as if she gets flowers and the occasional box of candy quite regularly."

I yearned for the childhood habit of putting my hands over my ears. Then I would miss what was surely to come.

Micah's voice was steady and unemotional as he continued his narration. "The chocolates were all from the same Belgian candymaker. The same one that poisoned Nurse Ross. She always shared them with the staff and residents without incident. No one would have suspected anything was amiss."

"Surely there are purchase records, something to prove who sent it." I was on firmer ground now. No one could blame Magdalen for receiving a gift, could they?

"They're checking that out now. One thing they verified, though. She always saved the candy for others. Made a habit of it." Micah locked eyes with Pruett when he said that.

The key to solving homicides often lay with the victim herself. I knew that from personal experience as well as crime literature. I asked myself what we really knew about Nurse Carole Ross. One thing I had observed: she liked to snoop. Perhaps she'd uncovered the manuscript or knew about our quest. If so, had she shared that information with friends or a lover? Learning the answer was a task suited to the particular talents of the winsome Wing Pruett. His claque of superannuated fans would bask in the attention and spill anything they knew about poor Nurse Ross. He grinned when I proposed the idea but didn't reject it. That boy knew his impact on all spectra of the fair sex. I gave him points for honesty at least.

Micah reached into his briefcase and retrieved his iPad. From his grim expression I foresaw that more bad news would soon follow. "Something else," he said. "The sheriff mentioned this but didn't elaborate. Still, I 'm afraid it's something to consider."

He fumbled around in his briefcase, found his glasses, and adjusted them, slowly, carefully. My side view of Babette suggested she was losing patience fast and might soon explode. Fortunately, she controlled her emotions by clinging to Clara, giving her a nose kiss and a big hug.

"Sara Whitman. I think you recall the name." Micah nodded encouragement at us, as if he were addressing particularly bright pupils. "Apparently there was a fracas between Magdalen and her." He shrugged. "Who knows what prompted it? Anyway they had a heated exchange. No blows, of course, but Magdalen may have threatened her. At least that's what Dr. Fergueson said."

This time Babette jumped in. "That proves what?" She snorted. "Two old tabbies spittin' at each other—BFD. Bet it happens all the time at those places. Nothin' much else to do."

Micah kept his tone unemotional. That heightened the impact of his words all the more. "True. However, this spat got way out of control. Magdalen apparently threatened to kill Mrs. Whitman. Two days later she died."

Suddenly I appreciated Sheriff Aleita's dilemma. My thoughts seemed disloyal, but I could not dispel them. When two deaths follow verbal threats, a pattern begins to emerge. I recalled how easily Magdalen had "borrowed" Nurse Ross's car and found her way to my house. That required an agile mind, physical dexterity, and technical skill. Age was no barrier to antisocial behavior despite our culture's tendency to idealize sweet little old ladies. Magdalen Melmoth was tough as an old army boot, but I still doubted her capacity for evil. On the other hand, I would describe her more as saucy than sweet.

Babette pinched my arm, almost causing me to spill my drink. "Hey! Watch out! What's wrong with you?"

Naturally no apology was forthcoming. My pal firmly believed in the adage about the best defense being a vigorous offense. "Stop woolgathering," she said. "We need all our wits about us if we plan to help Magdalen."

That galvanized Pruett into protector-of-womanhood mode. He knew better, but that didn't stop him from trying. "Listen, you two. Stay away from the Falls. Let Micah and me handle things. After all, there may be—no, probably is—a murderer on the loose. Forget about that Therapy Dog stuff."

I met his eyes with a fierce and fiery glare of my own. Pruett knew me well enough to gauge my reaction.

Babette sputtered with indignation. "Wing Pruett, you sexist pig. Perri and I started this adventure and we plan to finish it. So, if you're thinkin' of layin' down the law—just forget it!"

Silence enveloped the room as four adults and three canines assessed the situation. The dogs leaned forward, ears pricked, eyes alert. Pruett and Micah had a different reaction. They laughed.

"I guess they told you, Wing." Micah's eyes glittered with amusement.

Pruett rubbed his cheek and shared the joke. "Put me right in my place. Ouch!"

Babette simmered down, enjoying the impact of her action. "What can I do to help?" she asked.

I had an idea. "Look. Irene strikes me as a pretty cool customer. Find out her take on that Sara Whitman and anything else that might be relevant at the Falls. Why did Sara plan to leave the place? Something must have upset her. Meanwhile I'll dig into this paperwork. The manuscript might still be the key to all the mayhem at that place."

Micah finished his drink and rose. "What's my job—in addition to saving the skin of our favorite senior citizen, that is?"

I was so glad he asked. "Can you vet the staff with the professional societies in the state? I agree with Magdalen about Dr. Tully, but he may be a creep and nothing more sinister. Dr. Fergueson, Nurse Ross, and that new guy may have something worth knowing in their backgrounds."

Micah agreed. He and Babette left at the same time, although I can't swear they left "together." Meanwhile Pruett made himself useful by helping me with some pet chores as well as the dishes. We connected with Ella via Skype and got the good news that she would return that next week. Later on Pruett once again proved his expertise in other areas too personal to mention. I admit that I cherished this domestic side of him. What a startling contrast it made to the dazzling sophisticate who haunted DC hot spots and dominated the society pages! I dared to dream that maybe—just maybe—our relationship could work out.

Chapter 16

Babette couldn't wait to get started. Early the next morning—way too early for me on a Sunday—she phoned with plans for meeting Irene Wilson. "I already called her," she said. "Instead of visiting at that mausoleum we agreed to meet in town for a fancy meal. You know—ladies who lunch. Big brunch." She took a breath. "My treat, of course. Irene has to watch her pennies. That Falls place is superexpensive."

Although I was bleary-eyed, my synapses were still firing. Babette needed firm guidelines to keep her on track. Meanwhile Pruett rustled around in the dark, searching for his robe and slippers, stubbing his toe in the process. He muttered a few creative expletives so loudly that Babette overheard them.

"See you got lucky last night," she said, heaving a very audible sigh. "Wish I had. Micah said adios and rode out of Dodge in a hurry."

To avoid a diatribe on perfidious men, I congratulated my pal on her initiative and ended the call. My pets were milling about demanding attention, and before long Zeke would start braying for his breakfast. I intended to exercise Raza as well. Thirty minutes of trotting, cantering, and galloping the Arabian could clear my head like nothing else. Fortunately I had perfected the morning routine and was able to meet everyone's needs in record time. Pruett met my urgent needs by producing two large lattes complete with foam.

Both of us had prior business commitments, so our time together was short. We put aside our involvement with Magdalen and focused on our own work. He planned to interview a disgruntled congressional aide with a tale to tell. My leather products were featured at a juried craft show in the DC Convention Center and I had high hopes for significant sales. I would tackle Henrietta's documents afterward.

The hours passed quickly, and before long I was speeding up the George Washington Memorial Parkway toward home laden with cash and buoyed by significant sales. As usual, my dogs accompanied me on the trek. I'd found that few things deterred car thieves like two hovering Malinois guarding the contents. The weather had turned blustery and I yearned for a pot of tea and a roaring fire to mute the chill. When we reached home Keats and Poe immediately sped around the property doing their daily run and cavorting with Zeke and Raza rather than joining me indoors. I put on the kettle, lit the logs in the fireplace, and bounded upstairs in search of Magdalen's papers. I was positive I'd placed them on my desk in the study, but they were nowhere to be found. Perhaps Pruett had taken them into the living room after all. Some primitive instinct caused me to clutch the banister as I started my descent. That action probably saved my life. I stumbled over Thatcher and tumbled headfirst into darkness.

* * * *

Thank goodness for my hard head. The first thing I saw when I awakened was Babette Croy bending over me, towel in hand. Some sticky substance was dripping down my face, and I realized with a start that it was blood. My blood.

"I declare, Persephone Morgan, you are an accident in the makin'. You scared me half to death."

Typical Babette. Everything, and I mean everything, was about her.

"Here. Help me up." I leaned on her arm and gingerly rose to my feet. Nothing was broken, which seemed like a minor miracle unless you counted the wound on my scalp. Head wounds bleed profusely, so despite the mess, I wasn't too alarmed.

"Now don't worry. Pruett's on his way." Babette smirked. "I called Micah too. Just in case. Sometimes a lawyer comes in handy."

I tried to protest, but a wave of nausea put a stop to that. Pruett wasn't obliged to save me from harm. We didn't have that type of relationship. Did we?

"Did you faint?" Babette asked. She narrowed her eyes. "You're not pregnant, are you? Tell me right now. Pruett is such a wonderful father."

"Certainly not! For your information I fell down those stairs." I felt certain she didn't believe me. Babette the romantic much preferred the pregnancy theory to clumsiness. The gravity of the situation finally registered with my pal. After checking the locks on my doors Babette pointed to Keats and Poe, mystified. "How could anyone hurt you with these two guys around? They were outside when I got here."

I explained the situation, stressing that an intruder had probably rummaged around before I arrived.

That didn't satisfy Babette. "What about your burglar alarm? It wasn't on when I got here."

Although I'm very security conscious, it was possible—no, probable—that in the rush to leave that morning neither Pruett nor I had activated the alarm. A stupid but understandable mistake.

Babette played nurse while I lay on the sofa assessing my wounds. My livelihood depended on the use of my hands; fortunately neither one had been damaged. My knee was not so lucky. It had swollen to twice its normal size and throbbed painfully. Nothing was broken or sprained and I could walk with a bit of help. After Babette cheerfully recited the injuries I might have sustained, ranging from death to a broken neck, I felt fortunate indeed.

I must have dozed off because I awakened to the murmur of voices. Pruett and Micah each sat in my leather wing chairs like Praetorian guards while Babette perched on the arm of the sofa. I carefully raised my head and smiled at them, inciting a near riot.

"Don't move," Pruett said, rushing to my side. He folded me into his arms and gently kissed my forehead. "Another bid for attention, eh, Persephone?"

"She's not pregnant," Babette said. "I asked already." Both Pruett and I blushed at that one, but Micah maintained a lawyerly silence.

After taking a sip of tea, I explained my theory. "I think someone was riffling through my desk. Magdalen's papers are gone."

Micah and Pruett exchanged looks and were immediately challenged by Babette. "Okay, you two. What are you hidin'? Come on. Spill."

Micah reached into his briefcase and removed a sheaf of papers that looked very familiar. "Recognize these? I found them stuffed in your trash bin outside."

I felt mixed emotions: relief and confusion. Why had the intruder risked so much only to discard the documents? It didn't make sense. "My money! Check my wallet, please." Pruett gave me a strange look but retrieved my tote bag from the counter. I dove into my purse, checking the side pocket for my haul from the trade show. It came to over one thousand dollars, a significant budget and ego boost and a needed addition to my bottom line. I sighed as my fingers touched a comforting bulge of bills.

"Call the cops," Babette said. "Some sex maniac may be on the loose. No decent woman in Great Marsh will be safe 'til he's caught."

Although Great Marsh had its share of both decent and decadent females, I doubted that sex was the motive unless an intruder found me too repulsive to molest. Besides, we couldn't really prove anything. My injuries were my own fault.

"Must we call them?" I asked. "Such a fuss for nothing."

Pruett and Micah exchanged looks again. Their crossed arms and frowns predicted what the answer would be, and I lacked the energy to fight them.

"Come on," Pruett said. "We're taking you to the urgent care place first. Your head's still bleeding; you need some staples. Micah and Babette can wait here for the police." He wrapped the towel around me turban style and gently lifted me from the sofa. "I'd better call Aleita too. This may be connected to the situation at the Falls."

My one comfort was the thought that at least they couldn't blame this on Magdalen Melmoth.

* * * *

By ten p.m. I was back in my own bed decorated with ten staples, a knee brace, and a thundering migraine. Mercifully the authorities had come and gone without major disruption and Babette had attended to the needs of my pets. Pruett insisted on spending the night. In fact, he declared that he would not leave the premises at all until I was able to fend for myself. Call it a cliché, but every cloud does indeed have a silver lining.

Exhaustion should have taken its toll, but it didn't. For some reason every time I closed my eyes another question swirled through my febrile brain. It made no sense and yet I couldn't shake it. If someone had burgled my home, what in the world did he or she want? I groped for my flashlight, hoping to hobble out of bed without disturbing Pruett. I'd forgotten that he had lightning-quick reflexes. He leaped up before my feet touched the floor and switched on the light.

"Are you okay?" he asked. "Need any help?"

"Can't sleep," I said. "Go back to bed." Keats and Poe responded immediately, plying me with doggy kisses as if they had been derelict in their guard duties and wanted to atone. Thatcher, the cause of my injuries, remained unrepentant. She glared at me and turned away from the light.

"Hold on. If you don't behave, I'll call in Babette. She's keen to practice her nursing skills."

That threat gave me pause. The last thing I needed was my well-intentioned BFF hovering over me, checking my temperature and plying me with tea and soup. Solitude was required, or at least some respite from Babette. I needed to think.

Pruett knew me too well. He slipped into his jogging suit and held out his arm. "Come on. Be a sport. We'll both sift through those papers. Maybe we can make sense of it. Two heads are better than one, or so I hear."

"Depends on which heads are involved." I couldn't help grumbling even though he made perfect sense. My head ached and the staples itched.

In the end we negotiated a truce and were soon ensconced in my study with a cozy fire burning and a pot of tea steeping. Pruett had pronounced homebody talents that both astonished and delighted me. He brewed a mean pot of tea and was a wizard at producing cinnamon toast.

We divided the material and dove into it. Most of the items were mundane, artifacts of life lived in a different era. The daunting task of sorting through a mountain of minutiae was enough to bring anyone to her knees. These days we'd label Henrietta Melmoth a hoarder. The woman saved receipts for household expenses, report cards, even correspondence with her dressmaker, but not one hint of a manuscript.

After toiling for two hours Pruett stood up and yawned. "I'm beginning to think this Oscar Wilde chase is a chimera. After all, we have only Magdalen's word and a few tattered pages of script."

I couldn't help laughing. "Chimera—pretty fancy language for five in the morning. Impressive."

He made a mock bow. "I live to delight you, my liege."

I swatted him away as I spied an official-looking document at the top of his pile. "Hey. What's this?"

"Henrietta's will. We've seen it before. She leaves everything to her daughter. No surprise there."

Some niggling doubt floated through my mind. "Better let Micah see it, though. Did Henrietta die before Declan or after? It might make a difference."

Pruett shrugged. "Easy enough to find out. Ask Carrick or check the courthouse." He yawned and headed for the bedroom. "I better get going. My editor isn't thrilled with this project, you know. Thinks it's a waste of my oh-so-valuable time."

His remark was a throwaway, but it made me think. Maybe we were all wasting our time. I was certain of only one thing: Magdalen genuinely believed in the Oscar Wilde connection absent one scintilla of proof. How to explain that? Family lore always emphasized the positive and her parents might have greatly admired Wilde. Perhaps they'd even encountered him in Paris and become friends. Sebastian may have penned *Sybil Vane* as homage to his hero. Without a copy of the novel it was impossible to say.

I sipped another cup of strong tea and plotted my course. Ministering to my pets came first, as Thatcher snarkily reminded me. She was capable of emitting ear-piercing shrieks when her needs went unmet. I hoped to avoid that if at all possible.

When Pruett appeared he was barbered and dressed for corporate combat. He planted a kiss on my forehead and headed for the door before delivering an ultimatum. "Don't leave this house by yourself, Persephone. Promise me."

"I have a business to run, you know. I can't stay immured in this place forever."

His smile was radiant. "Exactly. That's why I've arranged for you to have company." He checked his watch. "In fact, she should be here any minute."

Right on cue, the Range Rover swept into the driveway. Babette Croy was on the case.

Chapter17

She bustled into the house laden with food. "Don't thank me," Babette said before I opened my mouth. "You know I'm always here for you. When Wing called I came running."

The aroma of something tasty reminded me that I was hungry. In fact, I was starving. My generous pal had packed a basket full of sliced turkey, cranberries, gravy, and mashed potatoes. Comfort food supreme. Who cared if it was only seven a.m.? Both of us tucked into the feast as if we were starving Pilgrims at the first Thanksgiving. After we finished I divided the remaining scraps among the dogs and Thatcher.

"Yum," Babette said after emitting one very ladylike burp. "That hit the spot. Now I'm ready to do some detectin'. I have a plan."

I watched my pal carefully. "Just what did you have in mind?"

She flashed me the innocent look that had fooled so many men. "Time to pull out the stops and ask for help. Expert help."

Her explanation made perfect sense. Our group scheduled its monthly Therapy Dog update for the third Wednesday of each month. The session was local, lasted only an hour, and was led by Kate Thayer. Why not leverage Kate's expertise in another area: English literature? After all, the woman had been a top librarian at one of the country's most prestigious institutions.

Babette gave me her smug look. "Already touched bases with her and invited Kate to lunch as my guest. Right after our Therapy Dog meeting. Someplace extraspecial. I booked us a table at the Willard for tomorrow."

The Willard Hotel, directly across from the White House, was an iconic DC spot, both pricey and private. I gulped, thinking of the dent this meal could put in my bank balance. My feeble protest didn't fool Babette one bit.

"We just ate," I said. "Think of the calories."

"Oh pooh. By one o'clock tomorrow we'll be ravenous. Besides, think of it as an investment. Always get the best, I say, and the best is not cheap."

I resigned myself to fate and heaved an enormous sigh. With Babette's help I fed my pets and spent an hour riding Raza around the trails. Just being near the beautiful Arabian mare calmed me and helped me to think clearly. Kate Thayer was privy to literary gossip and might advise us on our next course of action. She also had the inside track on Rolf and his various enterprises. Naturally discretion would be called for and I would have to restrain Babette's exuberant impulses. She sometimes blabbered nonsensically without even being aware of the secrets being spilled. Pruett termed it "galloping glossolalia," a term he'd learned when researching religious cults. It meant speaking in tongues and accurately described my BFF in full stride, minus the spiritual side.

Just before noon the next day, we sped into the District garbed in our ladies-who-lunch finery. Mine was more modest than Babette's, but we managed to pass through the portals of the famous Willard without incident. Kate awaited us in the lobby looking slightly frazzled. Most people knew that the term "lobbyist" was coined by an irate Ulysses S. Grant to describe the pesky office seekers who swarmed about him at the Willard as he tried to enjoy his cigars. Smoking of any kind was verboten now, but the lure of two hundred years of history enveloped anyone entering the hotel in a warm embrace.

"Believe it or not I've never eaten here," Kate said. "Not likely on a librarian's salary. It's rather overwhelming. All this gilt and marble. Almost too much of a good thing."

Babette swept away her concerns with an imperious wave. "They're lucky to have three lovely ladies like us. We class up the place. Besides, Perri and I want to pick your brain."

We followed her into the elegant Café du Parc and were greeted with the ceremony befitting a big spender like Mrs. Croy. Naturally she was known by name by the staff and cosseted by the maître d'. He didn't bow and scrape, but his manner was certainly deferential. Babette frequented the most celebrated haunts of the capital city and had for years. We had absolutely no problem scoring a choice table.

After studying the menu and making our selections we got down to the business of the day. Librarians—even retired ones—were accustomed to dealing with the unexpected and bizarre. Nothing upset the unflappable Kate Thayer, even the bombshell dropped by her hostess.

"We're on the hunt for somethin' big," Babette said sotto voce, "and it's right up your alley. Tell her, Perri."

Kate raised her eyebrows but remained silent.

I gulped, attempting to frame a coherent sentence. "I'm sure you're familiar with the works of Oscar Wilde," I said.

"Of course. Historical fiction was my niche, but actually I'm a big fan of the man and his works."

Babette dove into the conversational pool immediately. "We think there might be somethin' new." She said no more, giving her coy look.

Kate frowned. "New? As in an undiscovered work?"

Fortunately our server arrived at that moment with the soup. That gave me time to regroup before Babette interfered again.

"Look," I said. "We've heard all kinds of weird things at the Falls, especially since the murder occurred. There's talk that an undiscovered novel of Wilde's might exist. Sort of a sequel to *Dorian Gray.*"

Kate's eyes widened. "You're kidding. There's been no buzz about it in literary circles or believe me, I would have heard. Who knows how these rumors start anyway? A new work by Wilde would inflame everyone here and across the pond. Around the globe actually." She leaned forward, temporarily forsaking her soup. "It would be worth a fortune too. Finding a treasure like that is the secret wish of every bibliophile I know. Unfortunately most of us can only dream of traveling to magical places. Our salaries never match those dreams and our pensions don't come close."

I gave an expurgated version of Magdalen's history, including the fragment of *Sybil Vane* we had read. Kate listened carefully while Babette took delicate sips of lobster bisque.

"If there's any truth to the tale, it would bring the literary establishment to its knees. I don't suppose you found anything else to support it?"

I explained that we were sifting through Magdalen's papers and those belonging to her stepbrother, Carrick, for any scraps of information. That made me wonder how many other people knew about the Oscar Wilde connection. Naturally upon hearing Carrick's name, Babette digressed into a lengthy discussion about Leonbergers and her new family member, the pup Prospero.

"I've heard of the Farraday kennel," Kate said. "Top-quality dogs. He finds it hard to part with them unless the buyer is fully vetted."

Babette preened after hearing that. "I guess I passed his test," she said. "Such a charmin' gentleman."

Despite the conversational detours I returned to the business at hand. Our window of opportunity would close with the last morsel of lunch and we needed Kate's expertise.

When she learned of my accident Kate reacted immediately. "Do be careful, Perri. Two people have already died if you count Sara Whitman and poor Carole. Who knows what lengths someone will go to if this manuscript actually exists?"

I still wasn't certain that the manuscript had inspired the murders or that Magdalen was the target. Carole Ross was privy to every secret at the Falls and knew where the proverbial bodies were buried. Had her behavior caused someone to eliminate her?

"You knew Nurse Ross fairly well, right? Did she ever mention it? Knowing Magdalen, she might have hinted about something."

Kate rolled her eyes. "Poor Carole. Limited social skills but a really good heart. Believe it or not, she was devoted to the residents."

Babette hooted rudely. "Coulda fooled me. That woman was positively unfriendly."

I ignored her and soldiered on. "We're worried about Magdalen Melmoth. She's so vulnerable."

Kate smiled. "Actually Carole—Nurse Ross—was worried about Magdalen too. She never mentioned any manuscript, though. Carole kept harping on about inheritances, real estate, and such. Not just Magdalen's. You hear so many things about old people being swindled. Some of those residents have fairly hefty portfolios and no close relatives. They're suckers for a sad story or a bit of attention."

"Like Sara Whitman?" Kudos to Babette for bringing that up.

"Hardly!" Kate rolled her eyes. "Sara was a crusty old soul. Pity the person who tried to fool her. Funny thing, though. When Sara told everyone she intended to divest of all her fixed assets, Nurse Ross went ballistic. Told her not to be a fool and to hold on to her portfolio. Sara became irate and told Carole to mind her own business. Said she had no relatives and would do what she damn well pleased." Kate coughed delicately. "Believe it or not she said she made a killing on some deal with her new partner. Sara and Magdalen were quite similar actually. Two very tough peas in a pod. Little wonder they fought."

I gulped but forced myself to forge ahead. "Surely not enough to incite murder. The police want to exhume her body and test for poison." I explained the official theory about pesticides used to eliminate gophers and the presence of strychnine. Babette mentioned the Falls' gardening shed, but before she could link it to Magdalen, I aimed a swift kick at her shins.

Fortunately, our entrees appeared as if right on cue, causing a temporary lull in the conversation. After taking a few bites of kale salad I sallied forth again. "Sheriff Page thinks Magdalen killed Mrs. Whitman and Nurse Ross. I'm so frightened for her."

"Fiddlesticks!" Kate tapped her knife on her plate for emphasis. "Magdalen is smart and feisty, not homicidal. Rolf mentioned that theory and I told him to go peddle his papers elsewhere. Man's a menace when it comes to gossip, but he has his uses. Just saying, he's the one you should ask about financial stuff, although not much else. His people skills are limited."

I'd wondered about Rolf's involvement; a hard-driving businessman seemed an unlikely candidate for a Therapy Dog group. Had Rolf used it to gain entrée into the Falls? A sea of vulnerable oldsters would make enticing targets for a profiteer. On the other hand, maybe the man just loved dogs and wanted to be of service. I couldn't discount altruism as a motive even though I loathed him.

Babette curled her lip. "I don't like that varmint. Thinks he's slick."

"Maybe." Kate nodded. "But the guy's kind of a financial genius. Real estate speculator, builder, you name it. He's been buying up properties like mad at a big profit, to hear him tell it."

I stayed neutral even though I shared Babette's distaste for him. Though Rolf's borzoi, Portia was delightful, so he got a few points for that. I filed away my doubts about him and tried a new gambit. "Magdalen is a very distant relative of Dr. Fergueson. But you probably already knew that."

Kate temporarily ignored her scallops and gave me a hard stare. "Look, ladies. My only interest is therapy dogs. I try my best to avoid the other drama. Gets in the way of the mission. Joan and I never discuss personal things."

I backed off, but Babette had no inhibitions. She leaned forward and flashed her pageant-winning smile. "Oh pooh. Librarians, retired or not, never miss a trick. You don't fool me. Now give us the scoop. Magdalen's goose is cooked and carved if we don't step in."

Most people find Babette hard to resist. Fortunately Kate was squarely in that camp. She heaved a sigh and finally capitulated. "Okay, although I stress that these are only impressions. Dr. Fergueson keeps that stiff, professional persona firmly in place. I've never even seen the woman laugh, but she tries to be fair with the residents. Most are really sweet, but some are a handful. I think she really tries to make their lives comfortable."

I knew without asking that Magdalen Melmoth was firmly in the latter camp. Feistiness was a virtue in my book, but to an administrator it might be less endearing.

"Dr. F called Magdalen difficult and Dr. Dreamy backed her up. 'Course my lady, Irene, says Mags is solid as a rock." Babette's comment left Kate looking bewildered.

"Dr. Dreamy? Who's that?"

I chuckled. Following the Croy commentary would bewilder any novice. Fortunately I was fluent in the language. "She means Jethro Tully."

Kate looked over her glasses and frowned. "He's not my favorite. Too patronizing and, as my dear mother used to say, up to no good. I admit that he's handsome if you like the smarmy type. Big favorite with the ladies. I thought at first that he was sweet on Dr. Fergueson, but now I'm not so sure." She shuddered. "Personally I wouldn't trust him to diagnose my pup Gomer let alone a house full of vulnerable seniors. He and Rolf are big buds, of course. Two of a kind."

I abstained from dessert, but Babette went whole hog. "Come on, Kate. Don't make me stand out. Perri watches her figure, but I go for the gusto. The crème brûlée here is fantastic."

Kate grinned. "I've seen Mr. Pruett, so I get it. No wonder you watch your figure, Perri. Smart girl. Plenty of competition out there."

As they gobbled their sweets, I got a sudden brainstorm. "Many residents at the Falls can't eat sweets. I suppose everyone knows that."

Kate savored a bite of dessert before responding. "Not really. At their age most do whatever they please, even the ones with diabetes. Not much to lose, I guess. Someone always has a tin of cookies or a box of candy around."

Still the person who sent Magdalen the box of chocolate didn't know her habits and expected that she would sample the treats. Was it an outsider or merely a casual acquaintance? According to Irene, Magdalen had a secret admirer who plied her with gifts.

Babette wrinkled her nose. "What about that new nurse—Edgar something or other? He looks like a real brute. Scary."

"Don't ask me," Kate said. "He came highly recommended. Dr. Tully knew him from before and vouched for him. I know he's an animal lover, though. Gomer adores him."

From what I'd seen of Gomer, that wasn't much of an endorsement. He loved everything and everybody, unlike my Malinois, who were far more discerning.

Conversation dwindled after that. Despite the elegant surroundings and haute cuisine, our lunch party left me mildly depressed. We had learned very little and wasted an entire afternoon for our trouble.

After Babette settled our bill, I made an impassioned plea to Kate. "Will you help us? Sound out your library pals about this Sebastian Melmoth connection? We scoured the Internet, but you must have sources we simply can't access."

Kate patted my shoulder. "Of course. Librarians are detectives of sorts, you know. A literary mystery is right up my alley. I'll see what I can find out."

As usual Babette had the last word. "Just remember. Be careful. Somebody's willin' to kill to eliminate Magdalen. Don't take chances."

* * * *

Pruett assumed custodial duty of me that evening, a welcome relief from Nurse Babette. She meant well but had never learned that the less-is-more philosophy applied to sickbeds as well as jewelry and cosmetics.

"Looks like those staples are mending," he said, gently brushing my bangs aside. "Hard heads have their uses, I suppose."

I ignored his feeble attempt at humor. My lunch at the Willard had left me in a cantankerous mood that hovered over me like a dark cloud.

"Maybe we're wasting our time on this Oscar Wilde quest," I grumbled. "For all we know Magdalen might be stringing us along. Lonely people want attention, you know, particularly older ones."

"I thought you liked tilting at windmills, Dulcinea." His smirk begged me to slap him silly, but as usual restraint was my superpower.

"For your information, Frat Boy, Don Quixote did the windmill tilting. Dulcinea was strictly eye candy."

Pruett bowed to my superior literary wisdom, but offered a different perspective. "Whatever her motives, something is definitely going on at the Falls and Magdalen is right in the center of it. Micah told me that she passed the psych evaluation with flying colors and gave Aleita more than she bargained for when they interrogated her." He chuckled. "They were expecting a docile old lady, but you know Magdalen. Fire and plenty of vinegar."

"Is she still a suspect?" I asked. "What about Sara Whitman? Are they still linking that to Nurse Ross's murder?"

Pruett spread his hands out wide. "Whoa, Leather Lady. One thing at a time. Micah didn't say this, but I think the police are stumped. Dr.

Fergueson keeps stonewalling them and no one can figure out a motive for the murders other than spite."

A wave of guilt assailed me. Some friend I was. How could I have suspected Magdalen of any involvement in the murder? If the *Sybil Vane* trail turned cold so be it. Bottom line: my new friend had something valuable that someone was willing to kill for. She had asked for my help and I couldn't abandon her.

We planned a quiet evening of reading and discussion, but it was not to be. An unexpected phone call galvanized both us and our pets into action.

I seldom answer my landline, especially at night. Customers use email or my cell phone and friends do the same. Not everyone gets the message, however. Every telemarketer in the world zeroes in on the dinner hour, inundating me with unwanted robocalls and promises of a magical impotence pill that Pruett simply has no need for. Tonight was different. The phone rang and an unfamiliar male voice, urgent and troubled, uttered my name. At first, I didn't recognize the caller. Then I realized it was Carrick Farraday, and something was very wrong.

Chapter 18

Carrick was so anxious, he skipped the amenities and plunged into a long, muddled narrative that made my head ache.

"Slow down, Carrick," I said. "Pruett's here, so let me put you on speaker. Are you okay?"

He took several deep breaths, and when he finally spoke, his voice shook. "Forgive me for disturbing you, Perri, but I think you'll want to hear this."

Pruett moved closer to the phone, pad and pen in hand. I noted that clever scribe was also recording the conversation on his iPhone as backup. "Go on, Carrick," he said. "No problem."

"I found it, or at least I found something important."

I closed my eyes, reluctant to break the spell by asking what the "it" was. Pruett had no such inhibitions. In his profession he had learned not to hesitate when a source was willing to spill information. "Ready when you are," he told Carrick.

"I was browsing through my library, just looking for something to read, you see. That's when I found it."

Once again I forced myself to power down. Otherwise I would be tempted to shriek something dreadful into the phone. Carrick would get to whatever "it" was in his own way and time. Sure enough, patience finally won the day. He described a fusty old volume that was concealed behind some of his father's papers.

"It's part of Henrietta's things, actually. She passed not long after my da, you know, and I haven't had the heart to sift through them. Funny thing. I was a grown man at the time, but I felt bereaved, like an orphan."

His anguish was spot-on. I'd waited a year before delving into Pip's belongings even though they weighed heavily on my mind. It felt like a betrayal, a final recognition that he was gone forever. Babette offered to help, but I resisted. Somehow that task was so painful and personal that I just couldn't bring myself to do it. Then I met Wing Pruett. That freed me to honor the past but also think of the future.

Carrick spoke so softly that I could barely hear him. "I have no right to bother you, but I figured you'd understand. Least I hoped so."

He still hadn't said anything, and my patience was wearing thin. Pruett, however, saw an opening and immediately sailed through it. "We'll be right over, Carrick. Don't you worry." When he ended the call a look of pure triumph suffused his face.

I gave Pruett my stoniest stare. "Are you crazy? Now we'll be up all night, and I for one have a business to run. You know, orders to fill, bills to pay."

He brushed off my objections like lint. "Don't be a spoilsport. You know, maybe you should alert Babette, and while you're at it I'll call Micah." He smiled coyly. "Of course, if you're really too busy, we can go without you."

Not likely! I started this adventure and intended to see it through to the bitter end.

As luck would have it, both Babette and Micah were otherwise occupied. Mrs. Croy was attending a gala at the Kennedy Center and Micah was presenting some dull-as-dust treatise on legal aid to his American Bar Association chapter.

Pruett seemed delighted to have the field to himself, even though it entailed sharing his Porsche with Keats and Poe. There was no telling how long this excursion would last, so I hastily filled water buckets for Zeke and Raza, and poured each of them an extra portion of feed to stave off the munchies. Thatcher's bowl was always filled in case that finicky feline decided to dine. While he waited Pruett pranced around the living room in a graceful movement worthy of Nijinsky. Clearly he was aching to reach Carrick to share his special find.

"You'll probably be disappointed by the big reveal," I said. "Best to lower your expectations." Pruett complained that I was a wet blanket, but from my perspective I was the only adult in the house. If Carrick produced the manuscript for *Sybil Vane,* I would rejoice. That outcome seemed highly unlikely.

Pruett bundled me into the Porsche Macan and ignored my grumbling. He planted a kiss on my forehead and fired up the GPS. "Things are finally coming to a head," he said. "Every time this happens my fingers start tingling. One way or another we're going to solve this thing, and tonight may be the night."

Keats and Poe leaped gracefully into the back seat, ready for adventure. After facing down terrorists and bombs, civilian tasks must have seemed mundane to those war heroes. Either way I was grateful for their company. If my unwanted visitor returned to the house, I wanted the dogs out of harm's way. With typical feline guile, Thatcher had the good sense to vanish whenever prowlers lurked or danger threatened.

Throughout the journey to Carrick's place, Pruett kept up a steady stream of conversation. Next week Ella returned, and he had plans for the three of us to celebrate. I suggested that Ella might bring her dog Guinnie to a Therapy Dog session. The gentle pointer had already mastered the Canine Good Citizen test and she would easily pass the temperament test as well. As an AKC Grand Champion, she was accustomed to being examined by strangers and mixing with other dogs.

"I'm not so sure," Pruett said. "Ella has schoolwork and horseback riding…" He didn't fool me. Something was bothering him.

"Okay. Out with it. Why don't you want Ella to join the program? Obviously it's up to you, but I'm curious."

Pruett was the ultimate Mr. Mom whose fierce devotion to his child was a trait I admired. He wanted to insulate Ella from danger. I got that. but an aversion to the entire Therapy Dog program still puzzled me.

He grasped the steering wheel in a death grip. "Until we resolve this issue, I don't want her anywhere near the Falls or that gang of weirdos. Something's not right about the whole thing."

No need to remind him that most of our Therapy Dog members were outstanding citizens bent on giving back to the community. The situation at the Falls was peculiar and certainly not typical of the many venues served by the organization. I took a deep breath before saying something that might ignite a feud. Our arrival at Carrick Farraday's kennel forestalled any further discussion on that topic.

To my surprise the entire property, including the outbuildings, was ablaze with lights. That seemed like unusual behavior for Carrick, who struck me as the thrifty type. My anxiety level ticked up another notch as I envisioned a number of unsavory scenarios. Pruett sensed the same thing. He squeezed my arm and said, "Steady now. We'll find Carrick and see what's going on."

Keats and Poe leaped to the ground, ears alert, ready for action. I gave them the Fuss command, to ensure that they stayed at my side in a perfect heel. Despite the warm temperature I shivered as we neared the entrance to Carrick's home. A sudden movement startled me and Pruett, but the Malinois weren't bothered one bit. They recognized Paddy, rising slowly from the porch step, shaking his giant head. That sight comforted me. Surely nothing was amiss if this canine patriarch looked so untroubled. A moment later the screen door creaked open and Carrick emerged. His disheveled appearance was startling—thick tufts of white hair stood straight up, his eyes were red, and his face was smudged with soot.

Pruett spoke first. "Everything okay, Carrick? You had us worried."

The older man flushed. "Didn't mean to alarm you. It was good of you to come." He gestured toward the house. "Please. Join me."

We gathered in the library where, despite the warmth outside, a fire blazed. The wide pine planks of the floor were littered with books and papers, a far cry from the neat and tidy space we had seen previously. A tray laden with a carafe of brandy, three snifters, and a plate of scones covered the coffee table. Carrick smiled when he saw me eye the treats.

"Can't take credit for those," he said. "Just never mastered the culinary arts. My stepma was the chef around here. Henrietta could bake like a charm." He poured each of us a drink and raised a toast. "To those magnificent Melmoth ladies, Henrietta and Magdalen." We obliged him by clinking glasses and took seats by the vast stone hearth. Paddy sighed and stretched out next to Carrick while Keats and Poe stayed Velcroed to my side. After a few routine inquiries about Daisy and her brood, we got down to the business at hand. Pruett sat quietly, hands folded and long legs crossed. Despite this outward calm, his eyes telegraphed impatience and a quest for the bottom line.

"Tell us all about your discovery," he said. "Perri's jumping out of her skin with curiosity."

Carrick took a mighty gulp of brandy and spoke. "Of course. Forgive me for woolgathering. Like I said, I was prowling about the library shelves when I found something odd." He reached under the sofa cushion and produced a thin hardcover volume plus some outsize pages of heavy vellum. I felt my chest constricting. Could it be? Had we found the treasure that would ignite the literary world? I glanced at Pruett. His face wore the inscrutable look so valued in his profession. Until he saw proof, he refused to commit himself. Good thing Babette wasn't with us. Knowing her, she would immediately have tackled Carrick to gain access to the prize. Come to think of it, that might not be such a bad idea.

Carrick slowly rose. He carefully handed the book to Pruett and placed the written pages in my lap. I peeked over Pruett's shoulder, eager to see the title. My hands shook, but Pruett's stayed rock solid. The volume in question was bound in red Morocco leather, with faded gilt around the edges. Despite the rigors of age, both the title and author's name were clearly visible. It read *Sybil Vane* by Sebastian Melmoth. I gasped, unable to say a word.

Pruett gingerly opened the book, mindful of the fragility of its spine. The frontispiece featured a profile image of a lovely woman with long, flowing locks and a saucy smile. The inscription read, "To Henrietta, my salvation, my Sybil Vane." There was no other narrative save the date of publication, December 1936.

That set off all manner of alarm bells in me. Oscar Wilde was long gone by that date, although it was possible Fingal had published it afterward. There were many possibilities, but such speculation served no purpose other than to clutter my mind. I looked to Carrick for some explanation—anything—that might clarify the situation.

"That's Henrietta," he said, pointing to the frontispiece. "A beautiful woman inside and out. My da adored her and so did I." He turned aside as his eyes filled. "So many memories. I know Mags will cherish this as I do."

Pruett had many dimensions to his character. When pursuing a story, however, he was the ultimate stoic. Sentiment was cast aside in place of ice-cold logic. "Have you read this, Carrick?" he asked.

The older man shook his head. "When I found it, all I could think of was calling you. Read the letter on Perri's lap. Should answer some of your questions."

Pruett leaned over, and together we read the letter, hearing the long-ago voice of Henrietta Melmoth Farraday. It was addressed to Carrick and Magdalen, crafted with the precise penmanship so typical of women of her era.

"To my dear ones, Carrick and Magdalen, I wanted to share one final goodbye with you before my time on this earth expires. As you know, Declan, my beloved spouse, recently passed and left a legacy to me that will now pass to you both. Love of the land is in the Farraday blood, as it was in that of my family, the Kingsburys. I implore both of you to enjoy this beautiful place you have called home for so long and live in peace.

"Your father left you another gift, Magdalen, one that I hope you will cherish and share with others. His literary genius produced the volume entitled Sybil Vane, *a book that exceeds even that of its famed predecessor. You didn't know him, but your grandfather was a great man who was cruelly treated by the world. Perhaps someday those who persecuted him will realize the error of their ways. Until then, guard this work as the treasure it is. Your loving mother, Henrietta Melmoth Farraday."*

Pruett cleared his throat before speaking. "Well. That's a very interesting document, but it raises as many questions as it answers." He turned toward me. "What's your take on it, Perri?"

I didn't answer right away because Pruett was right. Henrietta never mentioned the name of Magdalen's grandfather, although one could infer from the description that he was the great Wilde. Or not. Furthermore, she hinted that *Sybil Vane* was the product of Fingal Melmoth, Magdalen's father. Only one thing seemed clear: Carrick and Magdalen were to share the real estate that now comprised the Farraday homestead and kennel.

"Did Henrietta have a will?" Pruett asked.

Carrick shrugged. "Frankly I didn't pay much attention. This property is in one of those family trusts. My lawyer says that takes care of me, and I guess Mags too, as long as we live."

I knew there were all kinds of real estate trusts with provisions that differed state by state. Neither Pruett nor I was qualified to judge this one. Micah was the one with the legal expertise, but even he deferred to experts when it concerned real estate.

"Is Magdalen aware of this?" I asked. "She never mentioned it to me."

"Heaven only knows," Carrick stammered. "I figured Mags was out of the picture, maybe even gone forever." He grinned sheepishly. "Not very responsible of me, I guess. After all, I'm no spring chicken myself."

Pruett suggested that because Micah represented Magdalen, he might get involved. "This seems like something for the lawyers to pour over," he said. "Real estate trusts are complicated."

Carrick heaved a big sigh of relief. "Good idea. Let them sort it out. I need to see Mags more than ever now. Would you arrange that, Perri?"

I put aside my own business concerns and the irony that my simple act of altruism had morphed into a major entanglement. True, the Therapy Dog organization's goals were to provide comfort and solace to people under stress. But nowhere in their manual did anyone mention money, manuscripts, or murder. The tangled affairs of the Farraday clan had left me mired in quicksand and sinking fast. Now I was the one under stress!

"Still with us, Perri?" Pruett jabbed me with his elbow. "How about getting together at the Falls tomorrow? My calendar is free and that's your usual day."

Carrick's face brightened. "Sure, now that would be a blessing. Maybe I could bring Paddy with me. He's registered as a Therapy Dog, you know, a bit out of practice but still in the game." Paddy raised his giant head upon hearing his name and yawned. My enthusiasm was lukewarm, but fortunately in his euphoria, Carrick didn't sense that. I pasted a faux smile on my face and agreed to make the arrangements. Meanwhile Pruett was busily recording the pages of *Sybil Vane* on his iPhone. Fortunately the work was not too voluminous, and he was able to finish his task in short order.

"Why don't we take the book home with us?" Pruett asked. "That way you don't have to worry about it."

Carrick's shoulders, which had sagged under the weight of his discovery, suddenly straightened. He patted Pruett's arm. "Terrific. Let me wrap it for you."

When Carrick bustled off to another room I rolled my eyes at Pruett. "Mr. Considerate. You qualify for sainthood."

He flashed a smile at me that could shame a saint and wisely remained silent. Possession was nine-tenths of the law or, in Pruett's mind, 100 percent. I knew he had no intention of letting that book out of his sight.

After Carrick carefully wrapped the novel in brown paper and tied it with string, we finally said our goodbyes. It was almost midnight and I was exhausted. Pruett, on the other hand, seemed energized. He bounded to the Porsche with all the abandon of a teenager on his first date.

Despite the late hour, I texted Babette about our plans. To my surprise, she called back immediately.

"OMG," she said. "You found it. You actually found it!"

"I thought you'd be fast asleep," I said. It took at least five minutes to explain the basics to my friend, including the letter from Henrietta and the *Sybil Vane* story.

Babette was virtually bouncing back and forth, or at least it felt that way to me. Naturally she agreed to accompany me to the Falls the next day.

"Wouldn't miss it for the world," she trilled. "Funny thing. I knew you were up to somethin'. You know how keen my instincts are, Perri. ESP, spidey sense, and all that. Besides, I want to pick up Prospero this week. Ooh, everything's coming together just perfect!"

After far too much discussion we agreed to convene at my place the next day, or actually the same day at around noon. It was already well past midnight when our call ended.

"Will Micah be there? He can catch a ride with me," Babette said. She trotted out her coquette routine, but it was too shopworn to work on me.

"Pruett's handling all that. Now get some sleep. You'll want to look your best."

An appeal to her vanity worked every time, especially when an eligible male was involved. Babette signed off immediately, leaving me to doze while Pruett drove through the night. When we arrived home I took one final peek at Raza and Zeke and lumbered off to my nice, cozy bed. Pruett was still busily texting someone or other as I eased into slumberland. I was sound asleep before he joined me.

Chapter 19

I was a whirling dervish the next morning, caffeine-fueled and task-oriented. Between feeding my pets, responding to customers, and packaging my finished products, I had little time to anguish over the afternoon to come. Naturally Pruett was an oasis of calm as he sat sipping espresso and reading the latest headlines.

"You see more of the FedEx man than you do me," he joked. "Should I be jealous?"

"We have a relationship," I said. "He's the main man in my life. So dependable, and faithful to a fault. By the way, what kept you up so late last night? Should I be jealous?"

"I texted Micah, and the Goose. Needed to set things in motion before this process got away from us."

My puzzled frown made him laugh. Who in the world was the Goose?

"You know. Professor Bruce Douglas. My old roomie. The English Lit freak."

Ah. My synapses finally started firing as I recalled our conversation. "You sent him some of those pages you copied, didn't you?"

Pruett grinned. "Just a few as a teaser. Believe me, he'll be on pins and needles when he reads them. Big coup for his university if it's real. Every member of the publish-or-perish fraternity dreams of something like that."

I learned that Micah would join us despite his reservations about the Farraday real estate trust. His concern was understandable. An attorney specializing in those matters would have to review the document before any conclusions could be drawn. I wondered what Magdalen's reaction would be. That land was worth a pretty price based on the offers Carrick had already received. Two million dollars could turn a lot of heads and change some lives as well.

I checked my watch. There was just enough time for a quick gallop with my favorite girl, Raza. Pruett was nodding off on the sofa as I left to saddle up the elegant mare and enjoy sixty minutes of pure bliss. As usual, Raza greeted me as soon as I came into view. She coyly arched her neck and shook her fine, silky mane in a gesture reminiscent of a practiced coquette. I gently rubbed her muzzle and spoke softly to her as I adjusted the blanket, cinch, and saddle. She understood every word; of that I had not the slightest doubt.

Zeke, my pygmy goat, immediately added his two cents worth by emitting a piercing shriek that was as close to a civil greeting as the little guy ever got. I wasn't complaining. Since Raza became his stablemate, Zeke's entire personality had been transformed. No more perpetually grouchy goat was he. I wholeheartedly welcomed his crusty, curmudgeon self as a vast improvement.

Soaring through the brush with Raza was more therapeutic than ten visits to any shrink in town. All my doubts and worries vanished when the two of us cantered, trotted, and galloped along the trail. I did a quick status update. Now that we possessed the Holy Grail, aka *Sybil Vane*, one way or another, Magdalen's quest was over. Experts would determine the authorship of the work and, more than likely, debate its authenticity. Either way that particular threat to Magdalen had been neutralized. I also felt a secret sense of pride at reuniting her with her long-lost brother. Pruett rebuked me for being a romantic. In his experience family reunions were seldom the ecstatic scenes portrayed in novels. He was probably right, but due in part to my own status as an orphan, I still cherished the notion of a happily-ever-after ending—for Mags if not for me.

For a time, I even brushed aside thoughts of murder. Perhaps Nurse Carole's death had been an unfortunate accident or something totally unrelated to Magdalen Melmoth. I knew better, but while soaring over fences with Raza, anything seemed possible. Later, while giving her a brisk rubdown, reality slapped me smack-dab in the face. Someone—someone with lethal intent—had taken a life, coolly and deliberately. Those poisoned sweets were as deadly as any bullet. More so actually. A bullet usually mows down one target, but any number of people might have munched a Belgian chocolate and paid the price. For that reason I favored publicizing our literary find as soon as possible. Full disclosure would insulate Magdalen from at least one potential danger. Anyone seeking the manuscript would realize that the Oscar Wilde crusade had ended. Naturally if the killer had another motive, it would do nothing at all.

Pruett was waiting impatiently when I returned. His eyes had an overcaffeinated gleam from too little sleep and far too many espressos. The moment I stepped into the living room he pounced.

"Come on, Perri. Chop-chop. Today is a big day and I for one don't intend to miss out."

I gave him a big thumbs-up and raced to the shower. Whatever happened, my time with Raza had been worth the price. An almost Zen quality suffused my mind as I applied honey-scented shower gel and lathered up. I firmly believed that the answer to everything resided at the Falls. With a little bit of luck and a bit of probing I would find the answer. Magdalen was the key, whether she acknowledged it or not. If we were lucky, her reunion with Carrick might spark some memory that would enlighten us.

I toweled off and quickly donned my duds for the day. Because red was the color of valor and leadership, I chose a crimson shirtdress and paired it with my best leather boots. I peered into the mirror and was pleasantly surprised. Not a siren, but definitely a force to be reckoned with. Pruett's eyes sparkled as he twirled me around.

"Very nice, Ms. Persephone. Some old geezer might try to steal you away. I'll keep a close watch."

High spirits made me respond in kind. "Don't forget Dr. Tully. I just might turn his head as well, not to mention any other eligible male in sight."

Babette's noisy arrival curtailed any further banter. The Range Rover stopped suddenly, disgorging Clara, Babette, and Micah. Micah's face bore a slightly stupefied look that suggested he had just won a battle for his life. Babette's exuberant driving tended to do that to passengers.

She bounced up to us wearing her sauciest grin. "Okay, y'all. Ready to rumble?"

Micah was more interested in the novel. He gingerly fingered its pages and took a quick look at the contents. "I have to admit I felt a tingling inside when Wing phoned me. After all, we could be touching history here."

Babette raised her eyebrows but remained silent. I suspected that was not the tingling she had in mind for Micah. Luckily she was on her best behavior despite the fact that classic literature was simply not her thing. She consumed romance novels as if they were bonbons and could quote chapter and verse from her favorites. Hot guys and happy endings were her preferred formula, not the moralistic precepts contained in more serious works.

"There's something else to consider," Micah said with a lawyerly frown. "The legal heirs of Oscar Wilde might very well object or claim some of any proceeds. Things could get messy very fast."

Babette wrinkled her nose. "Oh pooh! Why are attorneys such spoilsports? Just when we were on a roll."

Everyone laughed, and after exchanging a few more pleasantries our caravan headed for the Falls. Pruett confirmed that Carrick and Paddy planned to meet us shortly after noon. My fingers were crossed that all would go well, particularly because Magdalen had been oddly calm, almost stoic, when I broke the big news to her. I expected tears, elation, or at least some emotion. Gratitude would have been a nice touch too. Instead she'd responded in a neutral voice that gave away absolutely nothing.

"Thank you, my dear," said Magdalen. "I'll expect you this afternoon. Perhaps we can all have tea before your program starts." That was it—nothing else. Not a thing. Most people would be exuberant or at the very least relieved that their quest had finally ended. Then again, Magdalen Melmoth was not like most people.

Pruett sensed my disappointment straightaway. "Don't look so glum," he said. "I told you reunions were seldom the stuff that dreams are made of. Magdalen's whole life has revolved around this Oscar Wilde thing. Now that you've solved the puzzle what does she have left?"

I bit my tongue before spitting out a reply that would cause hard feelings. Was he suggesting that I shouldn't have interfered? If Magdalen kicked the proverbial bucket now, was I to blame for granting her wish?

I maintained a sulky silence as we motored to the Falls. Of course, it was childish to blame Pruett because Magdalen was an ingrate. Reality hit me in the face like a bucket of ice water. I had my entire life before me, but Mags was eighty-five, with not many more innings left in her ball game. Now she might believe that she had fewer things to live for. Charity. Tolerance. I tried to abide by those virtues. When I opened my eyes Pruett was staring at me with a snarky smile on his face.

"Feeling better?" he asked, tickling my chin. "The Falls is a no-pout zone, as I'm sure you know. Therapy dogs are supposed to bring joy to the masses. Can't have any clouds on the horizon. After all, this was a big victory for you."

He meant well, but his high spirits and faintly patronizing comments annoyed the tar out of me. A murderer still roamed free despite the efforts of the alluring Sheriff Aleita and our own slate of amateur sleuths. Who knew when he or she would strike next?

"Any word from your source about the murder investigation?" I asked with a saccharine smile. As my favorite teacher once said, butter wouldn't melt in my mouth. Pleasant can be poisonous too, or so the saying went.

"None." Pruett was a master at playing this game, while I was the rankest rookie. "I understand that all deliveries to the Falls are now closely monitored by the staff. Precautions, you know."

I suddenly realized that, to my knowledge, Dr. Fergueson hadn't been notified about Carrick's visit. Maybe it wasn't essential, but good manners would dictate that it should have been done. "Should we include Joan Fergueson in this tête-à-tête? She is a relative after all."

Pruett shook his head. "No way. Stay out of this family stuff if you can. It's always a sticky wicket. Besides, Carrick knows her number. Let him make that call. Didn't sound to me like they're terribly close."

He was right. I knew it and so did he. For once I intended to play it by ear and allow events to take their course. For all we knew Magdalen and Carrick might loathe each other on sight. It had been a very long time since last they met—almost six decades. Resentments can fester in far less time than that.

We camped in the parking lot while waiting for Carrick. With so much uncertainty I exhaled sharply when his weathered truck with Paddy's giant head hanging out the window pulled in beside us. Carrick's hair was neatly combed and his clothing newly pressed, almost as if he were a schoolboy awaiting a trip to the principal's office.

"I didn't sleep much last night," he confessed. "Too much anticipation, I guess."

I said something banal that scarcely seemed to register, but Babette took the direct approach. She flung herself into Carrick's arms and gave the older man a big hug. She bent down and did the same to Paddy. "Don't you worry one bit, Carrick Farraday. Magdalen will be over the moon when she sees a handsome duo like you and Paddy."

Her words seemed to revive him. Few people, male or female, could resist the relentless optimism of a Croy embrace. Clearly her instincts were right on point.

Micah added a pinch of legal wisdom. "I'll speak with Magdalen afterward and we'll arrange for that trust to be evaluated. No sense in waiting."

We approached the front door of the Falls tentatively, as if each of us dreaded the possible repercussions of our great find. In the lobby I spied Kate Thayer and the unlovely Rolf Hart queuing up to visit with their clients. She waved, but all Rolf offered was a giant scowl. As soon as possible, I intended to update Kate on our progress. She deserved that courtesy; we'd plied her with a lavish lunch and asked for her help.

Before we reached the elevators, Joan Fergueson appeared and blocked our path. She was one tough cookie whose demeanor was hard to judge. The situation was uncomfortable for her, but Joan did seem vaguely pleased to see her uncle. Carrick embraced her immediately and murmured her name.

"Joanie. How are you, my girl? It's been too long."

She stiffened but didn't pull away, even after Paddy nuzzled her hand. "So nice to see you, Uncle." Hardly a warm greeting, but I expected no more from a cold fish like Dr. F. Despite her position, she lacked the empathy gene, a quality that was sorely needed in a place like the Falls.

Pruett stepped forward and cut the reunion short. "Excuse us, Dr. Fergueson. Carrick is eager to see his stepsister." She bit her lip and seemed about to refuse until Pruett played his trump card. "You know Micah Briggs, Ms. Melmoth's attorney."

Micah gave a lawyerly nod, all business and one notch short of brusque. He shifted his briefcase and edged closer to the elevator. Micah's actions left no doubt that whatever it took he intended to see his client.

"We'll speak later, Joanie," Carrick said. "I'm sure you must be busy."

Joan's shoulders slumped and she stepped aside. Our team notched a small victory in round one of what promised to be a contentious bout. I didn't delude myself, though. We'd scored a TKO at best. Dr. F would regroup and be back in the ring sooner rather than later.

Without further ado our party of five adults and four dogs entered the lift and pressed Magdalen's floor.

Chapter 20

Pruett was wrong this time. Despite his dire predictions, the reunion of Carrick and Magdalen was a textbook sibling lovefest. There was no need for words. The moment their eyes met he held out his arms and folded her into a tight embrace. The glow on Magdalen's face erased decades, giving onlookers like me a glimpse of the lovely young woman Carrick had adored. Our reactions varied. I took a deep breath, Pruett and Micah shifted from foot to foot, and Babette openly wept. Our canine crew showed the most poise: They sat at attention, silently eyeing the outpouring of human emotion.

I felt uneasy, as if I were a voyeur spying on such an intimate moment. Naturally Pruett had no such reservations. He moved against the back wall and closely observed the scene, committing each detail to that recorder in his brain. He was probably framing his headline already.

"Would you like some time alone?" I asked. It was a reasonable question. After all, neither Carrick nor Mags was a youngster. Time was their implacable foe.

Magdalen shook her head. "I for one am eager to see it—the novel that has haunted me for so long."

Carrick gave a sardonic laugh. "Same old Mags. Always did take the lead. Got right down to business." He plumped the sofa cushion and settled down. Paddy sat at his feet, resting his leonine head on his master's knees. "Might want to read your ma's letter first, though. Sets the stage and all."

Magdalen closed her eyes, as though she was seeking strength. "Of course. Mother kept a cool head in any situation. Her guidance was always sound." After Micah produced the letter Magdalen scrutinized each word, as if it might suddenly disappear. Her lips trembled and, in a gesture more evocative than speech itself, she reached over and clutched Carrick's hand. After several minutes Magdalen dabbed her eyes with a handkerchief and said quietly, "I'm ready for *Sybil Vane* now."

It would take some time for her to peruse that novel and Babette and I had our Therapy Dog meeting to attend. We excused ourselves, leaving Pruett and Micah to stand guard. On our way out Babette tapped at Irene's door to say hello.

As usual, Irene was impeccably turned out in a neat shirtwaist dress and heels. Her eyes glowed as she spoke of Magdalen. "Can you imagine it? What are the odds that Mags would find her brother and the novel? Nobody could believe it when I told them about it."

Alarm bells suddenly clanged in my head. "Who did you tell, Irene?" My tone was a bit more forceful than I had intended and she shrank back as if I had struck her.

"Did I do wrong? I only mentioned it to a couple of staff members. They were happy for Mags."

Babette immediately leaped to the rescue. "Don't worry, darlin'. We're just being extra careful 'til that murderer is caught." She beamed at Irene and asked, "By the way, who'd you tell?"

It turned out that Irene had spread the good word to several nurses, attendants, and at least one physician, Dr. Jethro Tully.

I bit my lip to keep from shrieking. Maybe it was my fault. I should have asked who hadn't heard the news about Magdalen. The list might have been shorter.

Sometimes—quite often actually—Babette's skill at duplicity stuns me. My pal is second only to Pruett at deception but gaining on him daily. She put her arm around Irene and chuckled. "Betcha Dr. Fergueson got all flustered hearing the news. Mighta had a fit of the vapors."

Irene gave her a puzzled look. "Oh, I don't know about that. I didn't see her today. Dr. Tully did rounds. He had that new fellow with him. I forget his name. You know, the big one, and someone from your Therapy Dog group as well."

The specter of Nurse Edgar Williamson looming over Irene caused me to shiver. No wonder she spilled everything she knew. Kate vouched for him, but so what. A man of his size could snap Magdalen's neck like a dry twig. I swallowed my concerns and allowed Babette to resume the lead.

"You mean that Rolf character was roaming around here? I think he's a creep. Slippery as an eel." She drew Clara closer for emphasis.

Irene seemed to agree, but being a well-mannered lady, she stayed silent about Rolf and focused on the positive. "I love his dog, though. Portia. She's so elegant." The poor woman started dithering and wringing her hands in an effort to placate us. I quickly realized that further interrogation would qualify as cruel and unusual punishment, or elder abuse at the least.

We thanked Irene and quietly made our escape.

* * * *

Babette pinched me as we waited for the elevator. "Well, that went well, Perri. You're sure good at scaring the tar out of old ladies. Who's next—little kids?"

My pal was a first-class pincher with the grip of a pit bull. I winced as she held on and didn't let go.

"Hey. Cut it out! That hurt. Besides, now at least we know the cat is out of the proverbial bag. I bet everyone at the Falls knows Magdalen's secret."

She glared, unwilling to let me off the hook. "Irene is a lady, Perri. Genteel. You've got to use finesse if you want to worm stuff out of her."

Gritting one's teeth can be dangerous, but I did it to avoid giving Babette the tongue-lashing she so richly deserved. Finesse and Mrs. Croy were total strangers to each other. How ironic that she scolded me about it. On the other hand I should have been gentler with Irene. Once again I realized that I lacked the grandparent gene. Give me a recalcitrant army private or an ornery poodle any day. I could handle them with ease.

We scooted out of the elevator and reached the conference room just as the Therapy Dog meeting started. Kate was in charge, although you'd never know it from the number of times Rolf interjected with his pearls of wisdom. I was surprised to see Nurse Edgar Williamson standing at the back of the room, his brawny arms crossed and a scowl decorating his face. Was he Joan Fergueson's spy or an informant for the dishy Dr. Tully?

"Today we have a full house," Kate said. "Let's do a general meet and greet before we start the show. Dr. Tully said that some of the residents are disappointed when they don't get a chance to pet our dogs. You know how much that means to them."

I'd seen the joy that contact with our dogs brought to so many residents and heard them reminisce about pets they had loved. Their reaction was understandable. A life without the company of animals was so barren that I couldn't even contemplate it. As usual, guilt welled up within me. Spending a few hours here was a small price to pay for the happiness Keats and Poe bestowed on others. I resolved to err on the charitable side in the future. Persephone Morgan, crusader for the elderly!

Babette raised her hand. "Oh Kate. We have a new addition to our little group today. Paddy, the Leonberger."

Kate frowned, but Rolf went ballistic. "Now wait just a minute. You can't bring strange dogs in here willy-nilly. Insurance risks."

I couldn't wait to knock him down a few pegs. "Actually, Paddy has his certification and current insurance. You may know his owner, Carrick Farraday. He's Dr. Fergueson's uncle."

Kate immediately brightened. "Oh yes. I'm very familiar with Farraday Kennels. Wonderful dogs. How nice."

For some reason Rolf underwent an attitude adjustment too. "You mean that place out past Strasburg? I know him too."

Before I could hush her, Babette chimed in. "Bet you didn't know he's Magdalen's stepbrother. We had a real, old-fashioned family reunion just now." She staunched tears with a beautifully ironed handkerchief of Irish linen. So much for my plan to insulate Magdalen from potential danger. No wonder Irene and Babette were so compatible: two incurable magpies, birds of a feather.

Both Kate and Rolf said nothing, and if they were shell-shocked, I couldn't prove it. I glanced toward the back of the room, where the mountainous Edgar Williamson lurked, and chided myself about making snap judgments. True, the man was typecast as a villain; his size and perpetual scowl insured that. But some truly hideous beings such as Theodore Bundy were handsome, glib, and utterly heartless. Appearance proved almost nothing about the content of a man's character.

Kate spent a few minutes reviewing the day's program, then led us into the main meeting area where Carrick and Paddy waited. Introductions were brief and reactions amiable, with the exception of Rolf's. When Carrick extended his hand, the Realtor shook it without enthusiasm. Carrick, normally the most affable of men, acted stiff and uncomfortable. Fortunately the canine connection was more positive. Paddy and the lovely Portia bonded and became fast friends.

Babette jabbed my side with her elbow and whispered, "Did you catch that? Something hinky between Carrick and ole Rolf. Understandable, though. Man's a monster, and I don't mean Carrick."

I immediately changed the subject to her new pup, Prospero. Babette launched a nonstop monologue that lasted until our program began extolling the virtues of her new charge. Every seat in the function room was occupied and a sea of smiling faces awaited us. I reminded myself that these residents were part of the independent living section of the Falls and were both mentally alert and physically active. The memory impaired or physically disabled were housed elsewhere.

Irene and Magdalen had snagged front-row seats and waved at us from their perch. Predictably Wing Pruett was surrounded by a claque of admirers who clutched his arms and inflated his ego. Micah stood at the back of the room and solemnly observed the proceedings. His courtroom presence was impressive, but otherwise he was a shy, introverted guy.

After Kate introduced each of us and our dogs, we held a question and answer session. Most people asked the ages and breeds of our dogs and the type of training they had received. We stopped by each row to encourage participants to pet our dogs or raise any other issues. Naturally Keats and Poe were a big hit, but Carrick Farraday and Paddy stole the show. It occurred to me that the mostly female audience was as enamored of Carrick as of his dog. Men in the over-sixty age group were in short supply, and in his own way Carrick was a superannuated hunk.

Kate bustled up to me afterward and grabbed my arm. "Do you have it? Can I just take a peek? Please? I've never been even close to literary history before."

"Stop squirmin' and I'll get it," Babette said. Her gruff response was unusual for someone who valued manners above almost all else. She bent over Magdalen and retrieved the novel. Instead of handing it to Kate, she tantalized her by holding it to the side. "What do you suppose ole Oscar Wilde would say about this? Seems like he always had some kind of sassy comeback."

The answer to that was easy. Wilde famously had said, "I can resist everything except temptation." Even if *Sybil Vane* was not his work, just the possibility would drive a number of otherwise staid individuals beyond temptation to the brink of sanity. It was akin to a type of Lotto fever that afflicted everyone when the prize got enormous. Bibliophiles would regard a new work by Wilde as a far greater lure. Kate, for instance, acted as if she were in a trance. She treated the novel with reverence, mindful that the pages were fragile.

"That woman is Magdalen's mama," Babette said. "Pretty, huh?" Kate nodded, but it was obvious she hadn't heard a word. She was nose deep in the narrative, seemingly trying to memorize each page. When Rolf Hart jostled her, she totally shut him out. "Watch your step, buddy. I'm busy."

"Hmph," he said. "Doesn't look like much considering all the fuss."

Pruett responded in clipped tones. "You're a businessman, right, Rolf?"

"Yeah. So what?"

"Well, that little book's more precious than a million-dollar piece of real estate. Far rarer too."

The words "real estate" caused little dollar signs to appear in Rolf's eyes. At least I imagined they did. That's the problem I have when I truly loathe somebody: no room for objectivity or doubt. If I had even one scintilla of proof, I would have nailed Rolf for the murder of Nurse Carole and possibly the kidnapping of the Lindbergh baby as well.

"That reminds me," he said, staring straight at Carrick. "We met a while back when I was in your neck of the woods. As I recall, you turned down a prime offer for your property." His attempt at folksiness fell flat.

Carrick returned the stare with interest. "Can't say as I recall that." He turned to Magdalen. "Hey, sis. How about joining me for a cup of cocoa? As I recall, you love that brew."

"Indeed!" Magdalen looked up at him with a shy smile. "Can Irene join us, Carr? Please."

Before long the three of them linked arms, and with Paddy in the lead headed for the truck. "Don't wait up for us," Carrick said with a wink. "With two lovely ladies for company I intend to take my time."

The rest of us headed home. Babette clutched *Sybil Vane* in a death grip while I pondered everything that had happened that day. Hard to believe it was finally over and even harder to link the manuscript to the murder of Nurse Carole Ross. For all I knew there was no linkage. Magdalen might still have an enemy who was willing to eliminate her at all costs.

Pruett had promised to deliver *Sybil Vane* to his professor pal the very next morning with Micah in tow to tie up any legal loose ends. The process would be a lengthy one. I realized that scholars from around the globe would eagerly debate and study those precious pages. Questions about authenticity would fuel innumerable dissertations and academic fistfights for years to come.

I also pondered the changes in Mags from her animated speech to the very becoming pink flush that stained her cheeks. The authenticity of the novel might be irrelevant after all. The reunion of two long-lost siblings was what really counted. It was all about family. When I mentioned that to Pruett he gave me a wary look.

"Don't kid yourself. Hold on to your hat, Leather Lady, we're in for quite a ride. Even a whiff of fame does strange things to ordinary people. Trust me, I've seen it happen too many times. Plus, there's the potential for lots of loot too. We're talking a bonanza of bucks and fame for the lucky winner. Television appearances, lecture tours, and who knows what else. People have killed for less."

Arlene Kay

I considered myself a realist with a hardheaded, practical approach to life. When it came to Magdalen and Carrick, however, I cherished a secret hope that as in the romance novels that thrilled Babette, their lives would have a happily ever after. In every competition there was also a loser. I said a silent prayer that Magdalen and Carrick would weather the storm and emerge unscathed.

Chapter 21

For the next few weeks, life returned to normal again. Creature Comforts prospered, and my calendar was filled with dog and horse shows and a reunion with Pruett and his daughter Ella. We celebrated at Applebee's, her favorite restaurant, by digging into heaping plates of chicken wings. Ella spoke very little about the European jaunt and I didn't probe for information. Her glamorous parent, photojournalist Monique Allaire, always treated me with a thinly veiled contempt that stung. True, she was gorgeous, rich, and famous, everything I was not, but I had one big advantage over her. Despite her accomplishments, Monique was dissatisfied with life, whereas I thanked the Lord daily for every blessing I had. Pruett genuinely loved Ella, but Monique often used the little girl as a bargaining chip in a high-stakes game with him. I had no idea what her goal was, but in the perpetual feud between Pruett and Monique I was more than content to remain neutral and play Switzerland.

To a seven-year-old child, the world was much simpler. Forget the glories of Paris and London. Ella plied us with endless questions about Carrick Farraday and Babette's new addition, Prospero. I saw the look of despair in Pruett's eyes every time his daughter mentioned Leonbergers and knew that the die was already cast. Sooner rather than later, Pruett's elegant residence would inevitably house another canine resident. Ella loved all animals, but her doting daddy was still a reluctant convert who bravely confronted his discomfort around animals to please his daughter.

I hadn't seen Magdalen for several weeks, although the Sebastian Melmoth story dominated much of the local news. She was caught up in the whirlwind of change and spent most weekends at Farraday kennels. This was a happy time for her. A flurry of animated texts extolling the virtues of Carrick and his dogs assured me of that. Even the murder of Nurse Ross gradually faded into the background until another unexpected death brought Sheriff Aleita Page back into our lives.

After a relaxing trail ride with Raza and my dogs I returned to find Babette pacing back and forth in front of my workshop. I knew immediately that something was very wrong. Her hair resembled a tangled hornet's nest and her usually impeccable makeup was a cosmetic disaster. Only the presence of Clara and the pup Prospero provided any sense of normalcy. Before I dismounted she ran toward me waving her arms.

"Where the heck have you been, missy? Don't you answer your cell phone anymore? Pruett and I've been tryin' to get you all morning." In her excitement Babette combined a fit of tears with hiccups, rendering her speech nearly incomprehensible.

I grasped Raza's reins and walked slowly toward my friend. "Whoa! Calm down. What in the world is wrong?"

A rivulet of tears and mascara streamed down her cheeks, adding to the chaotic scene. Not a good look for a former beauty queen, or anyone else for that matter. Babette bent over and regained at least some composure. Meanwhile Clara and Prospero licked her cheeks in a show of canine consolation.

"It's awful," she sputtered as she fended off the dogs.

I leaned against Raza for support, imaging the possible scenarios. Had someone died? At her age. Magdalen was the most likely candidate, but her health seemed quite robust. My stomach clenched. Had something happened to Pruett or Ella? I considered grabbing Babette by the shoulders and shaking her like a terrier with a rat. Luckily for her, she mopped her face and finally made sense.

"Explain," I said, making the supreme effort at control.

"There's been another murder at the Falls."

"Magdalen?" I sputtered.

Suddenly the snarky side of my friend resurfaced. "Magdalen? Who said anything about her? Sheriff Page called Pruett this morning with the news. They just found Dr. Tully in his office. Dead. Murdered." She grimaced. "Waste of a real hunk if you ask me."

Jethro Tully murdered? Unbelievable. He was my prime suspect in Nurse Ross's murder, and the death of Sara Whitman as well. Glib, oleaginous men with perfect teeth, blow-dried hair, and manufactured smiles always aroused my suspicions. Another one of my prejudices, I confess.

"How was he killed?" I asked Babette.

She yawned and shrugged her shoulders. "I dunno, but Pruett said they know it was murder. That's good enough for me." The glint in her eyes told me that she was hiding something. How like Babette to parcel out clues and make me guess. Normally I refuse to play her game, but today was different.

"Who found him?"

More dissembling from my BFF, who preferred to avoid unpleasantness and focus on the sunny side of life. After several abortive efforts I lost patience with her.

"Who found him? Spill everything or I swear I'll tell Micah your real age."

She snapped to attention, as I knew she would. The age card was the ultimate power play when dealing with Babette, who famously claimed to be thirty-nine. Her driver's license didn't lie, though. Despite a wrinkle-free complexion, the lovely Mrs. Croy was closer to the big five-oh.

"Okay. I wanted to protect you, but here it is. Kate found him slumped over his desk with Magdalen standing right next to him holding the murder weapon."

* * * *

Babette had few details to share, but that didn't suppress her endless speculation. "Maybe he threatened her or tried to steal the novel and Mags went bonkers. She has a temper, you know."

It wasn't easy to ignore my friend when she went on a tear, but somehow I managed. I moved mechanically through the routine of grooming and feeding Raza and Zeke, keeping both dogs at my side for balance. Babette followed me back to the stable babbling something that simply didn't register. After finishing those chores I grabbed my iPhone and called Pruett.

He responded by providing a few impersonal details in a tone that told me he was not alone. "I'm heading over to the Falls now," he said. "Micah's already there, and so is Carrick. Meet me."

I peppered him with questions to no avail. Pruett can clam up with the best of mollusks when it suits him. After fueling up with espresso and removing the trail dust, I harnessed Keats and Poe and hopped into Babette's Range Rover, determined to unearth the truth whatever the cost.

* * * *

An air of impending doom shrouded the Falls. Dark clouds, a cool wind, and a trio of police vehicles accentuated the gloom. On the far side of the building Pruett's Porsche and Micah's Cadillac sedan nestled together like old pals. Carrick's truck was nowhere to be seen.

Babette shivered. "Ooh. Looks spooky, doesn't it?" She reached over and squeezed my arm. "Don't freak out. Just wanted to see if you were alive."

This time I chose to ignore her antics. My mind was filled to overflowing with thoughts of Magdalen and murder. It seemed unbelievable: Dr. Jethro Tully struck down in his own office. No person or convoluted theory would ever convince me that Magdalen Melmoth was a killer, let alone a triple murderer. There must be some rational explanation for things. Had to be. I texted Pruett and got an immediate reply. "Stay in the car."

Babette, who had no qualms about violating my personal space, moved over and read the message. "Well, of all the nerve," she huffed. "Wing Pruett thinks he's a king or somethin', givin' orders." She paused and dimpled. "'Course he's pretty close to one, isn't he, Perri? So manly. Real take-charge type of guy. Such a contrast with the wimps out there."

Before I managed to pinch her cheeks Babette pointed toward the entryway. "Look! Here they come."

Sure enough, Micah, Pruett, Sheriff Page, and a bedraggled Magdalen Melmoth plodded solemnly toward the patrol cars. Magdalen's shoulders slumped and her eyes stared ahead unseeingly. She and Micah clambered into the back of the prowl car, but Pruett rode alongside the lovely Aleita. He glanced our way and put a finger to his lips.

"Maybe she placed him in custody," Babette quipped. "Sure looks like that woman wants our boy in cuffs."

I gave her a sour look and focused on the issues at hand. Pruett never had explained his relationship with Aleita, and I'd never asked. After all, we were both adults who had led full lives before we met. I realized that his love life had been considerably fuller than mine, but so be it. The issues confronting us now presented more than enough challenges.

"Let's find Irene," I said. "See what she knows about this whole mess." That was easier said than done, though, because two burly deputies were posted at the entryway to the Falls. To a law-abiding type like me, the task seemed insurmountable unless we confronted it head-on. Babette had other ideas.

"Let me handle this, Perri," she said with a sugary smile. "Bet I can get us through that door. Feminine wiles do the trick every time with those kinda fellas." She winked. "Just follow my lead."

I warily approached the entryway, but she bounded up to the lawmen ahead of me. Believe it or not, Babette immediately produced a pristine white handkerchief and a lusty chorus of sobs.

"I must see my Aunt Irene," she said. "She called me this mornin' in a terrible state." She daintily dabbed her eyes. "Her heart's bad and I'm afraid she'll have another spell if I don't calm her down." Defying all odds, Babette shed actual tears, droplets that flowed gently down her cheeks.

The deputies looked perplexed, clearly stumped at how to handle the emotional storm. That's where I came in.

"Officers, I'm a therapy group member too. I can escort Mrs. Croy to her aunt's room if you'll allow it. We won't touch anything or bother anybody. I promise."

People often comment that I look both reliable and respectable. That may not be a compliment because descriptors like "sultry" and "seductive" have far more cachet. In this instance, however, my girl-next-door persona was a definite plus. Both officers hesitated, then waved us through. As we made a beeline for the elevator, I deliberately ignored the sly look of triumph in Babette's eyes. No need to encourage her already outrageous behavior.

When the elevator doors opened, Carrick and Paddy appeared. I motioned them back and pressed the button for the second floor. Carrick furrowed his brow as if he were totally confounded. Paddy remained placid.

"I'm sure glad you're here," he said. "Things have gone from bad to worse."

We filed down the corridor to Irene's apartment and waited while Babette phoned her. "Irene, come out and open this door pronto before those deputies nab us."

The door slowly opened a crack as Irene Wilson peered out. Discarding her usually impeccable manners, Babette pushed ahead. Irene reluctantly admitted the rest of our little caravan into her flat.

I studied her for a moment, expecting that the turmoil would have altered her appearance. Not so. Irene was the picture of well-bred chic in a paisley twinset, black pencil skirt, and double strand of pearls. Only the red rims of her eyes betrayed signs of trauma.

Babette immediately threw her arms around her friend and hugged her. "I was so worried about you and Mags. Tell us everything."

Irene's voice quavered. "I don't know much, that's the thing. We were having tea when Mags got a call from Dr. Tully." At that point Keats approached Irene and put his head on her lap. Stroking him immediately calmed her.

Carrick leaned forward "From someone in his office or the doctor himself?"

Irene shook her head hopelessly and said she couldn't really say. "I assumed it was the doctor, but maybe not. Why? Is that important?"

If Sheriff Aleita was fixing time of death, that call was a critical factor. Perhaps Magdalen was lured to the murder scene and set up by the real killer.

"What happened next?" I asked Irene.

She dithered a bit but finally recalled that Magdalen said it was important. Said the doctor found out something big about Nurse Ross's murder. "I should have gone with her, but she said not to bother. If only I had insisted..."

Keats sensed her distress and nuzzled Irene's hand. There was no time for recriminations, and after a second of canine consolation she continued her narrative. "I got worried when she didn't return, so I went to find her. I never did see Mags, only a crowd of people making a ruckus. Mrs. Thayer came out with Dr. Fergueson and asked us to return to our rooms. That other man, Rolf somebody or other, was there too with his dog, Portia."

Of course. Today would normally have been a routine day for Therapy Dog visits. I had begged off because of my workload and Babette had some other engagement. Apparently, Kate and Rolf had carried the load.

Carrick had managed a brief conversation with Magdalen before the sheriff arrived. She said that she found Tully there sitting at his desk, already dead. Blood was splattered everywhere, and it appeared that the doctor had been assaulted with the ragged edges of his glass water bottle.

"He loved that Pellegrino," Irene said. "Always the kind in the glass bottles. Wouldn't drink a drop of tap water or anything in plastic. No sir. Not him."

"Hmm. Can't quite see Dr. Dreamy being excited," Babette said, "even in his most intimate moments. Seemed like the ultimate cool cat to me."

When it came to the male of the species Babette's observations were usually spot-on and I'd learned to take them seriously. Come to think of it, part of Jethro Tully's charm—such as it was—had been his composure.

That left unanswered the big question: What possible motive could drive Magdalen Melmoth to murder Jethro Tully? My iPhone pinged as I pondered that question. Pruett—finally.

Just hearing his voice warmed me all over, a daunting admission from a self-sufficient woman like me, who prided herself on her independence. Had I become vulnerable to a man who could easily break my heart? The answer was a resounding yes. Fortunately I had long passed the point where that bothered me. Come what may, I was in it for the long haul.

"What's the latest?" I asked.

"I'm on my way over there now," he said. "I won't even think how you got past the cops. Meet you in Irene's apartment."

The other three brightened and looked my way, as if they too expected Pruett to know everything. Given his talent for secrecy and deception, they were destined for disappointment. Pruett might indeed have the answers, but he was likely to hoard that information until after his exposé was published.

"It's teatime downstairs," Irene said timidly. "Nothing fancy, but we might get some information." She blushed, as if curiosity were an unpardonable sin. "We can see Mr. Pruett arrive from the dining area."

"Great," Babette said. "I could use a couple of those scones they make. Delish! Bring the dogs too. That loosens tongues."

We marshaled our forces and trekked down to the residents' lounge. Despite or because of the murder, the place was packed. It wasn't really surprising. Most of those gathered there had precious little excitement in their lives and had lived long enough not to be shocked by much, even a stray body or two.

Kate, accompanied by Gomer, bustled up to us and waved us to a table. "Thank the Lord you're here. I need all the reinforcements I can get." I noted that a strand of hair had escaped her French twist, and her lipstick was a thing of the past. Gomer wore his trademark goofy grin despite the tension in his owner's face.

"Looks like you could use a breather," Carrick said, pulling out a chair for her. "Here. Sit a spell." I had to admit the man was quite a charmer. Kate's reaction confirmed that as she banished her frown and managed a smile. When Babette returned with a plate piled high with scones, each of us gratefully partook.

"What can you tell us?" I asked Kate. Her relationship with Joan Fergueson was closer than mine and she had been at the scene of the crime. I was confident that Kate the library maven was a keen observer who didn't miss a trick. It wasn't ghoulish curiosity. We couldn't help Magdalen without knowing all the facts no matter how painful they might be. Time to learn the truth and face the consequences.

Chapter 22

Before answering Kate took a sip of tea. "I don't really know much. Rolf and I were in the lounge setting up the program. Today's musical chairs day and you know how we arrange the circle." Musical chairs was a favorite performance at the Therapy Dog sessions. Residents loved it and the dogs enjoyed the treats that came with it. To motivate them, each participant received a prize, win or lose. Unfortunately at least four dogs were required for the game to function adequately.

"Anyhow, we had only two dogs, so I went to check with Dr. Fergueson. It was almost one o'clock, but the place was a ghost town." Kate blanched as she said those words. "I swung by Dr. Tully's office and that's when I saw her. Magdalen. She was standing over him, holding that broken Pellegrino bottle in her hand."

Babette was never one to mince words. "Was he already dead? We heard he got bashed on the head."

Kate nodded. "Slumped down in his chair, blood and water everywhere. But it wasn't his head. She...or somebody...slit his throat. I bent over to feel his pulse and it got all over me."

Irene gave a strangled cry and put her hand over her mouth. Carrick and Babette gasped, and I have to admit feeling a tad woozy myself. Clobbering someone in a fit of anger was unacceptable but understandable. Slitting his throat...? No way would I ever believe that Magdalen Melmoth committed such a brutal, horrific act. Besides, how could an octogenarian, even a fit one, overpower a healthy younger man? Impossible! Surely this crime required physical strength as well as cunning. That argued for a much younger and stronger killer, probably male. Someone cruel and brutal enough to slit his victim's throat. Suddenly that scone, oozing strawberry jam, seemed far less appealing.

"Did Mags say anything?" I asked. "She must have been in shock." Kate shook her head. "Just that someone else killed him. I told her to put down the bottle, lock the door, and come with me while we called the sheriff's office. She didn't give me any trouble. Agreed right away."

Carrick asked the kind of question that a prosecutor might pose. "How would you describe her manner?"

"Calm, detached, almost clinical." Kate swallowed hard. "Frankly that surprised me. Probably in shock, I suppose."

It didn't surprise me one bit. I knew from experience that tragedy affected people in many different ways. During my army stint I'd seen soldiers whose buddies had been shredded to pieces play a boisterous, all-night poker game afterward. Yet the next morning, when the impact settled in, they were virtually catatonic or sobbing like infants.

I could tell Carrick wasn't buying this homicidal image of his stepsister either. He cracked his knuckles, then steadied himself by stroking Paddy. His words were terse as he turned toward Kate. "Not Magdalen. No way. That girl couldn't bear to see any creature hurt, let alone commit an atrocity herself. Mark my words, she was set up."

No one contradicted him, although I'm positive the others shared my concerns. People change over the years, often for the worse. Carrick and Mags had been apart for over half a century. He really didn't know her anymore and couldn't predict how she might react when threatened.

"What about Rolf?" I asked. "Did he see anything?"

Kate furrowed her brow. "I can't recall. Everything was so hectic." She evaded my question rather neatly, and that gave me pause.

"Were you two together the entire time? Where is he now?" Carrick asked. He adjusted well to the role of Grand Inquisitor. Dostoyevsky's depiction of that character had always intrigued me, and Magdalen needed all the defenders she could muster.

Babette barreled right into the conversation. "Yeah, that varmint has some explainin' to do. I don't trust him even one inch. He's the sleazy type for sure. Wouldn't put anything past him."

More dissembling by Kate. "I didn't notice. The entire episode was so disturbing that I zoned out." She shivered. "The sheriff questioned everyone, though. Made us all feel like criminals. Rolf took off as soon as she finished with us. Pressing business, or so he said. Can't say that I blame him. Wish I had thought of that."

Irene touched my arm and pointed toward the door as Pruett glided into the room. The man had both a panther's grace and a cat's inclination to toy with his prey. Despite his alluring looks, when parceling out information Pruett was fully capable of deception. Moreover he appeared to relish it. Like the villain in countless dramas, he was garbed entirely in black leather, which suited him as it did few others. I ignored Babette's grin and Kate's nervous giggle of assent. Today I nursed a grudge that no number of sultry moves would erase.

Pruett stopped at our table and bowed. "Ladies, Carrick. May I join you?"

Babette hastily moved her chair to clear a space. "Sit right down here, Wing. We've been waitin' for you all day."

He patted her shoulder and eased onto the chair. When our eyes met Pruett telegraphed a message of caution. I gave him a brief nod and powered down. Sooner or later, in his own good time, he'd share whatever ghastly details he could.

Carrick crumbled his scone into dust. "Where is she? Did they arrest Mags?"

Irene gave a faint cry and bit her lip. She seemed on the verge of tears, barely holding things together. I reminded myself that despite her appearance, Irene was a woman in her eighties who was unused to a diet of mayhem. Come to think of it, I was feeling a bit frazzled myself.

Pruett explained that no arrest had yet been made and that Micah would remain there for the duration with Magdalen. That wasn't good enough for Babette. She scrunched up her face and fired a volley of questions his way. "Stop bobbin' and weavin'. What's the story? Did someone really slit his throat? Did Mags do it?"

Instead of angering him, that verbal assault made Pruett laugh. A big, hearty, masculine guffaw. "Whoa, lady." He held up his hands in surrender. "Give me a break. I'm starving and my throat's dry as dust."

Irene immediately filled a plate with scones and signaled the attendant for a fresh cup of tea. "Here, Mr. Pruett. We didn't mean to appear rude."

I recognized a delaying tactic when I saw it, but Irene was totally deceived. In my book, a brutal murder obviated the need for party manners and polite asides. Given my druthers I would have demanded an immediate accounting of events from this slippery scribe who knew far more than he revealed. Once again, self-discipline, my superpower, saved the day.

After my guy consumed several scones and two cups of tea he lay down his fork, used his napkin, and shared the news. "Magdalen didn't say much, except that she found Tully already dead. She grabbed the broken bottle without thinking."

That made sense to me. Despite everything we've gleaned from crime shows on TV, innocent people often act irrationally when faced with horrific situations. "What did Tully tell her when he phoned?" I asked.

"Nothing much. Just that he knew the motive for the murders and it had nothing to do with the novel." He shrugged. "Or words to that effect. Micah shut everything down before things went too far. He insisted that a cardiologist examine Magdalen because of her heart."

Babette chuckled. "Bet that got your girlfriend's knickers in a twist. Serves her right, huh, Perri?" I scowled at her while Kate gave only a faint smile. Pruett was momentarily nonplussed but quickly recovered.

"Oh, you mean the sheriff," he said. "Like most cops she wanted to press on, but Aleita is one cool customer. She arranged things with a doctor. No problem."

Carrick steepled his hands together. "Let me get this straight. Dr. Tully solved the murder, or thought he had, and it wasn't about *Sybil Vane*. Then what in the world could it be?" He bent down and hugged Paddy. "That eliminates Mags as a suspect, doesn't it? Probably some drug thing at this institution. You hear about that stuff all the time."

Irene's face brightened. Drug dealing was certainly preferable to believing her best friend was a cold-blooded killer. I could tell by their faces that Kate and even Babette were unconvinced. Pruett wiped all emotion from his face, treating us to his most inscrutable pose. He subscribed in theory to Buddhism, with a healthy appreciation of Sun Tzu included. That served him well when playing poker and probing for information. Not as effective for providing consolation to others.

"The police aren't ruling out anyone at this point," he said. "They'll wait for the forensic team and the coroner to weigh in."

"So, Tully was alive when he phoned Magdalen?" I constructed a mental timeline of the gruesome crime. "Irene, did she leave immediately?"

Once again Irene seemed startled. "Not really. Mags finished her tea and primped a bit. We were just finishing our lunch, you see. Mags valued her independence. She never jumped when one of those staff people gave an order even though she was excited about this one. Mags always made sure she called the shots."

Carrick nodded fondly, as if this was just the type of behavior he expected of his big sis.

I calculated that up to fifteen minutes might have elapsed between Tully's call and Magdalen's arrival at his office. Plenty of time for someone else to step in and silence him forever.

"Where was everyone else?" I asked. "You know, Dr. Fergueson and Nurse Edgar. I thought they stayed around when the residents had lunch."

Babette bounced in her chair. "Yeah, that's right. Wouldn't take but a minute for that big lug to slit someone's throat. Arms like ham hocks, that one. Never did take to him, no sir."

Pruett shrugged but offered no additional information. Based on my experience that meant he knew something else but wasn't about to reveal it in front of a group. At that point we adjourned. Babette accompanied Irene back to her apartment, while Kate grabbed Gomer and headed for the exit, leaving Carrick with me and Pruett.

"Let me ask you," Carrick said, "what state was Magdalen's clothing in? Looked pretty normal to me."

Irene had mentioned that Mags primped before heading down to the office, and that suggested a nice outfit. I immediately grabbed my iPhone and texted Babette. I was confident she would wring a full description from Irene by whatever means were necessary. No one could wring information from the unwary like my BFF.

Pruett played possum, but I knew better. If Magdalen Melmoth committed that brutal crime, surely she would have been covered in gore. I'd only gotten a glimpse of her when she passed by. It was impossible to judge because her black cape had been slung over her shoulders and she was flanked by Sheriff Aleita and Micah. A sudden ping on my phone told me that, true to form, Babette had once again delivered the goods.

"Okay, you guys, listen up. Mags wore a pinstriped shirtwaist dress with a cameo broach, a purse, and gloves. She was carrying that black cape of hers over her arm." I turned to Pruett. "Now it's your turn. Seems to me if she committed the crime, she'd be covered with Tully's blood. Was she?"

Pruett admitted that the sleeve of Magdalen's dress contained bloodstains. According to Mags, when she entered the room she bent down, picked up the broken Pellegrino bottle, and backed away from the body without touching it. That would account for the bloodstains on her dress. When Kate found her she was about to call for help.

Time to confront Pruett. I folded my arms and gave him my tough sergeant glare. "There's more, isn't there? Come on. We're waiting. Fess up."

Carrick resumed his Inquisitor role. "Please, Mr. Pruett. This is no time to hold back. If she's charged with murder, Mags may not survive the shock."

My guy looked almost shamefaced when he finally shared his secrets. "Okay. There's one other point to consider. Tully's office had been ransacked. Papers all over the floor and drawers upended. Someone—probably the murderer—was definitely looking for something."

That suggested to me that Magdalen was telling the truth at least about part of it. Jethro Tully knew something that would point the finger at Carole Ross's murderer and maybe clarify the death of Sara Whitman. His killer had been determined to find that information at any cost.

Carrick grunted. "They'll be dusting the place for prints and such if those television shows get it right. Should tell us something at least." He gave Paddy a gentle hug and got ready to leave. "I'll stop in and see how Janie's doing. Stay in touch with me. Please. I can't lose Mags again after all these years. If her attorney needs money…"

Pruett nodded and promised to contact Micah as soon as we got home.

Chapter 23

Our return trip was a solemn one. I was too exhausted to speak, and Pruett's febrile brain was probably focused on his forthcoming article. His phone rang only once, and he responded with a series of terse comments—none of which told me anything.

"That was Micah," he said finally. "Magdalen's under observation in the hospital for erratic heartbeat. He'll contact Carrick and swing by your place later. And in case you're wondering they didn't charge her—yet."

I closed my eyes and pondered his meaning. Sheriff Aleita had to be under enormous pressure to solve the murders. One homicide in a retirement community was disquieting, but two within two months set alarm bells ringing all the way to Richmond. Aleita might be tempted to take the easy way out by tagging Magdalen for the crimes figuring that at her age she might be spared a jail sentence. I sat up abruptly and met Pruett's eyes. "She's innocent. I know that, but everything revolves around her somehow. The novel, reuniting with Carrick… If Dr. Tully really found the truth, what could it be?"

For once, even Pruett was stumped. It was only six weeks since I'd first set foot in the Falls, but it seemed far longer. The saga of Magdalen Melmoth, her heritage was one of those tales that never ended. If only I'd remained at Creature Comforts, crafting fine leather products rather than getting involved. I understood my animal clients. Unlike some humans, they had no hidden agendas or homicidal tendencies. Between the literary quest and two brutal murders I felt mired in doubt. Would we ever untangle this skein of drama, deception, and death, or would it remain a mystery forever?

Pruett must have sensed my despair. He put his arm around me and turned on the old charm machine. "Hey, Leather Lady, perk up. We'll get through this puzzle like we always do. Oh. With all that's happened I forgot to mention something."

I looked warily at him. If he uttered even one more discouraging word, I swore I would scream my head off. Instead I hunkered down and gritted my teeth.

He gently massaged my shoulders. "Relax, why don't you? Every muscle in your neck feels tighter than a spring. It's nothing bad. My pal from the University called last night. I guess the entire English faculty went bonkers over *Sybil Vane*. Anyhow they're convening an international symposium to study it with Wilde scholars from around the world."

"Do they think it's genuine?" I asked. At last a crumb of good news to savor. I could hardly believe it. Sebastian Melmoth might become a household name after all.

Pruett grinned. "You know academics. Fun, fun, fun. They'll fuss and fight and write innumerable treatises about it. Careers will be made and lost. Charges and countercharges leveled. No verdict yet on the provenance, but Micah has found an attorney who specializes in copyright stuff. She'll make sure everything's kosher."

At least Magdalen's interests would be protected on that front. It should delight her, assuming she wasn't jailed for double murder. Double murder! The evening was balmy, but I shivered nevertheless. "I don't suppose Micah had time to research the real estate trust. Maybe that's the root of Mag's troubles."

Talk about a Hail Mary pass. If Carrick was correct, the tract of land belonged to both Magdalen and him. He certainly didn't plan to sell it, and as far as I knew she wasn't even aware of the provisions of her mother's will. Still an offer of two million dollars was nothing to sniff at and people had been disposed of for far less. There was one little problem about that, though. I couldn't for the life of me figure how Nurse Ross and Dr. Tully fit into the scenario. Perhaps Carole Ross was the intended victim all along and not just collateral damage. That gave me an idea. Rolf Hart was obnoxious and a braggart, but according to Kate, he was a real estate wizard. If I applied a bit of soft soap and played the compliant female, he might clarify things for me.

Pruett interrupted my thoughts. "We're home, Liege Lady." He grasped my hand and kissed it. "You know, I love the sound of that. Home. All we need is Ella to make everything complete."

He was right, but I dared not pursue it. Not today anyway, when events had conspired to turn everything askew. Instead I smiled his way and squeezed his hand all the while repeating that word to myself. Home.

* * * *

Once we arrived I had little time to spare. Zeke immediately started braying and even my Raza extended her beautiful head and eyed me in quiet protest. I released my dogs, leaped from the Porsche, and attended to both of them. Their food and water buckets weren't empty, but both had the need for a spot of exercise and a dollop of love. What a treat to see Raza cantering around the paddock with the grace of a prima ballerina. My helpers, Keats and Poe, romped with Zeke, giving the little pygmy goat his share of glory too.

Just as they finished their run, Micah's car pulled into the driveway. With his loosened tie and rumpled shirt, he emerged looking more like a pugilist than a legal eagle. His first words to Pruett proved the point. "Got any scotch?" he asked. "I'm knackered."

While Pruett did the honors, I attended to one very irate coon cat, who demanded that her meals be both fresh and on time. After Thatcher unleashed a verbal scolding at me, she brushed against both male guests and deigned to eat the kibble and tuna. As with most felines, Thatcher issued imperious demands that I hastened to satisfy. Ignoring her was not an option and I strove, often unsuccessfully, to remain in her good graces.

I rarely cook, but with all due modesty I admit that my omelets are second to none. While Pruett and Micah sipped their scotch, I whipped up a crab and cheese omelet that satiated us all. Afterward we addressed the elephant in the room: Magdalen Melmoth and her plight. I wasn't certain how much Micah could disclose, but he was remarkably forthcoming. Mags gave an official statement that differed very little from Kate's account. After Tully's call she had gone to his office and found him mortally wounded. She admitted to picking up the broken Pellegrino bottle but denied trashing the room. When the police searched her, they found no evidence of notes or any other material related to a possible murder and no fingerprints other than Tully's. The absence of evidence was hardly conclusive, but I felt a faint ray of hope. Surely someone else had preceded Magdalen, ransacked the office, and murdered the good doctor.

Micah and Pruett were less optimistic. Their downcast eyes told me that.

"What about her clothing?" Pruett asked. "I don't recall seeing much blood on it. I would have expected everything Magdalen wore to be splattered with blood."

Micah agreed that only the right sleeve of her shirtwaist contained traces of blood. Then he played the cautious lawyer. "Naturally until they test the whole garment we can't really tell for sure."

While he and Pruett debated the pros and cons of the case, my thoughts went elsewhere. Tomorrow morning I planned to contact Rolf Hart for investment advice. Because I had no excess capital and limited experience with real estate, I needed backup. One name immediately sprang to mind whenever the subject involved money. Despite her whimsical ways, Babette Croy was razor sharp when dealing with dollars. She'd made some shrewd investments that expanded her net worth into the high seven figures. Confidence schemes never succeeded with her—she could spot a scam at ten paces. I counted on that big bank balance to intrigue rapacious Rolf into granting us an audience. Pruett wouldn't approve, of course. So be it. An occasional assertion of girl power was good therapy for an entitled male like him. The real estate rendezvous would remain my little secret.

* * * *

Babette was elated when I outlined the plan and readily agreed to play her part. She groused about being excluded from the previous evening's gathering until I explained that the guys virtually ignored me. Her spirits revived instantly. "Isn't that just like men," she said. "Thinkin' they have all the good ideas. We'll show 'em." She suggested that we meet Rolf at her home rather than the Falls. That was an inspired idea I wish I had thought of. Describing Babette's home as a mansion really didn't do it justice. "Estate" was closer to the mark. All twenty acres breathed an affluence that would help to bait the trap for Rolf and loosen his tongue. We agreed to portray ourselves as potential real estate partners interested in properties in Shenandoah County. A dose of understated guile would be necessary to allow Rolf to guide us toward the Strasburg area. I might even suggest that Carrick was reconsidering his options.

"Girl, you know how I can pile on the manure." Babette smirked. "Rolf won't even know what hit him. Anyhow, it won't be hard to fake. Real estate happens to be a solid-gold investment."

I cautioned her not to get too immersed in her part. Self-restraint was not Babette's superpower and excess enthusiasm might result in an actual purchase. She waved off my concern. "Oh pooh, you are such a spoilsport, Perri. I know what I'm doin'. Besides I just might find me a bargain. Now that I have Prospero to consider, a big slug of land would come in handy." I knew that she was a conspicuous consumer with very low sales resistance.

The last time we went sleuthing, Babette left with a massive recreational vehicle dubbed Steady Eddie. That too had been a bargain.

Initially Rolf Hart's personal assistant gave me the runaround. He took our information, explained what a busy man his boss was, and reluctantly agreed to call back. It didn't take long. Somehow those zeros in the Croy bank balance magically cleared Rolf's schedule for noon the next day. That gave us plenty of time to plot our plan of attack. Babette arranged for her housekeeper to serve an elegant buffet on the terrace, complete with wine, crystal, and Limoges. I was confident that Babette's good taste and her cook's culinary skills would captivate our avid entrepreneur.

"Remember," I said, "Not a word to Micah or Pruett. This caper is our little secret. If Rolf suspects what we're up to, we've wasted our time."

Babette scratched her head. "What are we really up to, Perri? Just askin'. I want to play my part right."

Just my luck. My pal the diva was a method actor! I took a deep breath and once again sketched out the plan. If we excluded the Oscar Wilde novel, that left the oldest of all motives for murder—money and greed. According to Kate, Nurse Ross had quarreled with Sara Whitman about real estate. We also knew that Rolf had scouted the area where Carrick lived, trying to entice him into selling. If there was a connection, we might uncover it during our tête-à-tête with Rolf. At the very least he could provide some useful information.

We finalized our strategy and parted for the day. Babette fled to the talented hands of her hairstylist, while I indulged in my own type of therapy. I saddled up Raza, summoned Keats and Poe, and spent the next hour riding the trails and savoring the beauty of autumn in Virginia.

* * * *

The next day I dressed for success, or my version of it anyway. That task took far more time and caused more angst than I cared to admit. I'm a simple soul who dresses for function, not fashion. Unlike Babette, who regarded *WWD* as her bible, wardrobe issues tended to confound me. I opted for comfort over any attempt at style and had a closet filled with sensible rather than sensual garb. There were practical reasons for this. Working with leather demanded attention to detail, precision, and a healthy dose of creativity. I had little interest in trends, preferred *Modern Dog* over *Vogue*, and considered a dab of lipstick a makeup plus. Not today. I studied my wardrobe and finally chose a Palomino-colored tunic paired with leggings and my best pair of show boots. Fortune had granted me long, slim legs that showed to best advantage in that type of outfit. No sense in masquerading as a fashionista. Besides, if the affluent, horsey set in Middleburg, Virginia, and environs deliberately dressed down, how could I go wrong? I embellished the look with two pieces of jewelry: a Tiffany key necklace courtesy of Pruett and an antique gold broach that formerly belonged to Pip's mother. Oddly enough those touches buoyed my confidence, as if both the gifts and the givers were at my side.

Babette chose an entirely different route. By wearing a handsome suede ensemble, mile-high stilettos, and discreet diamonds, she reinforced her position in the social and financial firmament. Artfully tousled curls and flawless makeup completed the look.

When I arrived she gave me a quick once-over and the Croy seal of approval. "We make a great pair, Ms. Perri," she said. "That slimy salesman will be putty in our hands. Believe me, I know the type. The scent of money makes them woozy."

Frankly the thought of any part of Rolf Hart in my hands made me woozy. I told myself to buck up and forget all that. To realize our goals I had to suppress my natural distaste for the man and make it about business. Nothing personal.

We sipped lattes as we waited on the terrace for our visitor. Either caffeine overload or anticipation made me jittery and Babette was no help at all. She dithered endlessly about our plan and its likelihood of success. Would Rolf show up or merely brush off an invitation from two women? I checked my watch. Timeliness was critical in both business and social transactions. It conveyed respect for the potential client and the issues at hand. Surely a real estate wizard realized that, and if he didn't, Rolf Hart's business acumen had been vastly overstated.

Our answer came promptly at noon when the housekeeper presented our guest and the games began.

Rolf had opted for a nicely tailored business suit, a rep tie, and a pinstriped shirt. I gave him points for realizing that a well-groomed appearance was a gesture of respect for his hostess and the dollars she represented. In all fairness he was an attractive man—until he opened his mouth and spewed vile things about our military.

Babette immediately went into gracious hostess mode. "So glad you could join us, Rolf. We need a bit of business advice. Accordin' to Kate, you're an absolute whiz at anything real estate."

His manner was polite but distant as he settled into his chair as if he was asserting himself, reinforcing his bona fides as a bigwig before our discussion started. His slight slouch conveyed the distinct impression that he was doing us a favor. "Why don't you fill me in on your plans, ladies."

I tried not to bristle at his patronizing tone. Babette caught the whiff of sexism too and responded with a saccharine smile.

She leaned forward and pounded on the table. "We're talkin' money here, Rolf. Big bucks for you and us. Perri and I been watchin' the market and we want in on it." As a finishing touch, she poured our guest a glass of a very fine chardonnay and eased back in her chair.

That change of pace surprised him. His eye widened as he adjusted his expectations to this more daunting reality. Suddenly the ladies who lunch had morphed into serious businesspeople. "What kind of property were you thinking of?" Rolf asked. "You realize that the DC area is saturated." He shook his head. "Very few bargains left around here."

Time for me to play my part. "Exactly. We were thinking of rural areas in Virginia, ones with acreage and growth potential."

Babette leaped into the conversation. "Lots of those old farms are undervalued. Low taxes too." She decided to sweeten the pot. "'Course we intend to pay cash up front. Makes things simpler, don't you think?"

Rolf took a mighty sip of wine and nodded. "I have some thoughts for you to consider. Shenandoah County still has some bargains. We're talking serious money, though. Last one I sold went north of two million dollars."

"We figured that," Babette said. "Carrick filled us in. I'd sure love to get my hands on a piece of land like his. Maybe start my own kennel with Perri." She smiled my way. "This gal knows everything there is to know about dogs and horses."

Rolf got a wary look in his eyes, and for a moment I feared we had overplayed our hand. Fortunately a tide of greed surged to our rescue. "I tried that," he said. "Mr. Farraday was quite emphatic about his own property. Besides, there were issues—an irrevocable family trust—involved." He shivered. "Those things get messy, let me tell you. Only his descendants can inherit or make changes to the holding, you see."

"How nice for Mags and Dr. Fergueson." My expression was innocence itself, though the implication was clear. Rolf chose not to add anything, but it was obvious that he knew the issue at hand.

We paused as a platter of tasty dishes was placed before us. Maryland blue crab salad, avocado toast, and a tempting cheesecake quickly turned our thoughts from property to food.

"Dig in, Rolf," Babette said, displaying her dimples. "I love a man with a hearty appetite. Don't see much of that anymore. I'm a widow, you know."

I clamped my jaws shut to avoid shouting out. Technically my pal was a divorcée. True, Babette had been widowed three times, but her recent ex-spouse, the perfidious Carleton Croy, was very much alive and currently stalking other wealthy prey.

Rolf immediately flashed a toothy grin that flunked the sincerity test. "Oh, I'm surprised to hear that. A lovely lady such as yourself, I naturally assumed..."

Babette lowered her head, showcasing those magnificent eyelashes. She managed a brave smile and brought the conversation back to real estate.

"I bet lots of those old folks at the Falls own property they might sell. Let's face it, most of them are swirling the drain anyway. Land's the least of their worries. We might find us a bargain there."

Rolf shrugged but made no comment. That gave me the opening I sought. "From what Kate told us that lady who died, Sara Whitman, was a neighbor of Carrick's out in Strasburg. You knew her, I believe."

"Vaguely. She was very sharp. I enjoyed discussing real estate with her." Rolf cut himself another slab of cheesecake. "Your friend Magdalen tangled with her, I hear. Of course I try to avoid petty disputes. No point in it."

Babette and I both nodded in agreement. Any smart businessperson knew better than that. After all, potential customers came in all shapes and sizes. No sense alienating them. We made yet another foray into Rolf's business dealings.

"You bought a parcel of land from this Whitman woman, didn't you?" I asked.

He looked at his watch before answering. Obviously our questions were making Rolf a bit skittish. "Correction: I purchased land with Mrs. Whitman. We were partners in the enterprise." Another specious smile. "Much like you and Mrs. Croy here."

The tone of our conversation had changed from warm to frigid, but nothing deterred Babette. She clapped her hands and gleefully said, "I bet you had one of those 'key man' clauses too. Guess they call it 'key person' these days, but I don't get tangled up in that mess. Anyhow, that's what I want. After all, it's a smart play. Protects both of us in case something bad happens. 'Course we're both plenty healthy, but you never know."

Rolf smiled, a fleeting smile without mirth. "True. One should never take good health for granted. Things can change so rapidly."

Despite the warmth of the sun, I felt a sudden chill. His manner was perfectly pleasant and his words were innocuous. It was one of those sixth sense spidey moments that my dogs felt too. Keats and Poe went on alert and moved closer to me.

"What's your take on those murders, Rolf?" Babette held her head with both hands. "We're kinda leery of going back to the Falls. If some mad killer's runnin' loose, anyone could be next."

For a moment he hesitated, but the appeal to his ego proved too strong to resist. "I doubt that any of us is in danger," Rolf said. "Besides, those residents really love our therapy dogs." He leaned closer. "I have it on good authority that the sheriff will have things wrapped up very soon."

My vamping skills were rusty, but I tried my best. "Really? You have great connections at that place. Babette and I didn't get very far with Sheriff Page."

He gave us a taste of faux modesty and a coy look. "It was nothing really. I do have a lot of law enforcement contacts, however. I never said Aleita was my source. Your Mr. Pruett seems to have the inside track with her."

I could see that Babette had reached the end of her tether. Fortunately good breeding prevailed and she confined her frustration to a single oath. "Don't just sit there like a dummy, Rolf. Tell us who's on the griddle."

Rolf picked up his napkin and rose. "Unfortunately I'm sworn to secrecy. Let's just say it's someone you both know well." He placed two business cards on the table. "Ladies, this has been delightful, but I really must run. Let me consult my listings. Perhaps I can suggest a few properties for you to consider." His smile was now closer to a sneer. I doubted we would ever get that list or the chance to question him again.

After he left Babette poured herself another glass of chardonnay. "Well, darn. That was a waste of time and a good wine." She flounced into the house, followed by Clara and Prospero, while I joined them for the postmortem. I dreaded the inevitable storm of recriminations that was certain to follow. The duration of a Croy sulk was hard to predict, but I knew from long experience that my wisest tactic was to forge ahead and ignore the headwinds.

I was less pessimistic about our luncheon than Babette. Rolf had been wary but not totally unresponsive. We found out that he had purchased land with the late Sara Whitman and probably scooped the lot when she left this earth. Had that arrangement caused a spat between Nurse Ross and Mrs. Whitman? Was that the secret Dr. Tully uncovered? I wondered how many of the oldsters at the Falls were real estate partners with Rolf Hart. Perhaps Kate knew if he used the Therapy Dog program to influence residents. If so, it was the perfect guise for his shenanigans.

Babette spun around and faced me, hands on hips. "Well, Perri, it's up to you now."

"Huh?"

She exhaled forcefully and beamed her death ray glare my way. "Don't be dense. That Rolf character threatened us. Don't tell me you didn't notice."

I trod gingerly around that topic, mindful that Babette often got huffy when challenged. "I wouldn't exactly say he threatened us. Let's face it: Rolf is unpleasant at the best of times unless you're a potential customer with cash."

Babette exhaled forcefully. "Well, what in tarnation do you call us? We waved filthy lucre his way and he basically snubbed us. I say we struck out."

My silence was more eloquent than any rebuttal. This time she was right.

No one ever accused Babette Croy of being a quitter. After a brief period of reflection she was back in the game. Her eyes narrowed as she confronted me. "Don't be so wishy-washy, Perri. There's more than one way to skin a varmint and you know it. Pruett has an in with Sheriff Aleita; old Rolf was right about that at least. Make your sweetie play his ace in the hole or we might as well give up now."

I'm no quitter, but giving up sounded fine with me. Unlike Babette, I had a business that had been sadly neglected over the past month. My schedule included two dog shows and several major horse competitions. A tart response was on the tip of my tongue until I recalled Magdalen Melmoth, that spunky senior who depended on me. With that in mind I folded like a fifty-cent fan. "Okay. Enough already. I'll ask Pruett."

Babette didn't flinch. She folded her arms and growled, "When?"

"Soon. Okay, tonight. I'm not sure we should tell him about our session with Rolf, though. You know how tedious he can get." I envisioned the lengthy lecture I would get from Pruett about personal safety, interfering in a murder investigation, and any action that might compromise his sacred news story. That was something I was simply not up for after today's antics. Unlike Babette, the queen of histrionics, I avoided conflict whenever possible. I preferred to choose my battles wisely and listened to but ignored most unsolicited advice, electing instead to rely on my own good judgment. Pruett and I managed to respect each other's boundaries most of the time, although we had come perilously close to disaster on a few occasions. I vowed to avoid that tonight.

Chapter 24

As luck would have it, Pruett canceled our dinner date. He was full of apologies and less than convincing excuses. That emboldened me to broach the subject of Sheriff Aleita head-on. I mentioned Rolf's comment about an imminent arrest.

"What does the sheriff say about that?" I asked, clutching my iPhone in a death grip. If only I could see his eyes. Pruett couldn't fool me if we were face-to-face.

"You know more than I do," he said. "Aleita doesn't share that kind of information with the press. At least not with this member of the Fourth Estate."

I let the matter drop, but before we hung up, Pruett added something else. "Look, Perri, I'm not trying to deceive you. I'm on the trail of something big. As a matter of fact, I plan to meet with Aleita tonight. Strictly business. If I get the chance, I'll ask about Magdalen." He paused half a beat, then said. "Okay. I promise to ask about her. Satisfied?"

I kept my voice steady and unemotional. After all, I trusted Pruett. Didn't I? "Okay. I'll talk to you tomorrow. Stay safe."

We ended our conversation after that. I told myself to grow up and stop fretting like a nervous filly at the starting gate. What would be would be. Sheriff Aleita was a hot number, but then again, Persephone Morgan was no slouch either. I texted the update to Babette, summoned my dogs, and retreated to my workshop and the tactile comfort of leather.

Two hours of toil swept the clutter from my mind and focused my thoughts on the only issue that counted: extricating Magdalen Melmoth from the maw of the criminal justice system. I doubted she would be arrested, let alone prosecuted. Surely anyone could see that an octogenarian spinster, even a cantankerous one like Magdalen, was an unlikely double murderer. Still I worried that at her age the mere stress of a police matter might precipitate a health crisis. As I pondered these grim possibilities. the clarion call of my iPhone roused me.

Carrick Farraday's voice was subdued, but it worked like a tonic on my troubled mind. "Are you busy, Perri?" he asked. The slight touch of Ireland in his voice charmed me no end. Confession time: I'm a fool for a brogue. "I spoke with Mags a bit ago," he said. "Believe it or not, she seemed fine. If I didn't know better, I'd think it was just a normal day for her. That got me worried."

Micah must have worked his magic on the sheriff, unless it was some kind of trap. I clung to that ray of hope. If they had already released Magdalen, it had to be good news. Maybe another suspect was in the sheriff's crosshairs.

"She's back at the Falls?" I asked. Somehow I wasn't certain that was the wisest course of action. After all, it was already the scene of two homicides. Better to permanently insulate Magdalen from that house of horrors.

"Actually she agreed to stay overnight at the hospital while they evaluate her heart. Just to make sure." Carrick hesitated. "Tomorrow she's coming home with me. No one will harm her here. Not with Paddy and the gang standing guard."

Paddy was scarcely a guard dog, but I kept my misgivings to myself. No need to borrow trouble. "That's good news," I said. "Can I help in any way?"

More silence. Finally Carrick blurted out his concerns. "I need your advice. You're not a lawyer, I know that, but you have my sister's best interests at heart. I'm worried about money. Micah's fees must be mounting up and I doubt that Mags has much in savings. Joanie tells me that residents sign over most of their assets to the Falls when they move in."

I visualized Carrick wringing his hands as he spoke. "Anyhow, Mags is entitled to half this place, you know. Her mum's will said so."

Where was this conversation leading? I felt uneasy and inadequate to the task before me. "What were you thinking of?"

More sputtering and stuttering from Carrick. "I have some money saved and maybe I could refinance the place. There's no balance on it, you know. Or maybe get one of those reverse mortgage things I heard about on the telly. That real estate fellow offered me a pretty penny for the land. Almost two million dollars as I recall." Carrick's voice quavered as he mentioned the possibilities, and I could tell that he was agonizing over the choices. The Farraday property was part and parcel of his heritage, and Magdalen's as well. Even the thought of losing it must be heart-wrenching. I suspected that the "real estate fellow" in question was none other than the ubiquitous Rolf who covered central Virginia like a blanket.

"Carrick, stop! Why borrow trouble before we know what arrangements Micah and your sister have? She's quite business savvy, you know. Besides, the manuscript is another unknown. Who knows how much that might be worth?"

He heaved a sigh of relief. At least I presumed it was relief and not exhaustion. "Ah, you're a fine gal, Persephone Morgan. Just the pick-me-up this old man needed. I haven't had a sound night's sleep in a while but without this millstone hung around my neck I might finally grab forty winks tonight."

I promised to broach the subject with both Micah and Pruett as soon as possible and we ended our chat on an upbeat note by discussing Babette and her new pup, Prospero.

Afterward I recalled his reference to Joan Fergueson. That made me wonder. Joan had acted quite indifferent to Carrick and told me that she'd lost touch with him. Was she sidling up to her uncle all of a sudden or was it simply a normal exchange between two people who had reconnected? Any discussions involving money and Magdalen activated every suspicious bone in my body. I closed my eyes and did some deep breathing. Was I now responsible for her well-being and Carrick's as well? Quite a burden for a single woman with worries of her own.

Keats and Poe sensed my discomfort. They surrounded me and lay their soft, velvety muzzles on my knees. I looked into their eyes, slowly stroked their fur, and felt once again the magic of the human-canine connection. Small wonder that therapy dogs were in such demand. My lack of commitment and waning enthusiasm for the program gnawed at my conscience. True, I was a busy person, but that was more of an excuse than a reason. Our next session was already scheduled and I resolved to visit the Falls the very next day, spreading comfort and joy or something very much like it to the residents. What could possibly go awry? Besides, I just might learn something interesting.

* * * *

Babette grumbled at first about having to change her hair appointment. Apparently, some faux friend had asked her if she was going gray and that terrorized my poor pal into immediate salon therapy.

"Lookee here, Perri," she said, patting artfully colored strands of hair. "See any gray? Why, I pay good money to never see anything that color.

Ever. No matter what they say about silver power, gray is code for over-the-hill in my book."

I squeezed her shoulders and chirped words of consolation. "Your hair is always perfect. You know that. Just some jealous woman's fantasy. Besides, we're on a mission today, and that's lots more fun than sitting under a heat lamp covered with foils."

Babette snapped to attention. "You betcha. Just what are we looking for anyway?"

I filled her in on Carrick's dilemma and my conversion to the ranks of Therapy Dog enthusiasts. My hope was that we might learn more about Dr. Joan Fergueson, the formidable Nurse Edgar, Dr. Dreamy, and any other suspicious goings on at the Falls. Considering Babette's aversion to danger, I downplayed that possibility.

She gave me a hard stare. "Pruett know about this?"

My response was cool. I knew that by appealing to her contrary side, I'd win the day. Babette was a lukewarm feminist but a feisty one when roused.

"Why should he? We don't need his permission and we're perfectly capable of gathering information on our own without a man's interference."

A smile the size of Texas lit up her face. "Damn straight! We'll show him. Micah too. Those boys need a good comeuppance."

Our spirits were buoyed by optimism as we headed to the Falls the next morning. The plan was simple but focused: find the answer to several key questions, exonerate Magdalen, and corral the real killer. Simple? Admittedly they were stretch objectives, but why not aim high while we were at it? While the plan was tricky, I had to admit with all modesty that it was also rather clever. Under the guise of performing our Therapy Dog routine, Babette agreed to circulate among the other residents, encouraging them to gossip. Chatting up strangers came naturally to Babette and I had to admit she was far better suited to that task than I was. Her sunny disposition and gift of gab reached almost genius level and disarmed even the most taciturn person. Naturally she would enlist Irene's help too, and sprinkle the conversation with frequent references to Magdalen. I undertook the tougher assignment: interrogating Joan Fergueson, Nurse Edgar, and Rolf. Even the mention of Nurse Edgar's name terrified Babette, so she readily agreed to anything that kept her out of his sight. Although the man's size and grim visage were off-putting, I didn't fear him. Maybe he was just shy in the same way a sumo wrestler might be. I closed my eyes for a second, envisioning those meaty paws closing around my neck in a death grip. Then I recalled my secret weapons: Keats and Poe. I was safe with them by my side. Even a man-mountain like Edgar had to respect their mighty jaws.

Dr. Fergueson was a tougher proposition. The woman was an iceberg, indifferent to anything, even the winning ways of therapy dogs. Carrack painted a very different picture of her, but his views were tainted by fond memories of yesteryear with his uncle and assorted kin. A cynical person might question her sudden devotion to Carrack. That seemed inauthentic and awfully convenient. It neatly coincided with the real estate boom in rural Virginia and the seven-figure offers for Carrack's land. Joan had a glaring financial motive for her burst of family feeling. As Micah had explained it to me, the provisions of the family real estate trust made Joan the putative heir to Carrack's very desirable property when he passed. One thing stood in her way: a spunky senior named Melmoth. Magdalen's age gave Joan the distinct advantage, but it also required patience. For all we knew, Mags might live another decade or even more. If Joan hoped to challenge the trust and dispose of the property quickly, that would put a spanner in the works.

I had few illusions about Rolf or my ability to coax even a civil comment from his perpetually pursed lips. My goal was to pinpoint his whereabouts at the time that Dr. Tully was murdered. According to Pruett, Rolf had been vague about it when questioned by Sheriff Aleita. His excuse involved "scouting properties," a feeble but unverifiable one. Real estate was a peripatetic profession that allowed employees plenty of free time to maneuver. If Tully had learned something incriminating about Rolf's dealings, I knew that he was ruthless enough to neutralize the threat and anyone who posed it. One niggling point argued in Rolf's favor: Portia, the lovely Borzoi. The man's devotion to her seemed genuine. It wasn't enough to tip the scales, but it was definitely something to consider. I freely admit my bias toward any man, even a loathsome one, who loves animals. Rolf wasn't irredeemable, just unlikable.

Our quest was clear: determine who besides Magdalen had motive and opportunity to eliminate Nurse Ross and Dr. Dreamy. Although Pruett had assured me that Sheriff Aleita was doing that very same thing, I had my doubts. Cops—even comely ones—were more likely to seize upon an easy victim like Magdalen rather than looking farther afield. I couldn't allow that to happen.

When we arrived at the Falls our colleagues had already assembled outside, juggling dog leads, purses, and other paraphernalia. Frankly it was a more dispirited group than normal. Not surprising. Murder tends to dampen even the hardiest souls. Fortunately our dogs were oblivious to such concerns and were much more interested in a new addition to our pack. Babette had added baby Prospero to the mix even though he was far too young to be a certified Therapy Dog. I expected Dr. Fergueson to rush out and demand to see his bona fides, but she was nowhere to be found. Prospero's grasp of commands was sketchy, but the rambunctious pup proved to be a crowd pleaser. Soon he had an eager audience surrounding him. Some of the more somber residents responded by hugging the young Leonberger and clutching him to their chests. That gave Babette the entrée she sought to chat up a host of people. I felt confident that she would worm any information worth having from the mouths of the unsuspecting.

Meanwhile I angled closer to Kate and the unlovely Rolf, hoping to break new ground. Our dogs responded nobly by paying special attention to the more infirm and wheelchair-bound residents. Keats and Poe shook hands and gazed soulfully into the eyes of anyone who approached them. Shy residents got an extra nuzzle and headbutt that brought sunshine into the room. My boys made me proud.

"Makes everything worthwhile, doesn't it?" Kate said. "Gomer never met a stranger. That goofy guy loves everyone."

We had stopped for tea and scones in the dining room and I responded with my carpe diem moment. "Too bad Magdalen couldn't join us," I said. "She loves those dogs so much."

Kate gave a noncommittal "tut-tut," but Rolf immediately snarled a response.

"She's where she belongs. In a padded cell. That woman is a menace. I told Joan Ferguson to get rid of her long before all this trouble started."

I counted to ten, but it wasn't enough to calm me down. Self-control, my secret superpower, totally deserted me and a sharp retort flew from my lips. "For your information Magdalen is with her brother and not under any type of arrest." I restrained myself before I really got into Rolf's face. After all, my goal was information, not confrontation. I also cursed my stupidity. By opening my big mouth I might have inadvertently tipped off the murderer to Magdalen's whereabouts. Bad move!

Kate poured oil on troubled waters. "Be fair, Rolf. You can't blame Magdalen for Nurse Ross's death. No one forced that woman to wolf down six chocolates. As for Dr. Tully, Irene Wilson confirmed that he called Magdalen to his office. Anyone could have slipped in and killed him with that bottle before she arrived."

Rolf gave an evil smirk. "Next you'll be saying he slit his own throat. Well, I happen to know that Jethro Tully had his own theories about Carole Ross."

"Really?" Kate and I asked in unison.

"I never got the particulars, but Tully told me that he knew all about it and intended to go to the sheriff. Stupid of him, I know. Talk about tempting fate."

I narrowed my eyes and stared at him. Rolf's big reveal was late in coming and very convenient. I deliberately powered down and forced myself to smile. "When did he share that with you? Timing is everything, as they say."

"The same day your dear friend slit his throat. We spoke right after breakfast." I'm no shrinking violet, but Rolf had cornered the market on malice. The man was a virtuoso and proud of it.

"We got to be pretty close friends," he said. "Guy stuff, you know. Jethro had some cash to spend and he valued my opinion on real estate. We even bought a couple of properties together. He was nobody's fool either." Rolf preened. "Some men would drown in this sea of geriatric head cases, but not him. He had it all figured out."

Kate stepped back as if to insulate herself from the conflict. Not me. I leaned in. "Funny that he'd invite Magdalen to his office if he thought she was a murderer. The killer had to get awfully close to him to do the deed. I know I wouldn't risk it."

Kate's complexion turned ashen, and she buried her face in Gomer's wooly coat. Her reaction wasn't lost on Rolf.

"What's the matter, Kate, real life too tough for you? Smarten up. Get your nose out of a book for a change."

I suddenly recalled something. On that awful day, it was Kate who'd discovered Magdalen standing over the corpse of Dr. Tully. That grim scene could permanently scar the hardiest soul.

Naturally Rolf was impervious to anyone's finer feelings and plowed on with his narrative. "I figure it this way. Jethro wanted to be fair to her. Give her a chance to explain things. Come on, the old doll is over eighty. All she had to do was pretend to show him something, lean over his desk, and bam!" Rolf made a sickening motion across his throat and chortled. "Even vegetarians know how to use a steak knife."

Kate mustered her strength and faced him. "I was there, remember? Magdalen's shirtwaist was spotless. Unlikely if she'd just done such a thing. The papers on his desk were soaked in blood. If I hadn't been wearing an apron, I would have been drenched too." She shuddered. "Plus the murder weapon wasn't a steak knife. It was a broken Pellegrino bottle, or some kind of sharp implement."

"Details, details," Rolf said airily. "That's the cops' job. 'Course they wouldn't tell me anything. Betcha that cute little sheriff knows what's what. Right, Perri? Your guy seems pretty close to her. Ask him."

I clenched my hands behind my back. Better that than using them to strangle the miscreant in front of me. Fortunately at that moment the tinkling of a bell summoned us to the main living room. Time for part two of the Therapy Dog program to begin. I motioned to Keats and Poe before heading toward the side door to allow them to answer the call of nature. That landed me up close and personal with none other than Nurse Edgar.

Chapter 25

Edgar said nothing. He made no threatening gestures. But the mere sight of that man-mountain was enough to give me pause. I backed up and immediately went into fight-or-flight mode. Oddly enough, Keats and Poe neither bristled nor growled. Their keen instincts for danger had saved my bacon more than once, but today they were detached and untroubled. Truth be told, their dignity went flying out the window. My brave war dogs wagged their tails and beamed joyous doggy smiles at Edgar. Given the chance, they might have rolled over and begged for a tummy rub from the behemoth. I watched in awe as his features lightened, and he mumbled a soft, barely audible greeting to them. With great difficulty I collected myself and spoke.

"I'm sorry. This is totally unlike them. They're usually reserved with strangers."

Edgar flashed a smile that transformed his entire being. It was magical, like an outtake from *Beauty and the Beast*. "No problem. I love dogs and they sense that."

I introduced myself again, determined to capitalize upon this era of good feeling. "I'm sorry about Dr. Tully. I understand he was your friend."

The big man's face darkened. "Jethro asked me to come here and help out. We'd been friends since grade school. More like brothers."

I shook my head and tsk-tsked. "Such a charming man. I wouldn't have guessed he had an enemy in the world."

Nurse Edgar folded his arms in front of his sizable bulk and glowered at me. "He didn't."

In view of Dr. Tully's ghastly end that statement was either palpably false or delusional. "Someone killed him," I said. "That wasn't a friendly act."

Edgar jabbed a meaty finger my way. "Jethro had one glaring fault, Ms. Morgan, one that you seem to share. He was nosy. Arrogant and nosy. Thought he could outfox the cops and solve any crime. He was wrong and it cost him his life." Edgar made a kissing sound to the dogs and, with surprising grace for such a big man, pivoted toward the entryway. "Learn from his mistake and mind your own business."

* * * *

I admit it. That encounter shook me to my socks. I spent a moment collecting my thoughts, trying in vain to make sense of Nurse Edgar. Was he the malevolent presence I had imagined or merely a quiet, reclusive man trapped in a giant's body? Either way he was no one to trifle with. I knew Babette would have plenty to say about that and she didn't disappoint. As the group reassembled, she hustled toward me with Clara and Prospero in tow and a smug smile wreathing her face.

"Perri, get over here pronto," she said in a stage whisper. Babette possessed many gifts, but subtlety was not in her skill set. "Wait 'til you hear what I found out." Her big moment was delayed by the sudden arrival of Joan Fergueson, who stepped up to the microphone and began the program. I hadn't seen her since the most recent tragedy and the change in her appearance was startling. She'd shed the mantle of authority that enveloped her like a shroud in favor of an approachable, dare I say human persona—less Dr. Fergueson and much more Joan. Even her attire suggested something new, a change from the official uniform she favored. The formal skirted suit had been banished, replaced by a twinset—probably cashmere—in a cheery shade of yellow, accompanied by nicely cut slacks. A lovely triple string of matched pearls completed the ensemble. Even more astounding was her wide, inviting smile. I'd never seen the woman smile before. Wasn't sure she was even capable of it. Babette narrowed her eyes and whispered, "What the…?" She was in the presence of ladies, most of them quite elderly, so she wisely stopped there.

"I'm so glad you all came here today," Joan said. "We've suffered two grievous losses recently, but remember this. The Falls community is a family and we're here to support each other."

Someone in the back of the room called out, "Three losses. Don't forget Sara Whitman." Several in the audience nodded and at least one clapped.

Nothing dented the composure of Dr. Fergueson. I had to admit that in view of the circumstances it was impressive.

"Of course," she said. "We mourn every loss in our little community." She gestured toward our group. "These kind volunteers and their dogs are part of our support system. I urge you to take full advantage of it."

"Utter balderdash!" Babette hissed in a stage whisper. "It's all about the money." Fortunately her back was turned my way, blocking the sound from reaching anyone else. We took our places and formed a circle, ready to start the day's entertainment portion. Joan introduced us and our dogs individually and gave a capsule biography of each. When it was my turn, she first mentioned the wartime service of Keats and Poe. That earned a spirited round of applause from the audience and a bow from my dogs. Against my better instincts I started to warm up to the good doctor. Perhaps I'd misjudged her. Praising my dogs earned anyone extra points in my ledger. That warmth ended when she mentioned my involvement as a "detective." Naturally that inspired Babette to chime right in. She stepped out to the middle of the circle and patted Joan Fergueson's shoulder.

"You are so right! Perri tracked down two murderers. Almost got killed too." Babette ducked her head in an attempt at faux modesty. "'Course I helped her a bit. Clara too. And we won't even mention Wing Pruett's part in the whole shebang." That name excited a murmur among the audience. As Irene later pointed out, they might be old, but they weren't oblivious to a handsome man. I held my breath, hoping against hope that my pal would say no more. Naturally, being Babette, she didn't stop there. "Plus, I want y'all to know that Perri and I are on the case again. We won't let Magdalen Melmoth hang for somebody else's crimes. Count on it!"

No more happy talk from Joan Fergueson after that bombshell. Now she resembled an ice sculpture with facial features firmly frozen in place. Someone on my right side gave a sharp intake of breath and Rolf Hart issued a derisive hoot. As I watched the audience, I realized that the residents were thrilled, not traumatized, by the news.

Irene clapped her hands and trilled, "Oh, how exciting! It's like an episode of *Murder, She Wrote* with dogs!" Others joined in a hearty round of applause and offered their help and suggestions. In all, the incident was a disaster rivaling that of the *Titanic*. I closed my eyes, imagining the reactions of Pruett and especially Sheriff Aleita to our involvement. Amateur sleuths—even ones with a good track record— were the bane of law enforcement professions. I longed to slink away, but that would have caused an even bigger scene. Besides, blocking the main exit was the bulky form of Nurse Edgar, whose folded arms and scowl rivaled that of Zeus at his most unpleasant. No thunderbolts were hurled, but Edgar made no secret of his reaction.

One thing I recalled from my military experience proved to be our salvation. Someone—Sun Tzu, I think—said that knowing when to fight and when not to fight were both critical. This was definitely the time to brazen things out and go full steam ahead. "We're ready to begin our program now," I said with a grin that would shame a Cheshire cat. "Come on. Let the games begin!"

* * * *

We reconvened that evening around the long walnut table in my dining room, sipping my best brandy. Despite the surroundings, it was not a convivial group. Babette and I were joined by Pruett, Micah, and of course our four dogs. Thatcher jumped on the sideboard and sat aloof from the proceedings, judging me every minute and finding me wanting.

"Are you crazy? What were you thinking of?" Wing Pruett sounded more like a stern parent than a beau. Before the scolding escalated, I held out my hand and said, "Stop. Let's discuss this rationally and calmly."

Micah, ever the lawyer, went into arbitrator mode. "Perhaps you could explain the context for what happened."

"Context, phooey!" Babette snarled. "Ask Dr. Joan Fergueson. We were minding our own business, trying to bring joy to a bunch of oldsters, when she blabbered about the murders we'd solved. That set the cat among the pigeons." Those comments were true enough, but the self-satisfied smirk Babette wore gave the game away.

"God only knows how Aleita will react," Pruett said. "By implication you made her sound incompetent."

His defense of the comely cop gave me pause. Why assume I was the guilty party? I expected more of him, perhaps too much. Without acting too sensitive, I had to admit that Pruett had hurt my feelings. Fortunately Babette was spoiling for a tussle with him. She leaped from her chair, marched over, and immediately got into Pruett's face.

"Listen to yourself! You'd think that sheriff was your main squeeze instead of Perri. Besides, what has that crackerjack cop done besides measure Magdalen Melmoth for a noose? Huh? Take off the blinders, buster."

Pruett gave Babette a long, cool stare as the temperature in the room ratcheted up. Then he leaned back and laughed, a hearty belly laugh that immediately dispelled the tension. He shrugged and turned to his friend.

"See, Micah, I told you they were feisty. No one bullies these two ladies without paying a price."

I gave everyone refills while Babette distributed a platter of jalapeño poppers and fried calamari. "Good and hot," she said with a cheeky grin. "Help cool the passions around here. But not too much, I hope."

Frankly I shared that hope. Pruett and I had our own special brand of binding arbitration that I was eager to invoke.

Micah capitalized on the momentary lull and dipped a toe into the conversation. "Let's pool our information. Why not tell us what you two found out today? Then we can add our two cents. Sound right, Wing?"

Between crunches of calamari, Pruett nodded. "Agreed. And forgive me if I misspoke. You two have a knack for getting into scrapes and there's a murderer on the loose. A ruthless one at that. Guess I was playing the overprotective male again."

He was singing Babette's favorite tune. She gave both men a dimpled smile and turned on the feminine wiles. "No need to explain, boys. It feels good to know you're watchin' out for us. Doesn't it, Perri?"

My response was half-hearted at best, closer to a grimace than a grin. Better and safer to stick to a factual narrative. I started with a crowd pleaser: my encounter with Nurse Edgar. The reaction from all parties was explosive to say the least.

"You were alone with that varmint?" Babette shrilled. "Why didn't you call me?"

Micah's response was more temperate. "He's awfully imposing, Perri. Not someone to tangle with."

Pruett was uncharacteristically silent. That made me suspicious. He was hiding something and I intended to wring it out of him by any means necessary.

"Okay," I said. "Out with it. Edgar said he was Dr. Tully's friend. What did Aleita find out?"

"Naturally she checked him out immediately," Pruett said. "I mean, a guy like that is typecast as a villain. Turns out he told you the truth. Edgar is not only a legitimate nurse practitioner, he's also an ex-deputy sheriff from California and a licensed private eye."

Babette's eyes bugged out. "You're kidding. That hulk a PI?" I could tell that her image of a svelte, smoldering inquiry agent had been dealt a lethal blow.

"So," Micah said, "was Edgar on the case, whatever the case may be?"

"Yep. Tully called him in after Nurse Ross died, but he didn't get far. Seems the good doctor thought someone was planning to victimize one or more of the residents. No names were mentioned. Tully asked him to nose around and to keep his eyes and ears open. They never got a chance to thrash out the issues."

Once again I marveled at the superior instincts of my dogs. Edgar had frightened me, but Keats and Poe knew that he posed no threat to anyone except the murderer. Score one for canine intuition versus judging a book by its cover. My bad.

Meanwhile Babette was getting impatient, ready to burst at the seams. I knew how my BFF reacted under stress and it wasn't pretty. Volcanic was more like it. A timely intervention was in all of our best interests.

"I guess you're ready for me now," she said. Those downcast eyes and the humble act didn't fool me for a second. My pal had plenty of tidbits to share. She explained her assignment in excruciating detail, with special emphasis on the role of Clara and Prospero. "I swear, y'all, that pup was a superstar. Those ladies were like a bunch of groupies hanging on him. I peeled them like a grape."

"But what did you find out?" Pruett asked. His store of patience had worn thin some time before. He folded his arms, ignoring Babette's massive frown.

"Spoilsport," she groused. "Okay. Some of this is old news, but it bears repeating. Most of them thought Magdalen put on airs and made stuff up. Stuck up, someone said. Nuts, another said."

That puzzled me. "They knew about the Oscar Wilde thing?"

"Of course." Babette snorted. "Honey, nothin' stays secret in a place like that. Those old tabbies have all day to gossip and most of them are still pretty sharp. Mags was always dropping hints about the manuscript, stuff like that. It didn't take a genius to figure out her game."

I was afraid to ask the next question. "They didn't think Mags was a killer, did they? Please tell me that."

Babette shook her head.

Micah leaned forward. "And Nurse Ross? What was the consensus about her?"

Babette favored him with a dazzling smile. "That's the weird thing. They really liked that gorgon. Who knows why. She was rude and grumpy to us, right, Perri? They said she really cared about them and watched out for them. Not uppity like Dr. Fergueson or nosy like Kate. They kind of resent some of the Therapy folks. Oh, not us. But they felt like Kate and Rolf were always butting in, trying to chat up the residents and asking personal stuff."

That reaction didn't surprise me. One of the goals of the Therapy Dog program was to mingle with the residents, act friendly, and let them get to know our dogs. It was a delicate dance between intrusiveness and isolation that some were better able to navigate than others. Rolf very likely blundered into people's lives without respecting their privacy. I questioned his motives. My experience with Kate was quite the opposite. Like most librarians, she seemed to be the soul of tact and genuinely helpful. Perhaps the residents confused friendliness with impertinence. It might well be a generational thing.

"Anything else?" Micah asked, drumming his fingers on the table.

Babette hesitated. "Well. Some of those ladies said things went missing."

"What kind of things?" Pruett came to attention all of a sudden. Had he been a dog, his ears would have stood up straight. "Maybe they misplaced their belongings," he said. "You know how easy it is to forget things."

"Maybe, but this was jewelry and keepsakes. Expensive stuff." Whenever anything of value was involved Babette got that speculative look in her eyes. I was ill-equipped to assess anything like that, but she took her finances very seriously. I'd learned to defer to her expertise. "Check out some of the pieces those old dears wear every day," she said. "I scan the Weschler's auction website and a couple of others just to keep my hand in. Great bargains to be had on custom pieces. Believe me, art deco jewelry and old-world diamonds are pricey. We're talking thousands here."

Pruett frowned. "I'll check with Aleita, but it's doubtful that any police reports were ever filed. Joan Fergueson would keep that quiet if at all possible. Nothing dampens recruitment like rumors of theft."

There was more to come. I could tell by the smug smile on Babette's pretty face. "Okay," I said, giving her my stern sergeant look. "Out with it. Spill the beans."

"Someone did file a police report," said Babette, "and you'll never guess who."

I guessed the answer before she said the name, but why deprive her of her big reveal?

Babette cleared her throat. "Sara Whitman, that's who. The week she died. And that's not all. She'd just had her physical with none other than Dr. Jethro Tully. Some women confide in their doctors, don't they?"

Chapter 26

For a minute there was total silence. Pruett took a deep breath, Micah's eyes widened, and I sat mute. The dogs, even the pup Prospero, sensed the gravity of the situation. They stared at us, ears up, eyes alert, waiting for our next move. Thatcher, ever the drama queen, shared the excitement by stretching her legs and purring loudly.

"What's the matter," Babette teased, "cat got your tongue?"

All at once we pummeled her with questions. Was she certain? How did the police react? Did Sara name anyone or tell Dr. Tully anything?

Finally Babette held up her hands. "Stop. Here's what I know. Sara didn't name anyone in the report—worried about lawsuits, she said—but she told her pals that she definitely knew who the culprit was, and she had help getting to the bottom of things. If her jewelry was returned pronto, no harm no foul. If not, it was time to call in the cops."

At moments like this I was tempted to grab my friend and shake her like a rag doll. Pruett and Micah knew better and played it cool. Babette hoarded information like a miser did gold. She was Lady Bountiful, sharing scraps with the starving peasants. Threats were useless and begging did absolutely no good. One simply had to wait her out.

"You guys are just spoilsports," she groused. "No fun at all. She never got that jewelry back, of course, because she died. Satisfied? And I'm pretty sure that help she mentioned was the late Dr. Tully."

That would certainly provide someone with a motive for murder, or in this case for several murders. Money, filthy lucre, the bane of all evil. Lust for it had fueled wars and all manner of crimes since the world began. Had the quest for greenbacks also seeped into the Falls and poisoned that otherwise tranquil setting? I closed my eyes and meditated. Immediately the only image that arose in my mind was that of Rolf Hart. I was honest enough to confront my prejudices. He was a villain in my mind, but in all fairness that didn't necessarily make him a killer.

Pruett excused himself, reached for his phone, and stepped out of the room. I was certain he was contacting the sheriff and who could blame him?

Micah, ever the attorney, focused on the practical. "Any idea what jewelry was involved? Most valuable pieces are photographed and insured. Easy enough to check."

Babette shook her head. "Her friends only recalled one thing she wore all the time: a humongous emerald ring surrounded by diamonds. Set in platinum and very valuable. Sara loved it because it was her grandmother's. Called it her retirement policy."

I hesitated to ask the next question. Couldn't bear it if Magdalen's name came up. "Did the ladies mention Magdalen? I know she and Sara quarreled."

Babette gave an emphatic shake of her head. "Nope. Everyone knew Mags had zero interest in jewelry, or money for that matter. All she ever cared about was that stupid manuscript and her family's literary legacy. She bored everyone silly braggin' all the time. Irene was her only real friend." Babette teared up. "Kinda sad actually."

My reaction was different. I heaved an enormous sigh of relief. Magdalen was no killer, but it was comforting to have it confirmed by those who lived with her. Once again Babette's ability to inveigle information from almost anyone had served us well. Perhaps the missing items had feathered someone's nest quite handsomely, someone who would kill to protect that secret. Pruett eased back into the room without saying a word.

"Anything to share?" I asked.

"Yeah, we're supposed to be a team." Babette folded her arms and scowled at him. Even Micah gave Pruett a wary look.

Faced with a united front, Wing Pruett bowed to the inevitable. "Okay. Okay. I gave Aleita a heads-up about the jewelry. She'll check out the police reports and the insurance angle. Bear in mind, though, that high-end merchandise can change hands through private sales without leaving any record."

After each of us got an assignment we agreed to reconvene the next evening at Carrick's homestead. I was eager to quiz Magdalen about some things and to update both Carrick and her on our findings. Meanwhile Pruett promised to check with his university pal on the manuscript, while Micah continued to comb real estate transactions in Virginia. Babette favored us all with a mysterious smile. She vowed to grill her society friends and the upscale jewelers in the area about recent acquisitions, especially those involving emeralds. That worried me because she might easily put herself in danger or risk alerting the thief. When Babette focused on a mission, zeal sometimes overrode good sense.

"Not to worry," she said. "Irene gave me this photo of Sara and lookee there." It was an exceptionally clear image of a diminutive woman sitting soldier straight with her hands folded in front of her. On her left hand she wore a stunning emerald ring.

"Wow!" Micah said. "That's really something."

Pruett praised Babette's ingenuity and I had to agree. The theft angle was certainly worth pursuing. If anyone had the informal contacts to scour the local market, it was Babette Croy. Her personal collection of gems, which grew by the year, could fund a small republic. Retailers leaped at the chance to assist such a client.

My guests left all at once, giving me time to tend to my pets and process everything that had happened. Beautiful Raza rubbed her velvety muzzle against me as if she knew the conundrum I faced. Zeke was less patient. The little goat headbutted me until I finally agreed to groom him. Then, having won yet another battle in our continuing war, he calmly munched his hay and bedded down for the night.

I spent a few hours in my workshop, finishing some sorely neglected projects, and clambered into bed before midnight. Instead of the deep, dreamless sleep I sought, my night was troubled with vivid images of broken bottles, tempting chocolates, and blood—so much blood.

* * * *

Pruett phoned promptly at nine the next morning. I was hunched over the dining table, groggy, mainlining espresso, and fending off Thatcher, who insisted on hogging my seat. No friendly greeting came from my lips, no sir. I growled a barely audible sound that startled him.

"Wow! Someone had a rough night," he said. "My message won't exactly lift your spirits, I'm afraid."

Keats and Poe hovered around me in doggy solidarity as I listened. *Not another death*, I prayed. *Please Lord.*

"Go on," I said. "What's wrong? Is Magdalen okay?"

"Nobody's dead. It's the manuscript, Perri. They've had a crew of Wilde experts analyze everything about it and the results aren't good."

What a disappointment. Apparently the experts concluded that *Sybil Vane* was an elegantly written novel in the style of Oscar Wilde, an homage but probably not an original written by the great man himself. Several scholars speculated that Sebastian Melmoth may have crossed paths with Wilde, even befriended him when they both lived in Paris. That might explain the poet's occasional use of Melmoth's name, as a sort of tribute to his friend. Nothing more.

"Magdalen has to be told," I said. "Tonight's as good a time as any, I suppose."

Pruett agreed and added another thought. "It still has possibilities, though. Several publishers are interested, and it should provide academic fodder for years to come. You know how they love to debate arcane issues. The Melmoth family might still get recognition."

Small consolation for a proud woman like Magdalen, who had lived in the shadow of the great man for so long. On the other hand, perhaps it would be liberating. Now she would be free to celebrate her real grandfather's talents without constantly questioning her origins. Easy enough for an orphan like me to say.

I texted Babette and Micah to confirm our departure time but didn't mention the manuscript. No excuses. It was a case of procrastination with a purpose. Babette tended to go off-track rather easily and it was far better to keep her focused on the jewelry quest rather than the manuscript. Micah and Pruett were thick as thieves, so he probably knew the score already. Guy stuff.

To clear my head and lighten my heart, I saddled up Raza and settled in for a soul-soothing gallop on the trails adjoining my house. As usual, Keats and Poe accompanied us. They formed a type of honor guard and were an effective deterrent to any predators—human or animal—who might stand in our way. Despite the beauty of the crisp fall day, my thoughts strayed to the drama surrounding my encounter with Magdalen Melmoth. Everything was drawing to a close and that was comforting even though it had yet to reach a satisfactory conclusion. Her dalliance with the ghost of Oscar Wilde had ended, but the unsolved murders at the Falls were a thundercloud that hovered over Magdalen and the rest of us. The outcome was painfully clear. Despite my best efforts, I had to concede that I had failed. It was high time to step aside and let the professionals handle the case. After all, why kid myself? Babette and I weren't Holmes and Watson. Not by a long shot. I told myself that it was a thirst for justice that drove us and not ego. Three people—productive members of society—had lost their lives. I was realistic enough to know that sooner or later inertia would take over and the murders of Carole Ross, Jethro Tully, and Sara Whitman would be relegated to that cold case pile in the sky—unsolved and dismissed.

Another thought riled me. Somewhere quite near to me a ruthless killer prowled about laughing at our amateur efforts. I really hated that.

Our ride concluded with the comforting ritual of untacking, cool down, and grooming. Raza loved the attention, even though Zeke disrupted everything by braying and generally acting up. Raza nuzzled me as I rubbed her coat, curried, and combed her. I marveled at how delicately she sipped her water, just like the princess she was. Some philistines told me that my pet duties were too onerous. Get out and enjoy life, they said. Poor fools. In my view a life bereft of animals was an impoverished one. My pet family provided more love, loyalty, and support than most of the humans I'd ever encountered. Even irascible Zeke had some endearing ways when he wasn't headbutting me or shrieking.

Before Pruett and the gang arrived I did some grooming of my own. Nothing spectacular, just a soothing, sudsy bath followed by a brief nap and a change of clothes. Despite such efforts, my anxiety level continued to climb. Would Magdalen be devastated by our news or take it in stride? She was one tough cookie who was hard to read despite her apparent openness. Then I recalled something that Babette had said. If Magdalen's obsession with Oscar Wilde was commonly known at the Falls, why would the killer strike out at her now? Perhaps Nurse Carole Ross had been the target all along. Her habit of gorging on sweets was probably as well-known as Magdalen's aversion to candy. Gossip, most of it quite harmless, was common currency in residential facilities. Hadn't Irene said as much? I knew with all my heart that Magdalen had no part in the murders. Motive was the sticking point. Unless she was unhinged—and I refused to believe that—Magdalen Melmoth had no reason to eliminate Carole Ross, Dr. Tully, or Sara Whitman. It made no sense at all.

I had no time to ponder my theories before Babette, Micah, and Pruett arrived promptly at six o'clock, ready for action. We packed four adults and four dogs into my old Suburban and headed toward an uncertain outcome. As usual, it was Babette who started the conversational ball rolling.

"What's the latest on that book?" she asked. "I'll bet Mags is beside herself by now."

Pruett cleared his throat and explained the *Sybil Vane* situation. "We just found out today. Tonight we'll have to tell Magdalen the bad news and I'm not sure how she'll react. After all, she's lived with this delusion for years."

Micah grimaced, but Babette scoffed. "Don't fool yourselves. Old Mags is sound as a bell. I'll bet she already has some inkling of this. Besides, you can still write a heck of a story about the whole mess. Give her braggin' rights at the old folks home."

Pruett paused, considering his options. "Babette, you're a genius! I can frame it as a human interest piece centered on Magdalen's family quest. Should make great copy."

Because I was the driver I was too distracted dodging homicidal motorists and roadwork to join in the happy talk. When I did my words stopped the discussion cold. "Hold on. Haven't we forgotten something here? A little thing like the murders. How do they fit in to this human interest piece?"

Pruett hesitated. "Look, Perri. Realistically we may never have that answer. Time to back off and leave the murders to the professionals."

Self-restraint was indeed my superpower. I bit back the tart response that hovered right on the tip of my tongue, the little reminder of just how inept that crackerjack Sheriff Aleita was. Only a jealous woman would mention that, and I rose above petty insults. Mostly.

Micah poured oil on troubled water by pointing out the progress we had already made. "I did my due diligence," he said. "Found some very intriguing information about real estate transactions."

Predictably Babette refused to be outdone. "You're not the only one," she crowed. "Wait 'til you hear my scoop about the jewelry. I outdid myself this time."

Lights appeared as we drew nearer to Carrick's compound. By consensus we agreed to defer any further discussion until we were able to share our news with everyone. I had no idea what the evening would bring.

Chapter 27

A welcome party awaited our arrival. Carrick, Magdalen, and Paddy peered anxiously out the front door as our caravan alighted from my truck and approached the kennel. Keats, Poe, and Clara stayed at our side in a perfect heel, but Prospero scampered ahead to greet his sire. Babette found it difficult—nay, impossible—to discipline the pup and instead smiled indulgently like the proud pet parent she was as he romped free.

"Isn't he adorable?" she trilled. In truth, Prospero was a hot mess.

Pruett muttered as if he had another less positive description for the rambunctious pup. Fortunately the greetings by our hosts drowned out his comment. Carrick's face was wreathed in smiles I had not seen before. Perhaps despite the tragedies, the influence of his long-lost sister had brightened his life. Magdalen's expression was more difficult to read. She looked curiously unchanged in her neatly pressed shirtwaist and canvas flats, quite the same as the first time I met her. Her composure was such that I wondered if she already knew the fate of *Sybil Vane.*

"Come in, come in," Carrick said as he enveloped Babette in a hug. "Glad to see young Prospero lookin' so fine. The other pups are all gone now, so the nest is empty."

Flames from the fieldstone fireplace warmed the main room and the beautifully carved mahogany sideboard featured an array of comestibles.

"Help yourself," Carrick said. "Mags outdid herself tonight. Hard for an old bachelor to compete with."

Pruett and Micah eyed the crystal decanters of whiskey and sidled up to the Jameson. Carrick grinned and poured each of them a dram in glasses that to my untutored eyes looked like Waterford.

"Nice touch," Babette said, nodding her head.

Magdalen flushed with pleasure. "They were my mother's. Came over from Ireland with us and stayed in remarkable condition. I used her recipe for the chicken pot pie as well."

We filled our plates and sprawled in the comfortable leather club chairs that ringed the room. After some preliminary chitchat, discussion turned to the business at hand.

"We have news on several fronts," Pruett said. "But first, how are you doing, Magdalen?"

She sat on the edge of the chair with her spine upright and her shoulders soldier straight, a carryover from the Victorian strictures against poor posture. "Much better in these surroundings, cosseted by people and pets I love. Dear Micah has kept me out of jail, and Carrick fusses over me like I am an invalid." Mags glanced fondly at her brother. "So, thank you for asking, Mr. Pruett, but I am fine. Quite able to hear your news."

I noticed that Carrick had abandoned the role of genial host and now gripped the arms of his chair like a condemned man awaiting the death sentence.

Pruett played his part admirably. His dispassionate, matter-of-fact delivery recalled Jack Webb on the old *Dragnet* show. "Just the facts, ma'am."

"It's a fake. Is that what you're sayin'," Carrick stammered. "I just can't believe it. Our mam was so certain."

"Not necessarily. You know those academic types," Pruett said. "They never agree on anything. Like dogs scrapping over a bone."

Magdalen's expression remained unchanged, as if she were an alabaster figure sculpted from stone. When she responded her speech was measured and calm.

"I understand, Mr. Pruett. Thank you for all your efforts. I suppose our killer wasn't interested in my manuscript after all. I fear I've wasted your time. *Sybil Vane* is not a fake, however. It is a genuine Melmoth and I am proud of that."

"Don't be discouraged," Micah said. "Publishers are interested in *Sybil Vane*. Quite a number of them. Some are university presses, but one or two are larger commercial ventures." He leaned over and squeezed her hand. "I can represent you or refer you to a reputable literary agent if you prefer. Naturally you'll want to think about it first."

This time Magdalen reacted swiftly, and her wintry smile said it all. "At my age, Micah, time is a luxury I can't afford. Let's go full steam ahead. If it's not the work of Oscar Wilde, at least my father's name will gain some recognition." Her voice quivered. "He was a good man, a talented man. He deserves that."

Carrick broke the tension by quickly proposing a toast to her long-lost relative. After we hoisted a glass and gave a hearty cheer, the subject turned to real estate and lost gems. Naturally Babette went first. She explained her mission in more detail than was necessary but finally cut to the chase.

"I spent two whole days visitin' high-end jewelry stores," she said. "Lawd, it was exhaustin'. Luckily most of those owners know me, so that loosened their tongues." I ignored the smug smile on my BFF's face. No doubt she had probably sweetened the pot by making a few strategic purchases at each establishment. The Croy formula for ensuring retail loyalty seldom failed.

Magdalen frowned as she listened to Babette. "Really? Jewelry thefts? Naturally I heard some of those ladies grumbling about lost articles, but I never took them seriously. Complaining was just a way of life at the Falls. Almost a competition at times. Besides, gems never interested me much. They always seemed so trivial."

My thoughts turned to Sara Whitman and her missing ring. Magdalen dismissed jewelry as trivial, but to many the rings, bracelets, and earrings from the past were important artifacts, part of their family heritage, as meaningful as *Sybil Vane* was to the Melmoth clan. From everything I'd learned, Sara Whitman avoided sloppy sentiment. Like Magdalen, she'd been one tough customer given to action, not idle talk. Her threat to contact the police proved that. Had it gotten her killed?

Babette continued. "My cover story was simple. Genius really." After preening a bit she finally resumed her narrative. "I showed them a blowup of Sara's emerald and said I wanted one just like it. Pronto."

Once again I saluted Babette's expertise. No way could I ever have gotten away with a story like that. But then again, like Magdalen I had zero interest in high-end gems and no track record as a purchaser.

Micah hunched over and put his hands on his knees. "Okay. What happened?"

"Just when I thought I'd failed, one of my sources saved the day. It seemed a consignment of custom pieces came in. Estate items, or so the seller said. He showed me photos of the goods on offer and the emerald ring was smack dab in the middle of the pack."

Carrick gasped and I felt every muscle in my body tense up. Had we actually done it—unmasked the murderer? Pruett sat absolutely still with his arms folded as if he had heard this tale before. I couldn't understand his reaction or lack thereof. Didn't we all share the same goal?

Micah spoke first with an urgency I had seldom heard from him before. "Who was it? Did he have a description of the seller? Come on, Babette, you're killing us here."

She hung her head, avoiding our eyes. "You see, there's a problem. My guy never actually met the seller. Someone sent him an email with shots of the items. When he said he needed to examine them and see the provenance, the seller got antsy and never kept the appointment. He tried emailing, but the account was closed."

"Any idea how much that haul would have fetched at auction?" Carrick was no expert in jewelry, but he understood cold hard cash.

Apparently the expert had given a very rough estimate in excess of two hundred thousand dollars if everything checked out.

Babette bit her lip, and I knew she was close to tears at that point. Pruett rode to the rescue once again. "Good job," he said. "Maybe we can trace the other items on that list to see if they correspond to those lost at the Falls. Micah can use his insurance contacts too. I know someone who can probably trace the IP address." He winked and said, "Nothing stays secret anymore."

I was proud of him for throwing her a lifeline. Despite her outlandish ways, Babette was very sensitive. Her feelings were easily crushed and as her best friend I should have done something to comfort her. Too bad I couldn't think of even one comforting thing to do.

Carrick reached down and stroked Paddy. "I got to admit I'm stumped. What does missing jewelry have to do with these murders? Mags wasn't involved. Like most fellows my age, I don't know diamonds from paste. Now if Joanie were here, she'd know. That girl always loved sparkly things."

Pruett and I exchanged glances. "Suppose Nurse Ross got wind of the thefts and confronted the thief," I asked. "Things could easily have gotten out of hand. You said she loved to snoop, didn't you, Magdalen?"

She nodded. "Truthfully she thought she was our protector, but Carole's approach was ham-fisted. A good soul, but subtlety wasn't her strong suit."

I pictured Nurse Ross blundering headlong into a confrontation with the thief. Good intentions aside, that strategy was very risky. After all, Sara Whitman went public with her threats and she died. Apparently Carole Ross had been undeterred by the scent of danger or the lure of chocolate.

"Got your laptop handy, Carrick?" Babette asked. He pointed to a handsome mahogany writing table complete with computer and printer.

"Mags has the computer skills in the family," he said. "She's been organizing my kennel info all week. I'm what Jonathan Swift would call a Lilliputian when it comes to technology."

Magdalen rolled her eyes. "Another great Irishman from another age. Send me your list, Babette, and I'll print it out." While they organized that, Carrick played host again. I was the designated driver, so I refused a refill, but the gentlemen were quick to accept his offer. "Nothing like fine Irish whiskey and beautiful women." Pruett glanced my way as he said that. I'm realistic about my appearance, but a compliment still lifted my spirits.

After some urging Micah shared his real estate finds. "I'm not convinced that stolen trinkets are the answer," he said. "Gold and silver hold value, but property is fungible and much more reliable." His eyes glowed. "A real wealth generator. Lots of transactions in your area, Carrick. But you already know that."

The older man nodded.

Micah reached into his briefcase and unfurled a spreadsheet. "Take a look at these parcels."

Pruett, Carrick, and I hunched over the table studying the figures. The addresses meant nothing to me, but one name stood out in most of the acquisitions: Venice Enterprises.

"Who or what in the world is that?" Pruett asked.

"Still digging," Micah said. "It's a shell corporation registered in the Cayman Islands. May be all legal and proper, but someone took some trouble to complicate matters. Once we find the corporate officers things will become clearer."

I recognized names of several of the property owners and they led right back to the Falls. Was the evil genius behind Venice Enterprises also affiliated with the Falls? Naturally one name sprang to mind: Rolf Hart. I told myself to power down until more facts emerged. After all, just because a man was arrogant and obnoxious didn't mean he was also homicidal. Or did it?

When Magdalen rejoined us, she posed the pivotal question: Where do we go from here? Under the circumstances her poise astounded me. After all, as far as the authorities were concerned, Magdalen was still their chief suspect. They didn't consider her a flight risk, but no other suspect was on the horizon. Sheriff Aleita was still pursuing leads but appeared no closer to resolving the murders. According to Micah, the lack of progress and the interest fueled by the media frustrated the sheriff and made her wary. Police harassment of an octogenarian woman, even one as feisty as Magdalen Melmoth, didn't play well in rural Virginia, so Aleita was proceeding with caution.

Pruett seemed amused by the dilemma. He stood before Magdalen, hands on hips, and said. "You know the players better than we do, Magdalen. What's your suggestion? Should we leave it alone or try something else?"

Magdalen didn't miss a trick. "Ah, Mr. Wing Pruett, you're thinking of your investigative piece, aren't you? What good is a mystery without finding the culprit?" Her eyes challenged him to deny it, but he stayed silent. Tension rose in the room as each of us did too. Our dogs went on alert, their eyes searching faces for behavioral clues. Even Paddy abandoned his normal sprawl and acted more alert. For my part I was willing to forgo the detective work and return to the simple life of a leathersmith. Grand Marsh was looking awfully good at this point and I had plenty of clients to attend to. The quest for Oscar Wilde's legacy was over, so I had done my part.

Unfortunately Babette had not gotten the message. "Here's what I'd do," she said. "Start from the beginning."

My response was simple but inelegant. "Huh?"

She waved me off. "Not the book stuff. That's over. Sorry, Magdalen."

"Not to worry, my dear. I'm in good hands with Micah." Magdalen furrowed her brow. "I was thinking, Isn't tomorrow your regular time for Therapy Dogs?"

We nodded.

"Well then, I suggest you report as planned. Perhaps Mr. Pruett can spare some time as well." She gave him a coquettish look. "Those ladies seem to open up to you. Now that they know you're all officially on the case, I believe they'll share some theories about the crimes with you. One never knows if something of value will emerge."

Babette immediately agreed to vet the list of jewelry against those reported lost at the Falls. She assured us that custom pieces were far easier to identify than the mass market offerings in most shops. "Men really knew how to spoil their wives in those days," she sniffed. "Not like the junk you see today." She unleashed a diatribe against malls and the chain stores they perpetuated, which ended only when Pruett held his arm outstretched and bowed his head. "We get it," he said. "I feel suitably chastened and promise never to set foot in one of those stores again."

My task was more subtle but equally challenging. I agreed to chat up Sara Whitman's friends and anyone with information about the day Dr. Tully died. Recollections varied and I had found that people often recalled things later that had seemed unimportant at the time.

I could tell Carrick was uncomfortable with the plan. Probably a case of divided loyalties. After all, his niece might well be impacted by anything we did, particularly if she was involved in the skullduggery. Come to think of it, Dr. Joan Fergueson might well be the architect of the crimes. She had the brains to plan and execute the thefts, access to the entire facility, and information about each resident. For Carrick's sake I hoped she wasn't involved.

After he reluctantly agreed not to alert Joan, we left on our homeward trek. The strategy was sound and our spirits were buoyed by a surge of optimism. I kept my fingers crossed. Luck would play a part in the undertaking, and sadly that lady might not be on our side.

Chapter 28

The weather gods cooperated nicely the next morning. Sunlight bathed the Falls in a brilliant golden glow that accentuated every carefully tended shrub. The idyllic scene contrasted vividly with our somber task, although our dogs and the residents seemed not to notice. Babette and I arrived first. I had dosed myself with a supersize mug of green tea, but I could see by the overcaffeinated gleam in her eyes that my friend had gone the espresso route.

"As soon as we do the meet and greets, I'll make tracks for Irene's place." Babette tossed her blond curls. "Irene rounded up some of her pals for a little coffee klatch. Nothing formal. Just girl talk."

She assured me that the invited guests had all lost or misplaced valuable items and were keen to retrieve them. "Leave it to me." Babette chuckled. "I'll wring every ounce of information out of them before I leave. You know how cagey I can be."

Silence was platinum in these instances, so I merely bowed my head and smiled. There was no reining in Babette when she got the bit between her teeth. I'd learned it was far wiser to cross my fingers and trust her.

I signaled to Keats and Poe and joined the throng surrounding Kate and Gomer. Today was sing-along day, and many residents arrived early to claim choice seats. Oddly enough Rolf was nowhere to be seen.

"Where's your partner?" I asked Kate.

I noticed she was leaning heavily on her cane today, trying to manage Gomer, her guitar, and other gear without falling. "Need some help?" I asked. "Gomer can be a handful sometimes."

"Sure. I'm not proud." She grinned as her goofy pup wrapped himself around my legs. "He must think you're a maypole. Rolf's around here somewhere. I think he went into Dr. Fergueson's office."

I arranged a row of chairs in front of the audience and helped Kate and Gomer to the center. Meanwhile Keats and Poe joined me in greeting the residents as they entered the room. By now I knew which ladies were timid around dogs and which ones eagerly embraced them. One tiny woman garbed in shades of gray reminded me of a wren. She asked for permission, then bent over and gave my boys each a big hug. "I'm Therese," she said haltingly. "Therese Ellis. May I speak with you after the program? I don't want to sound foolish and it's probably nothing, but I have no one else to tell. It's about Dr. Tully."

I checked the area to ensure that no one else was present and agreed to meet Therese on the veranda after the program ended. My spycraft was a tad rusty, but I still recalled the basics of covert operations. Rule number one: keep details to yourself if you want to avoid trouble.

Therese hemmed and hawed for a moment before leaving. "I don't suppose you could bring Mr. Pruett with you? Men have such sound judgment about these things."

Once again my superpower came to the fore. I reminded myself that Therese was from a generation that revered the patriarchy and assumed that only males could protect them. Apparently she'd forgotten the grisly fate that had befallen Dr. Tully, a man who failed to safeguard even his own life. I managed a sickly smile and promised to include Pruett in our meeting. With that she slipped away once more, cloaked in anonymity and drab attire.

Promptly at ten a.m. the doors to the office complex swung open and Joan Fergueson, accompanied by Rolf and Portia, emerged. Call me crazy, but I thought I detected an extra bloom in Joan's cheeks. Even Rolf looked almost pleasant if you counted a snarky grin instead of his trademark sneer. Kate and I exchanged glances but said nothing. Babette and Clara took their place as somewhere in the back of the room another guest arrived. A genteel murmur swept through the audience as Wing Pruett found a seat between two beaming dowagers.

"Her finger," Babette said in a stage whisper. "Check out old starchy drawers' right hand." As Joan grasped the microphone I did just that, noting an eye-popping diamond of at least three carets that sparkled seductively in the sunlight. Small wonder she herself looked especially bright. Carrick said only last night that she had always liked a bit of glitz. I had little time to ponder the obvious: Joan Fergueson and Rolf were an item. Did their partnership extend to other areas of life as well?

I approached Rolf as he lined up with Portia. "Congratulations," I said. "I hope you'll both be very happy. Will Joan be joining your real estate ventures now?"

True to form he stared coldly at me and said nothing. It was awkward and unpleasant but not unexpected. Rudeness didn't bother me. I'd faced far worse and survived intact. After a brief standoff, Rolf gave a terse and frosty response. "Frankly our personal plans are none of your business. If you're still interested in discussing property, call my office. Heel, Portia." He summoned his borzoi with a brisk command and moved next to Kate.

We went through the preliminary introductions as our dogs, the true stars of the show, performed their routine. Afterward, before refreshments were served, those residents who wanted to pet, hug, or otherwise interact with our guys were free to do so. Initially the size and dignity of Keats and Poe had made some residents wary, but soon even the more timid souls realized how genial and loving my boys were and joined their many admirers.

When tea and scones were wheeled into the sunroom I seized my chance to confront Joan. Pruett was surrounded by a claque of women, so I had no doubt he was up to his task. Babette had disappeared and I assumed she had joined Irene to further their plot.

"Congratulations," I said in what I hoped was a cheery, nonthreatening tone. "Your ring is lovely."

For once Joan Fergueson's smile appeared to be genuine. She thanked me and held out her fingers to display the ring. Rolf was absent from the scene, so I pressed my advantage. "Carrick said just last night how much you liked jewelry. Does he know your good news?"

Her expression changed from pleasant to peevish as she frowned and stepped away from me. "I haven't discussed this with my uncle. He's mistaken, by the way. I have little interest in most jewelry. This is different of course." She excused herself and sped to the other side of the room, leaving me to wonder if the lady protested too much.

Kate signaled me to join her at her table. I filled a plate with goodies to share and pulled out a chair.

"Did you know about them?" I asked Kate. "Rolf and Joan, I mean. Seemed like her reaction was a bit over the top."

"Love is strange," she said wryly. "Rolf never seemed like the romantic type to me, not that I'm much of an expert in that field. Never been married myself." She eyed the ring again. "That's some statement, though. Must have set him back at least twenty thousand dollars."

That amount seemed staggering to me, but Kate was very matter-of-fact. I mentally calculated how many dog leashes it would take to earn even half that sum.

"Wow. I can't imagine wearing something that valuable, although I guess some of the ladies here wouldn't have any problem with it." Kate chuckled. "No indeed. These ladies are old-school. Furs and jewelry galore. They expected it in their day and their husbands supplied the goods. Custom made, not your average chain-store fare. Just take a look around if you don't believe me."

How right she was. Most ladies in the audience were bedecked and bedazzled with an assortment of earrings, pendants, and rings. Enough loot to tempt a thief and perhaps a murderer.

Kate's eyes twinkled as she said, "Your Mr. Pruett might just surprise you with one someday."

Although I had long passed the stage of maidenly blushes, her sudden reference to Pruett made the blood rush to my cheeks. I quickly changed the subject. "Apparently Sara Whitman had quite a sparkler. Emerald, I heard."

"Search me. By the time I met her that ring had disappeared and all hell had broken loose. Dr. Fergueson was apoplectic and Carole Ross was buzzing around like the queen bee looking for her hive. Even Jethro Tully got into the act. Rolf told me all about it. He and Sara were thick as thieves, you know."

Just as I put a dab of honey and butter on a croissant, Pruett pulled up a chair and joined us.

"Ah, Perri, I thought you didn't have a sweet tooth," Pruett teased. His own plate overflowed with goodies that he wolfed down without compunction. "Lots of temptation around this place. No wonder Nurse Ross couldn't resist that candy."

Kate bit her lip and cast her eyes downward. "What a tragedy. I wonder if they'll ever solve Carole's murder, let alone Dr. Tully's. It casts a pall on this place, hasn't it? I was tempted to change Therapy Dog slots for something less bleak, but I didn't want to leave you in the lurch now that Rolf's thrown in the towel."

Pruett jumped on that bit of news immediately. "Really? He doesn't seem like the squeamish type."

Kate explained about the upcoming nuptials, all the while eyeing Pruett's face. His reaction or lack thereof must have disappointed her. My guy was a sphinx when the occasion demanded it. A bell rang, signifying the start of the musical program, and Kate slowly hoisted herself up. Pruett immediately offered to carry her guitar and gear while I wrangled Gomer into a manageable trot. As we joined those gathered in the sunroom, I noticed Babette and Irene as they slipped into seats in the anteroom. Both wore particularly smug smiles that suggested their quest had gone well.

Kate's performance was always a crowd pleaser. Today's requests included several selections from the folk song era, as well as traditional tunes from long ago. I found myself tearing up when she played, "Leaving on a Jet Plane." It had been one of Pip's favorites and I treasured every line. When the program concluded Babette, Pruett, and I agreed to reconvene at my house after our discussion with Therese. Babette could barely contain herself but finally agreed to wait in the Suburban with Clara and Prospero.

At first I thought Therese wasn't there. My eyes scanned the veranda searching for her and fearing the worst. Pruett spotted the tiny figure as she scurried from the shadows and approached us.

"Thank you for coming." Her voice was barely audible and she couldn't meet our eyes. "I don't want to be a nuisance."

Pruett immediately launched a charm offensive. "Nonsense, dear lady. It's very brave of you to come forward." He motioned to a nearby bench and guided Therese toward a seat.

After some dithering the lady came to the point. On the day of Dr. Tully's murder, Therese had a dizzy spell. "Nothing major," she said, "but worrisome nevertheless." She went to his office without an appointment hoping for a quick word. "Dr. Fergueson would have had a fit if she knew, so I kind of crept around the corner. She's a stickler for rules, you know, but Dr. Tully was always so very kind." Therese dabbed at her eyes with a linen handkerchief and seemed on the verge of a crying fit.

To forestall that Pruett quickly interposed a question. "About what time was that?"

"Right after noon. Around twelve fifteen. I remember hoping that everyone would be at lunch. Nothing is private around here, you see, and I didn't want anyone making a fuss over me." Therese swallowed before continuing. "His office door was only partially closed. That's how I heard the voices."

As I recalled, Kate had discovered Jethro Tully's body before one p.m. I forced myself to ask the one question I most feared. "Did you recognize who was speaking?" I steeled myself for the worst, terrified of what her answer would be. If Magdalen was the speaker, it was game over.

Therese continued her narrative. "That's just it. I could only hear fragments of the conversation, mostly Dr. Tully." She smiled. "He had such a resonant voice, you know, so like my dear father."

"Any idea who Tully was speaking to?" Pruett asked.

"I don't know." Therese hung her head again. "Just that it could have been a woman, or a younger man. Things got loud. Both of them raised their voices."

Patience may be a virtue, but I was fresh out of it. I ignored Pruett's frown and plowed ahead. "Did you recognize it? It wasn't Magdalen, was it?"

She frowned as if I had committed a social faux pas. "Oh no, my dear. This voice was younger. When Dr. Tully called whoever it was a thief, you wouldn't believe the foul language they both used. I'd never heard some of those things before. Horrible words. Magdalen would never be vulgar." Obviously the salty talk had scandalized poor Therese, who was used to more subtle ways of sabotaging an antagonist. Murder by innuendo and gossip was a practiced art at places like the Falls and frequently resulted in a more acceptable but still lethal death by a thousand cuts.

I thought of Nurse Edgar, a large man with a somewhat high voice. Under stress he could sound feminine. Rolf, my favorite suspect and villain, would certainly know a slew of curses to hurl at an adversary and I knew from experience that he was both unpleasant and aggressive. Only two women were in the running: Dr. Fergueson and Kate. Neither seemed the violent type, although I knew that looks were frequently deceiving. All four had access to residents and the opportunity to grab some of their valuables. If on the other hand someone was swindling the seniors out of their property, one suspect leaped to the top of the list. I knew my objectivity was in doubt. I really wanted Rolf to be the culprit and that clouded my judgment.

"Therese, give me your opinion. I can tell you've given this some thought." Pruett leaned over, as if they were confidants sharing secrets. "Were they talking real estate, jewelry, or something else?"

She furrowed her brow, trying mightily to please him but to no avail. "I'm sorry, Mr. Pruett, but I just don't know. Dr. Tully mentioned a betrayal of trust."

Pruett came to attention. "Could it have been a real estate trust he was talking about?"

Therese shook her head as if her desire to please was at war with the need for accuracy. "I'm sorry. Trust. That's just what he said, but I heard someone coming and got frightened. I didn't want them to find me eavesdropping."

Pruett tut-tutted and squeezed Therese's hand. "You've been very brave. The sheriff has to hear about this, you know. No need to be frightened. I'll drive you there right now myself."

Before she could object, he nudged her toward the door and into the parking lot, leaving me alone with plenty of questions.

Chapter 29

"Where is he?" Babette fumed. "We said we'd share our findings and I've been waitin'."

I calmed her down by suggesting that we call Micah and arrange a meeting at my place with or without Pruett. As expected, Micah's name worked like a magic potion. Babette's face was immediately wreathed in dimples and smiles.

"Great idea, Perri. We'll keep our lips buttoned until Micah shows up. I'm gettin' mighty fond of that boy even though he is a few years younger than me." She ignored the fact that he was actually a decade her junior and thrust her cell phone my way. In Croyland inconvenient facts were challenges, not problems. "Here. You call him. I don't want Micah to think I'm bein' pushy."

She had long since passed the pushy point, but in the interests of peace I wisely chose to ignore that fact. When I reached Micah he knew all about Pruett's trip to the sheriff and was already primed for action. Apparently his real estate quest had borne fruit he promised to share with us that evening. True to form, Babette insisted on going home to primp before our meeting. "Nothin' spells good groomin' like a manicure," she said as she inspected her hands. "You really ought to try it, Perri. If I hurry, I'll have time to change and drop by my nail spa before Micah shows up."

No use reminding her that for a leathersmith like me, a manicure was a waste of time and money. I kept my nails clean and neatly trimmed. That was the best I could hope for.

I had no time to ponder the events of the day. Once I arrived home Raza, Zeke, and an irascible Thatcher demanded my attention. While Keats and Poe roughhoused with Zeke, I checked my emails and attended to the neglected coon cat. Thatcher, like her namesake, was very much the iron lady who ruled the household with a velvet paw. Keats and Poe were respectful of her and even Zeke kept his distance. I merely tried to do her bidding.

To my surprise I received an email from Magdalen Melmoth thanking me for our efforts on her behalf and inviting me to lunch with her and Irene at the Red Fox Tavern in Middleburg the next day. Ironically although Babette was included in the party, Pruett and Micah were not. The wording was courteous but distant. I got the distinct impression it was a dismissal of sorts, although it might reflect the formal style of another age. Perhaps Magdalen blamed me for the failure of the *Sybil Vane* venture. That was hardly fair, but then again, life didn't always play by my rule book. Truth be told I had grown fond of Magdalen and felt wounded by a perceived snub. I told myself to grow up and sought consolation by saddling beautiful Raza and spending an invigorating hour cantering through the byways of Grand Marsh. Time spent with her was more therapeutic for me than an hour's soaking my hands at a nail salon. By the time I had cooled the mare down and curried and combed her soft coat, my fit of pique was completely forgotten. I had just enough time to groom myself and attend to customer invoices before the arrival of my guests.

* * * *

Babette arrived first, armed with several bottles of Chablis and an array of Chinese dishes from the local Szechuan restaurant. I applauded her generosity especially because my cupboard was almost bare and I hadn't planned to serve dinner. Babette, on the other hand, pointedly reminded me that the way to a man's heart was through his stomach. It was a route she was very familiar with.

While she bustled about arranging dishes and folding napkins, I shared Magdalen's invitation with her. Unlike me, Babette shrugged off any insult.

"Give it a rest, Perri. Magdalen's an old lady and that's the way they roll. I'm surprised she used email, though. An engraved invitation would be more her style." She proceeded to rhapsodize about the Red Fox, a place with plenty of interesting history behind it. "You realize that JFK and Jackie frequented it, and even Liz Taylor and that political stiff she married hung around there." My pal rolled her eyes. "If walls could talk, huh?"

I had no interest in reliving old history or in having another tedious luncheon, but to placate Babette, I agreed to the meeting. Middleburg was one of my favorite places, an ultrawealthy but distinctly horsey enclave where even the debutantes wore jodhpurs and boots about town. A number of local stores carried my products so I could combine a spot of business with our social engagement.

Just then Zeke issued another one of his hideous shrieks, alerting us to the arrival of Micah. The plucky lawyer was not alone; he was joined by the Sir Galahad of the printed page, Wing Pruett. Both men immediately headed for the sideboard and poured themselves and us goblets of Chablis.

"What a day!" Micah said. "Small wonder I avoided real estate law. Tedious beyond belief."

Babette sidled up to him wearing her most winsome smile. "Sit right down and tell us all about it, Micah. We're all ears."

Pruett raised his eyebrows but wisely said nothing. He braced himself against an onslaught by Prospero, who apparently found my guy quite irresistible. The pup was already nearing thirty pounds and growing by leaps and bounds. Despite Babette's half-hearted efforts to thwart him, he launched himself at Pruett with the force of a Scud missile.

"Isn't he just the cutest thing?" his fond mama asked. "Prospero I mean, although you're mighty cute yourself, Wing."

I hated to be a spoilsport, but time was ticking away. "They're both adorable. Okay? Now let's hear what each of us has to report. Ready, Micah?"

He gave a brisk nod and quickly summarized his efforts to unmask Venetian Enterprise company. "It took a while, let me tell you. Somebody knew what he was doing and intended to obscure ownership."

Babette shot him a look of pure adoration. "Bet that didn't fool you, did it?"

Modesty aside, Micah cut to the chase with amazing speed. "There are three corporate officers of Venetian: none other than Rolf Hart, Joan Fergueson, and the late Sara Whitman. From what I could tell, everything is in order. No funny business except for one anomaly."

We all leaned forward.

"Most of their acquisitions involved large parcels in rural Virginia, and from what I could gather the majority of sellers were affiliated with the Falls."

Now I realized the connection that had percolated in the back of my brain ever since we first heard of the company. Rolf Hart loved Shakespeare, particularly *The Merchant of Venice*. It recalled his college triumph in the title role of Shylock. Even his beautiful borzoi Portia was named for one of the main characters. No telling what role fiancée Joan Fergueson played in the drama.

Micah finished his part of the evening's entertainment with this tidbit: The corporation had a "key person" policy that provided that in the event of any principal's death, all proceeds were disbursed to the remaining two. "That's pretty standard. Ensures continuity." Micah paused. "And before you ask, the sellers got fair market value for their land with this exception. Unbeknownst to them, a major shopping and housing complex is slated to move into the area. Lots of acreage for over-fifty residential communities and more facilities like the Falls." His lawyerly instincts suddenly asserted themselves. "Nothing's certain, of course, and plans can change. If they don't, the investors in Venetian stand to make a bundle."

Babette puffed up like a cobra. "Is that legal? Cheatin' old folks out of money? Doesn't seem right."

Micah explained that unless someone could prove undue influence, the transactions appeared to be perfectly legal. "Caveat emptor, as they say."

"Not necessarily ethical, though," Pruett added, "especially if Joan Fergueson misused information she acquired through her position. That may have been what upset Nurse Ross and Dr. Tully."

We digested that information while ingesting the food Babette had brought. Righteous anger gave each of us a healthy appetite and before long every grain of rice and morsel of shrimp had disappeared. I didn't dare read the legend in my fortune cookie considering the dire thoughts I harbored.

Next Babette took center stage. She couldn't wait to share the information she and Irene had learned from schmoozing with their pals. "It was phenomenal, I swear. Just like an episode of *Murder, She Wrote*." She hesitated as the image of the title character sank in. "Naturally I'm a much younger version of Jessica," she said. "Maybe like her daughter or niece."

I didn't dare laugh. That would be unkind, and more to the point, it would delay us even more.

Despite the drama, Babette and Irene had apparently delivered the goods. Babette reached into her handbag and produced a neatly typed list of the missing items with a name alongside each.

"We struck gold," she announced. "Or in some cases, platinum. Everything offered to that jeweler belonged to one of those ladies. They couldn't believe it." She pointed at Pruett. "They expect the loot to be returned posthaste. That sheriff friend of yours can probably see to that."

I recalled again what Carrick said about sparkly things and Joan's love for them. There was enough sparkle in that collection to light up an entire room. Unfortunately although their audience racked their collective brains, no one had been able to pinpoint exactly when their treasures went missing or who was in the vicinity when they did.

My contribution seemed meager in comparison with the nuggets unearthed by my friends. I mentioned the engagement ring and the eye-popping price Kate had speculated about. Babette immediately cut in. "Big deal. That ring was nice enough, but I would have expected more from a moneybags like Rolf Hart. When it comes to diamonds you really can't go wrong, and size does matter."

The testimony of Therese Ellis made everyone sit up straight. After all, she was an actual earwitness to Dr. Tully's final minutes. Micah zeroed in on the timetable. "If she can be believed, Tully may have been murdered earlier than we thought. Magdalen got his call at twelve thirty and found him a little before one. That was verified by Kate's account as well."

"Too bad she couldn't tell whose voice that was." Babette curled her lip. "Friend or not, I say Nurse Edgar fits the part."

We reminded her that Edgar hadn't been present during Sara Whitman's tenure or prior to Carole Ross's death. She dismissed that stumbling block with a wave of her hand. "He could have been in cahoots with someone there. You know, the outside man. Mark my words, that guy has something to hide." She preened. "You know how keen my instincts are on these matters."

Pruett then added his two cents. According to the ladies he spoke with, Rolf Hart had zeroed in on anyone with property, particularly those without a vigilant family around them. Several residents complained to Nurse Ross about what they termed harassment. That caused Rolf to revise his strategy and include Sara Whitman in his recruitment efforts. She was well-liked, informed, and very persuasive. "Several of the ladies changed their minds after speaking with Sara," Pruett said. "She invested her own money, so they felt much more comfortable getting involved."

Micah was impatient. He crossed his arms and rocked back and forth in his chair. "Bottom line, did any of them back out of a deal before signing? Any coercion involved if they did?"

"Nope. That's the strange thing. Some of them got nervous, especially if their lawyers advised against selling. No harm no foul. One lady owned a prime package in Georgetown not far from my place. She told Sara right up front that she wouldn't sell."

Babette spoke. "Peer pressure. You want to fit in at a place like that and Sara Whitman was what they call a social influencer. I'll bet a lot of those ladies caved and you can be sure that Joan Fergueson was right in the mix."

Micah reminded us that sales pressure in itself was neither illegal nor a likely motive for murder. "Personally I'd focus on the jewelry theft. Much easier to pinpoint and quite unambiguous when you're talking crime."

I was curious about Sheriff Aleita's reaction to Therese and why Pruett hadn't mentioned it. Information sharing was often a one-way street with him unless someone demanded an answer. So I did.

He tried some evasive tactics until Babette marched over to his chair, folded her arms, and faced him squarely. "Out with it," she said. "What are you hidin', Wing Pruett?"

According to Pruett, Therese had fared quite well at the sheriff's office. Aleita listened respectfully to her, took notes, and had her sign a statement. Afterward the sheriff told him that although Magdalen was still the prime suspect, no substantive evidence had been uncovered. Now in light of Therese's information the timetable would have to be reevaluated.

As my friends debated the merits of both crimes, I also focused on that timetable for Dr. Tully's murder. Therese was adamant about her movements, and I believed her. She was timid and so wary of bending the rules that she would have closely watched the clock. Jethro Tully was alive at half past noon and dead thirty minutes later. A standing joke at the Falls stated that residents seldom missed a meal because it might be their last one. Someone had slipped into that office knowing that the area would be deserted. That same person had quarreled with Tully and used his own water bottle or some other sharp object to slay him. A "weapon of opportunity" was the police term.

Our little group had strayed a long way from that initial quest to find Oscar Wilde and I for one was ready to call it a day. Micah and Pruett agreed, although Babette offered token resistance. In the end we compiled all our research into a Word document and made copies that Micah and Pruett agreed to share with the sheriff. Let the professionals take over. Our quest was finished.

Chapter 30

I never had that lunch in Middleburg. Business needs and life intervened, forcing me to bow out of the event. Babette went, however, and by her account a good time was had by all. It was cowardly of me, but frankly I was ready to put the Falls, Oscar Wilde, murder, and even Magdalen Melmoth in the rearview mirror and motor on. The Therapy Dog program was still a priority, although I asked for a different assignment. To my delight, Keats, Poe, and I were assigned to library duty in Southeast DC. The official program title was "Reading to Dogs," and because reading had always been one of my passions, the concept excited me. If we could encourage kids, many of whom had difficult family situations, to escape into new worlds and burnish their skills, I was all for it. Books had expanded frontiers for me when I was a youngster, and with including dogs, things just couldn't get better.

Before embarking upon my new assignment, I checked in with Kate to ask for tips on library issues and get her perspective on the children's needs. Her manner was cordial but surprisingly aloof. In the past Kate had always been warm and welcoming, but I surmised that she wanted to put the Falls and everything associated with it out of her mind. Apparently I was included in that mix.

Babette accompanied me to the library for my maiden voyage. Naturally she brought Clara along as her wingman, although she wisely excluded Prospero from our group. The pup's exuberance was endearing but more than any library could handle.

We received a rousing welcome from both the library staff and the children. They hugged our dogs and scrambled over to the kids' corner, books in hand. Their eager eyes and wide smiles soothed my nerves and made the entire process feel worthwhile. Experts contend that reading aloud to dogs allows children to burnish their skills and even improve test scores. Initially several kids were tentative but soon overcame their reluctance when Keats put his head in their laps and gazed soulfully at them. Clara curled her body around two little girls who giggled as they stroked the border collie's soft fur. By the end of the session, both Babette and I were sold on the concept and ready to sign on for more. As we said our goodbyes, I saw a familiar face in the background. Kate waved us over and motioned toward the side door.

"I couldn't resist," she said. "Do you have time for coffee?"

Babette immediately leaped in. "Of course. We need to play catch up with you."

We adjourned to a nearby Starbucks and claimed a table. Kate insisted on treating, explaining the reason with a shake of her head.

"This is my apology," she said. "I felt ashamed about brushing you off today. It was unforgivably rude of me. That whole experience at the Falls was so painful that I tried to forget everything about it."

Over double lattes we revisited the events there. Kate updated us on the romantic saga of Joan and Rolf, whose wedding was scheduled for the next week.

"Funny thing," Babette said. "I didn't get my invitation yet. Must be lost in the mail." Kate chuckled but wisely said nothing. I knew I was persona non grata with the happy couple and Babette was a close second. Joan had always been cool, but Rolf actively loathed both of us. Hardly ideal for a wedding invitation.

"Any news about the murders?" Kate asked as she cautiously sipped her drink. "I figure Mr. Pruett has an inside track even if there's nothing in the media."

"Sheriff Aleita was still plugging away last I heard. At least they've backed off Magdalen for the time being." Most of my information came secondhand through Babette's contact with Carrick and Irene. I tried not to act aggrieved, but Magdalen's snubs still stung. I had grown to care for her and had done my best to help her.

"We gave her all our findings," Babette said. "The sheriff, I mean. We figured the motive was either that stolen jewelry or the real estate scams. I 'bout tracked down the gems too." She winked. "I think you know who that puts in the bull's-eye."

Kate remained impassive. Based on her reaction or lack thereof, I knew she must be a masterful poker player. "Dr. Fergueson resigned from the

Falls or so I heard." She hesitated, as if there was more to that tale. "No reason given."

Babette gave her a hard stare. "Come on. Out with it. What else do you know?"

"Well...it seems the newlyweds plan to build quite a mansion. In Great Falls of all places. Big bucks in that place. Rolf was always careful with his money, so it must be love."

Babette shrugged. "Nothin' wrong with a man showing his love, and a big homestead is one sure way. Jewelry doesn't hurt either." She spoke from experience, having gained real estate and other valuables from adoring males.

I agreed in principle, unless, of course, murder fueled the funding. In my heart Rolf Hart was still the prime murder suspect, even though in my brain I acknowledged my own bias against him. He was such an unpleasant man that he had to be guilty of something, even if it was only bad manners.

"I'm surprised you gave up," Kate teased. "What would Agatha Christie say?"

Neither of us responded. As I recalled, Dame Agatha lived to a rich old age. My fervent hope was that by avoiding murderers both Babette and I would also do so.

We finished our drinks and said our goodbyes. Kate headed toward the Metro, the most expedient method of transportation during rush hour. Babette and I didn't have that option. DC traffic was a mess and the route to northern Virginia was even worse. Before we reached my Suburban a young woman rushed toward us waving her arms. I recognized her as a barista from the coffee house.

"Your phone," she said. "It fell under your chair."

I patted my jacket pocket, comforted by the reassuring lump it contained. Nope. My phone was still there. Babette kept her iPhone in the humongous Chanel satchel she slung over her shoulder and guarded that thing like the pricey treasure it was. "Not mine," she said, reaching for the phone. "Let me see. I bet Kate dropped it. No problem." She handed the server a handsome tip for her trouble. "Thanks. We'll return this to our friend. Might as well do it now; we'll be tied up in traffic no matter what."

I retrieved Kate's address from my directory and plugged in my portable GPS. Cleveland Park and Southeast DC were about three miles and many millions of dollars apart as the crow flies. It wasn't my first choice, but I felt honor bound to return Kate's property to her. After all, most of us, even retired librarians, couldn't function without our cell phones.

Babette chattered nonstop and played with Kate's phone as I bobbed and weaved through traffic. Despite appearances to the contrary, my zany pal was a wizard when it came to manipulating data and deciphering computer glitches. I suspected she was also adept at hacking.

"Wow," she said. "Kate has one heck of a phone. Topflight. Pricey too. 'Course she should have a better password on the thing. I guessed right away it was Gomer. Funny she didn't have that facial recognition stuff. Some people just don't move with the times, I guess."

"Stop it. You're invading her privacy. She won't like that."

Babette scoffed. "Oh pooh. You're such a wet blanket, Perri. After all, we saved this thing from who knows what. Kate won't mind if I just take a peek. Who knows, she might have a secret lover. Maybe Nurse Edgar or Carrick."

Kate hardly seemed the type to conduct clandestine love affairs, but then again, I was no expert on her personal life. I could barely manage my own. As we glided up Wisconsin Avenue and turned on to a side street, I gazed at the variety of architectural styles and savored the surprisingly suburban feel of this urban enclave. Queen Anne, Dutch Colonial, Craftsman, and my person favorite, Tudor, dotted the streets. Residents kept them perfectly maintained; civic pride and a vigilant historical society watched over the neighborhood. Everyone knew that President Grover Cleveland had once resided here, although that was long before the area had blossomed into one of DC's most coveted locations. I slowed down as we turned on Newark Street and approached Kate's address. I adored Queen Anne architecture, so I loved her home immediately. It wasn't the largest property on the block, but with the wraparound porch, hipped roof, and bay windows, the delicately wrought yellow house captured my heart. I sensed that a great deal of work had gone into maintaining such a perfect place. Kate kept the exterior perfectly manicured with just enough greenery to be inviting but not overwhelming.

As usual Babette had the first word. "Wow! This is really somethin'. Not that big but still. Nice. Must be worth a pile of money."

We spent several minutes drinking in the scenery and admiring the area before approaching Kate's front door. To avoid canine overload, we left our three dogs napping in the Suburban. I rang the doorbell while Babette continued scrolling through the photos on Kate's phone.

"Cut it out," I said. "She'll catch you snooping."

Babette chortled and in typical fashion ignored my protests. "These pictures are a scream. Only our dogs look good. 'Course Pruett came out fine too."

Just as Kate opened the door, Babette gasped and grabbed my arm in a vise. "Stop. Perri, stop."

"What's your problem?" I asked. "Behave yourself."

Kate looked surprised to see us but managed a pleasant greeting and a gracious invitation into her home. Gomer disregarded Kate's commands and flung himself at us with youthful enthusiasm. I explained our errand as Babette reluctantly relinquished the phone.

Kate frowned. "I didn't even realize it was lost. What a relief! You two are my saviors, facing that traffic to return it. Come on in. I'll give you a guided tour while you're here." She ushered us into the living room

Praising the beautiful woodwork, dentil moldings, and tasteful Queen Anne furnishings was easy. If Kate was house-proud it was perfectly understandable, and I was a fan. My own style was far more casual, but I appreciated elegance when I saw it. Babette, however, was relatively subdued, a most unusual thing for someone with exquisite taste and intense love of décor.

"Have a seat," Kate said. "Might as well wait out that pesky traffic." She reached into a drawer, found her purse, and studied her phone. Something was definitely amiss. I recognized it and so did Kate. Babette stared at that phone as if she were a cobra mesmerized by a snake charmer. A silent Babette was indeed an anomaly and it worried me.

"What's wrong?" Kate asked her. "Are you ill?"

Babette shook her head. "Musta been that latte. Maybe the milk was sour."

I stood and beckoned to my pal. "Come on. I'll take you home. You're such a drama queen."

Kate rose quickly and blocked my path. "Not so fast, Perri. I think our friend has something to share."

"I don't know what you mean." Babette put on a brave front, but she couldn't meet Kate's eyes.

Kate dangled her phone in front of us. "Someone's been playing with this. What's that saying—one picture is worth a thousand words?"

I remained clueless. "She didn't mean anything, Kate. Just scrolling through your photos."

Kate's face underwent a startling transformation from genial to grim. She folded her arms in front of her and glared. "Why don't we ask Babette what she saw?"

Babette bit her lip and got a sudden surge of courage. Defiance replaced fear as she confronted her hostess. "You take a nice picture, Kate, when you're all gussied up. That emerald ring suits you just fine. You didn't see that one, Perri. I tried to warn you. Our little librarian has a taste for fine jewelry. Other peoples'."

I uttered something totally forgettable like "Huh?" Demure Kate, the helpful songstress and animal lover, couldn't be guilty. She was a bibliophile for heaven's sake.

"Don't be naïve, Perri. Didn't the army teach you anything?" Kate's scorn was both palpable and sinister.

Surely she wasn't a murderer as well as a thief. Either way, Babette and I needed to make a speedy exit. I glanced toward the front door, calculating the distance from me. I was agile, but Kate was not. Hampered by age and her cane, she would be at a disadvantage. I had no worries about Babette. Her sense of self-preservation was second to none. She could scurry toward salvation with the best of them.

My confidence dimmed when Kate's cane suddenly morphed from a therapeutic device into a lethal weapon. A sword cane! She wielded the sharp steel with authority, flaunting the fourteen-inch blade.

"Sit down, Perri. Let me think." Kate swayed back and forth, brandishing that cane.

"You don't want to hurt us, Kate. We're friends." Hollow sentiments that sounded absurd, but it was the best I could muster at the moment.

Babette had no patience for niceties. "Is that what you used on Dr. Dreamy? Tully, I mean."

She wasn't being humorous, but Kate guffawed anyway. "Of course. What a joke! As if I'd use that stupid Pellegrino bottle. I set up the whole thing to focus them on Magdalen. That hick sheriff fell for it right away."

It seemed like a cliché, but I had a vain hope that the more she talked, the better our chances of survival were. Unfortunately we had no hero to dash in and save us. Babette and I were on our own.

"I suppose Tully found out about your thefts," I said. "Nurse Ross too. She was the real threat."

Kate scoffed. "Nurse Ross—what a cow. She planned to contact the police, if you can believe it. As if those rich ninnies even missed their jewelry. I knew Magdalen didn't eat chocolate, but Ross? That was child's play. She couldn't wait to stuff her fat face."

How could that bland expression mask such evil? Why hadn't I ever realized that? I liked Kate. Admired her. Considered her a friend. Obviously my powers of perception left much to be desired.

Kate reached into a small walnut writing desk. Against my will I had to admire the workmanship and delicacy of the piece. Cabriole legs and pad feet made the little desk a work of art. I gave myself a reality check.

How crazy was I to obsess about furniture in what might well be my final hour on earth?

During this exchange Babette stayed preternaturally calm. I steeled myself for hysterics, tears, or other displays that never happened. Instead she seemed genuinely curious about Kate and her murderous spree.

"You fixed that other woman too, didn't you? Sara Whitman."

Kate nodded. "Sweet, sweet Sara. She was a sharp one. A little too sharp for her own good. Loved that emerald ring, she did. I had no choice about her. She actually threatened me. Can you believe that?" Kate flexed her left hand and gazed fondly at the emerald ring she now wore. "It's a beauty, isn't it? I sold the other items but just couldn't part with this one."

A shrink would diagnose my problem as a whopping case of cognitive dissonance. My mind refused to reconcile this complacent killer with the guitar-strumming, animal-loving librarian I thought I knew. "Why, Kate? You're an accomplished woman with so many options."

The look she gave me wreaked of pity more than anger. Kate twirled about, pointing her weapon at her treasures in a gesture reminiscent of a museum docent. "You just don't get it, Perri. All my so-called accomplishments didn't mean anything at the bank. The upkeep on this house alone is shocking, not to mention the things in it. I saw an opportunity and I seized it. Money. Filthy lucre. Don't knock it."

I dared not look at Babette. Only one outcome seemed certain and it wasn't pretty. Kate intended to dispose of us as she had her other victims. I watched closely, hoping for an opportunity to spring at her. "Killing us here will mess up your pretty house. Bloodstains are impossible to remove."

She paused to consider her options. That was when a miracle occurred. Babette leaped from the chair, clutched her heart, and collapsed, writhing on the floor into a heap. I played my part by screaming, "Oh my Lord! Help her. She has a weak heart!"

It was pure theater, but no one told Gomer that. The first instinct of therapy dogs was to comfort the afflicted. He bounded across the room at warp speed, pounced on Babette, and immediately applied his own brand of medicine: doggy kisses.

Kate lost focus, giving me enough time to spring at her and wrest the sword cane from her grasp. Deprived of her weapon, she imploded. When the police arrived they found a meek, cultured woman without a trace of malice. Just the type you'd want as a friend.

Chapter 31

My second phone call was to Pruett. He would never have forgiven me if a rival had gotten the big scoop and, in all fairness, he had been part of this story from its inception. His rendition of our exploits was masterful and before long the nation was enthralled by the tale of a literary quest, murder, and salvation by therapy dog. It earned him yet another Pulitzer Prize. Gomer, the hero of the day, basked in the glow of an adoring public and became the darling of the dog world. His goofy grin now appeared on posters and websites promoting therapy dog work.

Good fortune smiled on Magdalen Melmoth too. *Sybil Vane*, her father's opus, became an international best seller and was optioned by a movie producer. I was thrilled for her, even though we never again renewed our friendship. I had served my purpose and Magdalen chose to focus on other things. C'est la vie, as they say.

Naturally Babette took bows all around. She was lauded for her bravery under fire and credited with unmasking a triple murderer. I could hardly protest because this time her claims were true. It was rude and possibly illegal for her to access Kate's phone, but without that bit of nosiness we would never have solved the murders.

I was content to return to normal life, or what passed for it in Great Marsh. My business, pets, and friends meant far more to me than celebrity or fulsome praise. Besides, a spot of boredom was a welcome tonic. Of late adventure had sought me out unasked. Who knew what the future would bring?

If you enjoyed *Murder at the Falls*, be sure not to miss Arlene Kay's first Creature Comforts mystery

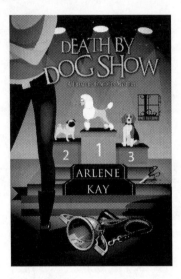

Army vet Persephone "Perri" Morgan has big plans, as her custom leather leashes, saddles, and other pet accessories are the rage of dog and horse enthusiasts everywhere. But when murder prances into the ring at a Massachusetts dog show, Perri must confront a cunning killer who's a breed apart.

Accompanied by her bestie, Babette, and four oversize canines, Perri motors down to the Big E Dog Show in high style. Perri hopes to combine business with pleasure by also spending time with sexy DC journalist Wing Pruett. Until a storm traps everyone at the exposition hall . . . and a man's body is found in a snow-covered field, a pair of pink poodle grooming shears plunged through his heart.

Turns out the deceased was a double-dealing huckster who had plenty of enemies chomping at the bit. But as breeders and their prize pets preen and strut, the murderer strikes again. Aided by her trusty canine companions, Keats and Poe, Perri must collar a killer before she's the next "Dead in Show" winner.

Keep reading for a special look!

Chapter 1

Road trips always rattled me. They carried me back to my army days in an airless transport truck, where I sat wedged between raunchy guys with mixed motives. I had to admit that they were expert practitioners of that international game—Russian hands and Roman fingers. In those times, a woman needed sharp elbows and an even sharper tongue to survive and thrive. Out of necessity, I had acquired both. They weren't a bad bunch. Like me, most of my fellow warriors were actually scared kids buoying their courage with a show of false bravado. As soldiers, we served our country and learned invaluable life lessons that strengthened us—if we survived.

Things were different now, of course, but those memories still hovered about the recesses of my mind every time I took a road trip. I closed my eyes and made a wish.

Please. Whisk me away on a magic carpet and make me vanish.

Naturally that didn't happen. We barreled down the highway in Babette Croy's superduper Class A motor home at top speed without missing a beat. Then, for the hundredth time that day, I wondered how in the world I would ever survive the coming week. Seven whole days in close quarters with my best friend and several thousand dog enthusiasts. The possibilities for mischief were endless.

"Are you okay, Perri?" The dulcet tones of seven-year-old Ella Pruett revived me and brought me to my senses. A mini-frown marred the sweet face of the moppet I had grown to love, flooding me with guilt.

"Of course. Don't worry about me. I was just dreaming." I winked to show her that everything was fine. Hunky-dory. Peachy keen. My trusty Malinois Keats and Poe immediately went on alert. They were canine truth detectors who could sense lies—particularly mine—at ten paces. That was their job during a three-year stint in the army, and retired or not, they hadn't lost a step. Most people confused Belgians like my boys with either German shepherds or shepherd/collie mixes. Nothing could be further from the truth, as police forces throughout the world now realized. Belgian Malinois are a distinct breed—streamlined, tireless workers with an unending appetite for action. I reached for them, looked into soulful doggy eyes, and gave each a nose kiss. In times of stress, nothing surpassed a furry embrace.

"Don't mind Perri, sugar. She's just a stick in the mud." Babette, my best pal and our designated driver, twisted around in the driver's seat and rolled her eyes, ignoring the threat of oncoming traffic and the blaring horns of outraged drivers. "I know," she said, "let's sing a song. Road trips are supposed to be fun. Look at it this way. By leavin' today, we'll beat the snowstorm and avoid all that nasty winter traffic. Plus, that gives us plenty of girl time together."

Babette was a guided missile—locked, loaded, and ready to fire. Fortunately, I distracted her by mentioning one of her favorite subjects: dogs. After all, canine competition was what had sparked our little caravan. Why else would two adults, one child, and four large dogs abandon Great Marsh, Virginia, and drive for six hours to the sooty embrace of the Big E Coliseum, also known as the Eastern States Expo Center, a carbuncle on the foot of western Massachusetts.

I didn't mind roughing it. Four years in the US Army had cured me of needless luxuries, but Babette was a different story entirely. My friend considered anything short of full cable, Italian sheets, and catered meals an unendurable hardship. Great wealth does that to a person, I'm told, although in my case it was strictly a rumor. My business, Creature Comforts, provided me with a decent livelihood and a satisfying creative outlet. I left the opulence to Babette and most of my neighbors in Great Marsh. That explained the luxury motor home. There were more modest models available, but Babette wouldn't hear of it. Second class was simply not in her vocabulary. This latest acquisition, the behemoth dubbed Steady Eddie, sported granite countertops, plush leather furniture, two steam showers, and accommodations for eight. At first, I'd been wary, but Babette surprised me. After all, not everyone could maneuver a metal monster through heavy traffic. My friend was petite but surprisingly adept at doing just that. Rule number one in the Croy friendship manual—never underestimate Babette!

"Miss your daddy, Ella?" Babette's coy tone gave her away. "I know Ms. Perri does."

Ella was the much-loved daughter of Wing Pruett, investigative journalist, hottie supreme, and my main squeeze. How to describe Wing Pruett? Sculpted features, thick dark hair, and a body most women (and men) could only dream about. No doubt about it. All six plus feet of my honey were as close to perfection as mere mortals could ever get. He was absent today but planned to join us later in the week after wrapping up his current assignment. He'd been uncharacteristically vague about the project, and that made me wonder. Despite Babette's prompts and none too subtle hints, Pruett refused to spill the journalistic beans. I surmised, however, that it had something to do with dog shows. That was a real puzzler. Wing Pruett, the man who fearlessly confronted evildoers of all stripes, was terrified of dogs. Cynophobia was the clinical term for an ailment I simply could not understand. Still, he had made great strides, mostly due to Ella and his interaction with my own menagerie. Few men would admit, let alone address, such a malady, but then Pruett was not most men. I missed him like crazy but kept that feeling to myself.

I turned toward my dogs to avoid Babette's scrutiny. Damn that woman. She sometimes knew me better than I knew myself. Truth be told, I missed Pruett every second that we spent apart. Simple logic told me that a country mouse like me was unlikely to hold his interest long-term, but raw emotion kept me firmly anchored to his side. After almost a year, things had only gotten better—for me at least.

"I see him every night on Skype," Ella said with that unassailable logic small children often use. "He blows kisses to me and Guinnie." Lady Guinivere, a champion pointer, was the love of Ella's life. "Ms. Perri too. Daddy always saves a kiss for her." I loved that child as if she were my own little girl. She wasn't, of course. She was the offspring of Pruett and renowned photojournalist Monique Allaire and had the black curly mane and soulful blue eyes to prove it. Monique was mostly absent from her life, but Pruett was the ultimate Mr. Mom. I knew that allowing Ella to join our merry band proved his trust in me, but it also conferred an awesome responsibility. That's what shattered my nerves and led to sleepless nights. Dog shows were busy places, and the Big E was cavernous—so many nooks and crevices where a little girl might wander off, get lost, or worse. Add a potential blizzard to the mix, and anything might happen.

"You won't go anywhere without me or Ms. Babette. Right, Ella? Remember. We promised your dad that."

She nodded solemnly. "I promise. Besides, Guinnie will protect me too." Her eyes shone as she stroked the pointer's silky coat. "And all the other dogs will help."

I crossed my fingers and took a deep breath. Babette and her border collie, Clara, were focused on agility contests. Babette was obsessed with winning agility competitions, and border collies—those bright, stealthy herders—won top honors in most agility contests. My friend tended toward extremes, especially in times of emotional stress. Since she had recently divorced the cretinous Carleton Croy, Babette was temporarily man-less, and a lonely Babette was a fearsome thing indeed. Thank heavens for the presence of an innocent child. That shielded me from hearing a litany of praise for Carleton's manly parts that Babette so desperately missed. She conveniently forgot that her ex had shared his largesse with any number of her friends and a few enemies as well. When it came to men, Babette had a fond but very selective memory.

Ella had her own dreams. She yearned to be a junior dog handler, a member of that select group of youngsters that dotted every dog show. After discussing the issue with Pruett, I promised to introduce her to some of the kids who participated in the sport. Fortunately, all juniors had to be at least nine years of age, so Pruett had two years to go before confronting the situation. Wing was ambivalent about animals, and I was certain that he hoped Ella's interest would fade.

"Remember," I told Ella, "I'm counting on you to help me with my store." I am a leathersmith by trade, an occupation that requires both creativity and precision. After careful study at art school and an apprenticeship with a master craftsman, I focused on designing products for the creatures I most loved. The majority of my customers were dog and horse fanciers, although lately I'd branched out to custom belts with mother-daughter themes. Any event at the Big E was bound to bring in a slew of business. Snowstorms and other weather mishaps encouraged even more potential customers to attend the show. They chose to brave the elements rather than risk a bout of cabin fever. That pleased me since by necessity I kept my eyes firmly trained on the bottom line.

The little girl beamed. "Yep. See, I got my belt on."

I nodded in appreciation of Ella, a truly wonderful child. I had never married, although I came close one time. Being childless wasn't a problem for me since my biological clock simply did not tick. Before meeting Pruett, I lacked the maternal gene, or so I thought. An affinity for animals came naturally to me, and my menagerie included two dogs, one cantankerous feline, and an ornery goat with bad manners and a temper to match.

Once Ella stepped into the picture, that all changed. At thirty years of age, I had finally embraced the role of child nurturer and caregiver. Go figure.

Babette slowed the trailer and pulled into a rest stop parking lot. "Let's take a break," she said. "I need to stretch my legs, and I know the pups could use some potty time."

Fortunately, we had the coach fully stocked with every possible type of provision, so food and drink were plentiful. Babette had made sure of that. After leashing the dogs, we stepped into the bright sunshine and walked toward the pet area.

"Heard they had some fireworks at last week's show," Babette said in a stage whisper.

I raised my eyebrows.

"Yep. A real dustup." She watched as Ella disposed of Guinnie's waste. "Yael Lindsay almost came to blows with that Bethany. You know her."

My goal was to sell products, not become mired in scandals. "Nope. Can't place either one."

Babette puffed out her cheeks in a pout. "Oh. You're no fun at all, Ms. Goody Two-shoes. Bethany is that slutty one. Slinks around the arena in super-tight duds that show everything and pretends to be a pet psychic. Don't see how that heifer can even move, let alone mentally communicate with dogs. Thinks she's the queen of agility too."

Something she said piqued my interest. "That's odd. Yael rules the pointer world with an iron fist. Strictly conformation events. Why would she bother with an agility person? Besides she's rather elderly for a fistfight."

"Aha!" Babette pounced immediately. "You know more than you let on. I knew it."

What could I do? I shrugged and gave her a guilty grin. Babette, master of trickery, had trapped me fair and square. "You know I steer clear of these feuds. At least I try to. Remember, I need to sell stuff to both camps."

Sales were a foreign language to my pal. She never even bothered to balance her checkbook, whereas I accounted for each penny with nuclear precision. Call it a legacy from my life as a foster child or just plain business acumen. Either one worked for me. Pip had always urged me to ease up and enjoy life without going overboard. Balance was his watchword.

I snapped a leash on further memories lest tears flood my eyes. Pip, my late fiancé, was gone. Had been these three years since melanoma had stolen him from me. He still resided with me in the home we'd shared, in the pets we both had loved, and in the memories I cherished. Those were the hardest things to suppress because I simply refused to. No matter where things went with Pruett, the late Philip Hahn, DVM, owned a part of me and always would. I told myself that he wasn't really gone. Pip had just left ahead of me.

"Hey, Earth to Perri." Babette tapped me on my forehead. "Stop mooning and get movin'. We've got a show to get to." She clapped her hands for Ella. "Right, Ella? Let's roll."

The remainder of our journey was uneventful, and we exited the Mass Pike and approached the Big E without incident. To my surprise, Babette had researched everything pertinent to parking and maintaining her motor coach right down to electronic and cable television hookups. Many dog show veterans chose the convenience of recreational vehicles over the rigors of motel life since upscale establishments banned or severely restricted dogs. The remaining "dog hotels" simply didn't measure up to Babette's high standards. Thus, the luxury coach—an inspired, if pricey, solution that paid dividends to me too. I groused about needless spending when my pal had purchased Steady Eddie, citing depreciation, inconvenience, and the numerous animal charities that needed the money instead. Opulence made me uncomfortable, a throwback to my hardscrabble childhood. Still, I was secretly pleased by the comfort and ease of our accommodations. Friendship with Babette conferred many benefits, and chief among them was sharing the spoils of wealth. Money aside, her loyalty and sweet nature were the primary attractions for me.

Although the Big E reserved a sizable area for large vehicles and trailers, choice slots close to the show venue were at a premium. I worried that our late arrival might relegate us to the far reaches of the fairground—Siberia, as the regulars termed it. If that were our fate, juggling dogs, leather products, and one lively child would present quite a challenge, especially during inclement weather.

Once again, Babette read my mind. "Don't fret, Perri. We've got a primo spot. I already arranged it." Try as she might, she couldn't hide the smirk that covered her pretty face.

"How'd you manage that?" I asked, mindful that a small child was within earshot.

Babette fluttered her eyelashes. "Charm and wit."

I crossed my arms. "What else?"

"Suspicious little twit, aren't you? Okay. You caught me. A well-placed bribe didn't hurt either. Just a generous cash gift to the guy in charge of the area." Babette stared me down. "Don't be an old prig, Perri. It's the American way. Once that snow starts, things will get crazy here."

"What's a prig, Ms. Babette?" Ella proved yet again that her hearing was exceptionally sharp.

Babette swung into a reserved slot closest to the show area. "Don't worry, pumpkin. Ms. Perri is just a stuffed shirt. We have to loosen her up."

Ella's big blue eyes sparkled. "My daddy says Ms. Perri is perfect."

Now it was my turn to blush and change the subject. I hated to acknowledge the firm grip that Wing Pruett and his darling moppet had on my heart. Orphans like me fear loss more than most folks. After being wrenched from my parents' arms and watching my fiancé slip away, I tried mightily to steel myself against further pain. Through a concentrated stealth campaign, Pruett had managed to penetrate those defenses and unleash my fondest hopes. Love does that to a body, but it's a deep and dangerous game.

"Come on," I said, dusting off my jeans. "Let's hook up this baby and walk around the grounds. I see a few familiar faces already."

Babette clambered out of the driver's seat and immediately made a connection. Our near neighbor, a muscular, middle-aged man with a thick crop of gray hair, held out his arm and helped Babette alight. She sized him up and went all girly on him.

"Why, thank you, kind sir. I can always use a little help." In true Babette fashion, she simpered. I really hated when she did that, but it was straight from the Croy playbook, with a bow to Scarlett O'Hara. Most men fell for it, especially when she showed her dimples. This guy was no exception.

I did a quick appraisal of Prince Galahad. He was tall, tanned, and neatly dressed in a pressed pair of jeans and checked shirt. There was nothing wrong with his body either, but I was more concerned with his motives. Call me protective, but Babette had zero judgment when it came to men. The unlamented Carleton Croy, husband number four, was an opportunist who was more interested in her bankbook than her loving heart. Similarly, any con man worth his salt would assess Steady Eddie and quickly realize the bucks that went with it. I leapt out of my seat, clutched Ella, and unleashed my dogs.

"Forgive me, ma'am. I should have introduced myself." Babette's admirer ignored me and kept hold of her hand. "Rafael Ramos at your service. Most folks call me Rafa."

Ramos's vehicle was a poor cousin of ours, a rusted Airstream that had seen better days. Naturally, Babette seemed oblivious to that as she zeroed in on our neighbor. I knew the signs and decided to immediately nip young love in the bud.

Babette was still in dreamland. "Rafa? Ooh. Just like the tennis player. That's fascinatin'!"

He shrugged and shook his head. "Don't I wish. Unfortunately, I'm not much of an athlete." His faux modesty aroused my suspicions. The muscles on this guy proved that he did some serious physical training.

"Hi, Rafa," I said, extending my hand. "I'm Perri Morgan, and this is Ella. Excuse us while we exercise our crew. We've got four hungry canines on board."

Ramos unhanded my friend and switched into helpful mode. "Of course. Be glad to help you with the connections on this big boy if you need anything. Sure is a beauty." He then proved that he was also a dog person. "Wow! Speaking of beauties, your dogs are phenomenal." He approached Keats and Poe with the palm of his hand open and lowered.

When they acknowledged him, he patted their silky heads and did the same to Clara and Guinnie.

"Do you have a dog, sir?" Ella asked.

He bent down and smiled. "Call me Rafa, honey. And the answer is yes. My breed is standard poodles. Don't have any with me this trip because I'm judging."

"You're a judge," Babette trilled as if he had said "brain surgeon." The throb in her voice sounded authentic and probably was. "How excitin'."

Rafael lowered his head in an "aw shucks" routine. "I just love doing the show circuit. Being around beautiful dogs and lovely ladies—doesn't get much better than that."

"Guinnie is a Grand Champion," Ella said proudly. "She's almost at bronze level." In dog show parlance, there were five levels of Grand Champion, and Guinnie was new to that elevated crowd. She had bronze, silver, gold, and platinum levels yet to conquer, but that didn't concern me one bit. With Guinnie's perfection, Ella's persistence, and Pruett's pocketbook, no obstacle was insurmountable.

Rafa nodded. "I can see why. Didn't I see her written up in the latest issue of *Canine Chronicles*?"

Ella's smile was luminous. She nodded and reached down to give Guinnie another hug. In deference to the little girl, I hoped Rafa wouldn't probe any further. Grand Champion Camelot Kennel's Lady Guinevere had come to us under tragic circumstances that were best forgotten. Like most pointers, Guinnie was a gentle, loving companion with plenty of brains. The important thing was the immutable bond between Ella and her dog.

"Let me take these guys for a run," I said, whistling to my dogs. "Ready, Ella?" We loped toward the backfields, leaving Babette to her new suitor. I know from experience when to fade from the scene, particularly when it involved a man. Their animated conversation told me that our absence hadn't even been noticed. No surprise there. Babette was a loyal friend, but any presentable man with a pulse could easily turn her head.

Ella, on the other hand, saw only Guinnie and the other dogs. Her big blue eyes shone with happiness as she romped with our pack of pups. Loving animals came easily to most children, and I harbored grave suspicions about kids who felt otherwise. Indifference to animals was just plain unnatural—serial killer material.

A sudden cacophony of noise rudely interrupted my thoughts. I clutched Ella's hand, steering her toward the trees and to the left of the warring parties. Neither combatant acknowledged us, but I suspect that, in the heat of battle, neither of them noticed us either. To my chagrin, these disturbers of the peace were adults, grown women, not marauding teens. Yael Lindsay, a well-preserved sexagenarian with seriously teased hair and an eye-popping diamond ring, shook her fist. "You listen here, Bethany. I run this show. That means no shenanigans by the likes of you. Hussy!" Her antagonist, agility master Bethany Zahn, was the seductress so vividly described by Babette. Maybe it was the black leather blanketing her from stem to sultry stern that gave Bethany away or the mane of unnaturally black curls that she twirled. Either way, she radiated sex appeal, snark, and a dollop of dominatrix.

"Run?" she sneered, hands on hips. "Honey, at your age you couldn't run if your life depended on it. Join a gym, why don't you? Better still, muzzle that horny hubby of yours. He's into agility in a big way, or so I hear." Bethany smirked at her own wit and sauntered off toward the show entrance without a backward glance.

I normally eschew gossip, but that little tiff fascinated me—until I recalled the urchin who clutched my hand. Ella Pruett trained her baby blues on me and asked, "Why were those ladies fighting, Perri? Daddy says that's not right."

Honesty was the best policy, especially when it involved a bright, inquisitive child like Ella, who was not easily fooled.

"Your daddy was right. Shouting never solves anything, honey. Some people never learn." I clapped my hands, causing Poe and Keats to snap to attention. "Come on. Let's run a race with these pups."

We sped down the field, trailing four dogs that easily outpaced us and leaving the snarling women behind. Canine quarrels were typically sparked by competition—dominance, food, territory, or sex. Humans were no different. Based on the scene I had just witnessed, one or all of those factors might have caused the dustup. I never dreamed that tragedy awaited us.

About the Author

Photo by Kim Rodriques Photography

Arlene Kay spent twenty years as a Senior Federal Executive, where she was known as a most unconventional public servant. Her time with the federal government, from Texas to Washington, DC, allowed her to observe both human and corporate foibles and rejoice in unintentional humor. These locations and the many people she encountered are celebrated in her mystery novels. She is also the author of the Boston Uncommons Mystery series as well as *Intrusion* and *Die Laughing*. She is a member of International Thriller Writers. Visit her on the web at arlenekay.com.

Printed in the United States
by Baker & Taylor Publisher Services